Praise for

"Lancet imbues *Tokyo Kill* with a vivid sense of Japan, from sections of Tokyo that only a native would know about to meticulous research into the country's history and legends. . . . Lancet hit the ground running last year with his superb debut, *Japantown*, and continues that winning streak with *Tokyo Kill*."

—*The New York Times*/AP

"A stellar novel of action, adventure, and intrigue. Jim Brodie is a true twenty-first-century hero. . . . On page after page of *Tokyo Kill*, skeletons bang on every closet door longing to be set free—and Barry Lancet delivers."

—Steve Berry, *New York Times* bestselling
author of *The Lincoln Myth*

"Brodie is immediately noteworthy as one of the more interesting characters in the thriller universe. . . . A book worth reading and a series worth starting."

—*Bookreporter*

"An impressive novel of spirited adventure and edgy intrigue. It's obvious Lancet has firsthand knowledge of Japan and has done extensive research regarding the historical elements. This, along with realistic characterization and notable plot development, makes *Tokyo Kill* a dynamic read."

—*FreshFiction*

"An excellent mystery that . . . offers some nuanced understandings of the China-Japan relationship."

—Forbes.com

"The author's familiarity with Japanese history and culture, combined with his storytelling skills, make this a first-rate mystery . . . a clear indicator that Lancet considers Jim Brodie a series-worthy character. He'd be right, too."

—*Booklist*

"Boasting surefire characters including the taciturn, thick-chested chief detective Noda and notorious crime figure called TNT who owes Brodie favors. . . . [Lancet's] series remains highly distinctive."

—*Kirkus Reviews*

"The book delivers on every level, both as a thriller and as a look inside an Asian culture with which many Westerners may not be familiar."

—ReviewingtheEvidence.com

TOKYO KILL

A Thriller

BARRY LANCET

SIMON & SCHUSTER PAPERBACKS

New York   London   Toronto   Sydney   New Delhi

Simon & Schuster Paperbacks
An Imprint of Simon & Schuster Inc.
1230 Avenue of the Americas
New York, NY 10020

First Simon & Schuster trade paperback edition December 2015

SIMON & SCHUSTER PAPERBACKS and colophon are registered
trademarks of Simon & Schuster, Inc.

For information about special discounts for bulk purchases,
please contact Simon & Schuster Special Sales at
1-866-506-1949 or business@simonandschuster.com.

The Simon & Schuster Speakers Bureau can bring authors to your live event.
For more information or to book an event contact the Simon & Schuster Speakers
Bureau at 1-866-248-3049 or visit our website at www.simonspeakers.com.

Interior design by Kyoko Watanabe

Manufactured in the United States of America

1   3   5   7   9   10   8   6   4   2

The Library of Congress has cataloged the hardcover edition as follows:

Lancet, Barry.
Tokyo kill : a thriller / Barry Lancet.
pages   cm
1. Antique dealers—California—San Francisco—Fiction.
2. Private investigators—Japan—Fiction. 3. World War, 1939–1945—
Japan—Tokyo—Fiction. 4. Murder—Investigation—Fiction. 5.
Chinese—Japan—Fiction. 6. Tokyo (Japan)—Fiction. I. Title.
PS3612.A547486T65 2014
813'.6—dc23   2014001390

ISBN 978-1-4516-9172-6
ISBN 978-1-4516-9173-3 (pbk)
ISBN 978-1-4516-9174-0 (ebook)

NOTE TO READERS: The two main systems for writing Chinese words in English
are Wade-Giles and Pinyin. Since most of the Chinese-related scenes take place
in China, I've chosen Pinyin, even though in some instances I prefer Wade-
Giles. In the case of Jiang Jieshi, I've worked both names into the text since
the Western reader perhaps knows him more commonly as Chiang Kai-shek.
The same goes for Sun Yixian, whose name often appears as Sun Yat-sen.

The reverse side also has a reverse side.

—JAPANESE PROVERB

DAY 1

TRIADS

CHAPTER 1

EIGHT people had already died by the time Akira Miura showed up at our door fearing for his life.

When the commotion broke out I'd been on a long-distance call to London trying to track down an original ink painting by Sengai, the renowned Japanese painter-monk of *Circle, Triangle, and Square* fame. The rumor had come out of the United Kingdom, so I was plying channels to nail down the potential gem for a client in San Francisco who would kill to get it, and kill *me* if I didn't.

People killed for a lot less. I learned this anew with each day spent at Brodie Security, the detective agency and personal protection firm established by my father in the Japanese capital more than forty years ago.

Had I been sitting in my antiques shop in San Francisco instead of behind my father's battered pine desk in Tokyo, I wouldn't have given the shouting match in the front office a second thought, but in Japan a loud altercation constituted a serious breach of decorum.

If not more.

Mari Kawasaki tapped on my door. "Brodie-san, I think you should get out here."

All of twenty-three but looking more like sixteen, Mari was the office tech whiz. When I came to town, she lent me a hand. We were a small operation and people wore multiple hats.

"Could I call you back later today?" I asked my London connection. "Something urgent has come up."

He said certainly and I jotted down his schedule, bid a polite good-bye, and stepped out onto the main floor.

Mari pointed across the room to where three hardened Brodie Security ops had herded a fourth man against a wall. The man cast indignant glares at them, and when my people didn't wither and fall back, he pelted the trio with the exasperated sighs middle-management salary-men usually fling at underlings.

That didn't work either.

Mari rolled her eyes. "He charged in here demanding to speak with you and refused to explain himself or wait at reception."

When the unexpected reared up at Brodie Security, containment came before all else. Our work brought us into contact with every manner of fringe character. Old-timers still talk about the right-wing lunatic who sprang from the elevator with short sword drawn and put two of the staff in the hospital.

"Calm down," one of the three men cooed. "If you would just return to the reception area . . ."

The salaryman was irate. "But it's urgent. My father is a sick man. Can't you see that?" He saw me and yelled across the expanse in Japanese, "Are you Jim Brodie?"

Since I was the only Caucasian in a sea of Asian faces, it wasn't a brilliant deduction. Our unannounced guest was handsome in the un-assuming way Japanese men can be. He was in his fifties and sheathed in the requisite business suit—dark blue in his case—with a white dress shirt and a perfectly knotted red silk tie. The tie had set him back some. What looked like platinum cuff links sparkled at his wrists. His attire was flawless, and under normal circumstances he'd be considered nonthreatening. But his expression was frayed, as if he were unraveling from the inside.

"That's me," I said in his native language.

He drew himself up. His eyes grew watery. "Kindly allow my father to intrude. He is not well."

All eyes shifted toward the paternal figure waiting patiently at Reception. He had a full crown of silver-gray hair and the same unassuming good looks: sculpted cheekbones, a firm chin, and the deep brown eyes women habitually swoon over.

He waved a wooden walking staff in salute, then began a tremulous foray around the unmanned half-counter that passed for Reception in our no-frills office. With singular determination he shuffled forward. His hands trembled. The cane shook. He wheezed with each step. And yet, there was something noble in the effort.

He had dressed for the trip into town. A brown hand-tailored suit that had gone out of style maybe three decades ago. As he drew closer the smell of mothballs suggested his attire had been plucked from a dusty clothes rack expressly for this visit.

Three feet away, he stopped. He squinted up at me with unflinching brown eyes. "Are you the *gaijin* the papers said caught the Japantown killers in San Francisco?"

Gaijin means "foreigner," literally "outside person."

"Guilty as charged."

"And tackled the Japanese mafia before that?"

"Guilty again."

For better or worse, the overseas murders and my run-in with the Tokyo thugs had made headlines in Japan.

"Then you're my man. Got notches on your belt."

I smiled and his son, who had sidled up on the other side, whispered in my ear. "That's his meds talking. Makes him emotional. Sometimes delusional. I only mentioned coming here to calm him. I never thought he'd actually do it."

His father frowned. He hadn't heard what was said, but he was astute enough to guess the content. "My son thinks I've toppled off the train because I've put on a few years. Well, I'm ninety-three, and until last December I could walk three miles a day without a damn stick."

"A few years? You're ninety-*six*, Dad. You shouldn't be charging around town like this."

The old man waved the cane under his son's nose. "You call this charging? There are tombstones in Aoyama Cemetery that move faster than I do, but upstairs my train's still running on straight tracks. Besides, when a man my age no longer wants to shave off a couple years to impress the ladies, *then* he's done for."

I was going to like this guy.

I said, "Why don't we step into my office? It's quiet there. Mari, would you show these gentlemen the way? I'll be there in a minute."

"Follow me, please," she said.

Once Mari had shut them in, I turned to a pale-faced detective nearest the entrance. "Anything else besides their showing up without an appointment?"

"Only the last name. Miura."

"Okay, thanks. Do you know where Noda is?"

Kunio Noda was our head detective and the main reason I came away from the Japantown case in one piece.

"He's out on the kidnapping case in Asakusa but supposed to be back shortly."

"Send him in as soon as he arrives, okay?"

"Will do."

I headed back to my office, where I exchanged cards and the customary bows with the new arrivals. The father's name was Akira Miura and he'd once been senior vice president of a major Japanese trading company.

The son with the pricey tie was a *fuku bucho*, or assistant section chief, at Kobo Electronics. His company was equally impressive but his position was not, especially for a Japanese salaryman in his fifties. You didn't start making good money until you hit *bucho*, the next step up for Yoji Miura, so either he was spending beyond his means or there was money trickling in from another source.

Taking my seat I said, "So, gentlemen, how can I help?"

Before they could respond, Mari knocked and entered. On a tray she carried green tea in decorated porcelain cups with lids. Guest chinaware. In Japan, courtesy rules.

"I was in the war, Mr. Brodie," Akira Miura said after Mari departed.

When a Japanese mentions *the war*, he or she means World War II. And only the youngest soldiers—now the oldest surviving veterans—were around today. Japan fought no further battles after the big Double Two.

"I see," I said.

Miura Senior's eyes zeroed in on me. "How much do you know about Japanese history, Mr. Brodie?"

"Quite a bit, actually."

My endeavors in the field of Japanese art made knowledge of the country's history, culture, and traditions mandatory.

"Did you know that in the old Japanese army you followed orders without question, or your commanding officer put a bullet in your head?"

"Yes."

"Good. Then you probably also know that my country conquered part of Manchuria and set up a puppet state."

I did, and he seemed pleased.

Japan had entered China aggressively in the early 1900s, then cemented its grasp by laying railroads, bringing in settlers, and setting up branches of its large conglomerates. In 1932 it famously resurrected the rule of China's twelfth and final Qing Dynasty ruler, Pu Yi, canonized in popular culture as the Last Emperor.

Miura said, "I was sent to the Manchurian front in 1940 as an officer. My men and I fought many battles. Then new orders shifted us to a frontier outpost called Anli-dong. Our assignment was to stabilize the region, and I became the de facto mayor of Anli and the surrounding area.

"We were outnumbered two hundred to one, but by that time the Japanese military had a reputation so fierce we retained control without incident. Although I preached nonviolence and it held, my predecessor had been ruthless. Any Chinese male offender faced a firing squad or worse, and his women became the spoils of war. Which is why I need you."

"For something that happened more than seventy years ago?"

"You've heard about the recent home invasions in Tokyo?"

"Sure. Two families slaughtered within six days of each other. Eight people were killed."

"You saw the police suspect Triads?"

"Of course."

"They're right."

Inwardly I cringed at the mention of the blade-wielding Chinese gangs. I'd run into them in San Francisco once when I lived out in the Mission. It hadn't ended well.

"How can you be so sure?"

Miura's handsome brown eyes flooded with fear. "In Anli-dong they told me they would come after us. Now they have."

HE had my attention. "How can you be so sure the Triads are target-ing you after all this time?"

"Because I know what was *not* in the papers."

"Which is?"

"Two of my men are dead all of a sudden."

My men. "And you told this to the police?"

"*Uma no mimi ni nembutsu,*" he said with undisguised disdain.

Might as well read sutras to horses. Meaning the Japanese police were too dense to understand.

"But you did tell them?"

He shrugged. "They insisted the killings couldn't possibly be moti-vated by 'ancient history.'"

During the war years, the Japanese police became an organ of ter-ror at home almost as much as the armed forces did abroad. After the surrender, the police were emasculated. A heavy-handed bureaucracy filled the vacuum, and to this day a cautious mind-set colors their every action, which leaves a lot of territory for the likes of Brodie Security.

"And you think otherwise because?"

"My gut."

His son smiled apologetically.

I ignored Miura the Younger but could no longer dismiss his earlier comments about his father's instability. "And what is your gut telling you?"

"That two of my men killed so close together is no coincidence."

I said, "Even assuming that what you say is true, how would Brodie Security be able to help?"

"Guard my house."

His son wanted me to humor him, so I said, "That we can do. But security takes men, in teams, and doesn't come cheap. Are you sure?"

"I'm sure."

I looked at his son, who nodded reluctantly.

"Okay," I said, "we'll put some men on you for a few days."

"I also want you to find out who butchered my friends."

"The murders landed on the front page. You can bet the police have made them a top priority."

He shook his head. "The police are idiots. I gave them a connection and they didn't even bother to check it. Both men served together because they grew up in the same neighborhood. The same place they were killed. It is not a gang of thieves targeting the neighborhood, as the police think, but Anli-dong Triads targeting my men."

There was a knock, then Noda barreled in without waiting for a reply. The chief detective was short and stout and built like a bulldog—broad shoulders, a thick chest, and a flat humorless face. His most distinctive feature was a slash across his eyebrow where a yakuza blade had left its mark. Noda's return swipe left a deeper mark.

I made introductions and brought Noda up-to-date. He grunted when I mentioned the Triads.

"What? You think Triads are a possibility?" I said, pushing the habitually laconic detective for a more revealing response.

Chinese gangs had been in Japan for decades. They could trace their roots back to the end of the Ming Dynasty in China, where they started as a political group aiding the government against the invading Manchus, and were hailed as heroes. Over time the glory faded. But the beast needed feeding. Triad leaders looked elsewhere to buttress their dwindling support and found the easy money—protection, extortion, loan sharking, prostitution, and drugs. First at home and, inevitably, overseas. In Tokyo, gangs inhabited the darker corners of Shinjuku, Ueno, and other enclaves. Yokohama Chinatown, thirty minutes by train, was a major operational base.

Noda shrugged. "Could be."

"And?"

"Tricky."

Frustratingly curt as usual.

Miura looked from Noda to me. "So you'll take the case?"

"Noda?"

He shrugged. "It's what we do."

Meaning Brodie Security had handled Triad cases before. That was the question I'd really been asking. I was still new to my father's outfit, having inherited half of the firm just eleven months ago. But showing my ignorance in front of a client was not an option.

"Okay," I said. "We can look into it. My father's people are very good at what they do."

"They'll need to be," Miura said, his eyes lingering on Noda with vague apprehension.

"How many men from your old squad are left?"

"Twenty-eight of us survived the war but most died long ago. Only seven showed up at our last get-together. Then Mitsumoto died of a brain aneurysm, and Yanaguchi caught the bird flu on a visit back to Anli last year. Before the home invasions there were five of us."

So only three remained.

"Where are the other two?"

"One left for a friend's vacation home in Kyushu. He won't tell me where. The other went to stay with his son in the countryside."

Noda and I exchanged a look. That the remaining members of Miura's troop had fled Tokyo—and one to the farthest western island of mainland Japan—bolstered the old soldier's claim.

I had a last question:

"If you ruled Anli-dong with an even hand, then why would someone want you and your men dead after all this time?"

He sighed. "It's the dirt. Whenever higher-ups came through they expected to be entertained. They invariably ordered us to 'weed out traitors' and 'set up inspections.' The first consisted of lining up any villagers in jail for target practice. The second involved examining local beauties in private. These were orders we couldn't refuse or they'd—"

"—put a bullet in your head."

Miura's shoulders sagged under an old guilt. "Without a second thought."

"I see."

"After the first VIP visit, the Triads threatened me. I told them I could only control those under my command, not above. They were unconvinced. 'If you wear the master's uniform, you can bleed for him too.' They didn't act then because they knew more villagers would suffer if any soldiers were attacked. But they told me they would come one day.

"Years later, when China finally allowed Japanese tourists into the country, a handful of us went back. We looked up the families we knew. We were shocked to see how poor they were, and still are today. We've returned many times, bringing them money and modern appliances like Japanese rice cookers. We ate together and drank together. We did what we could to make amends. But we couldn't help everyone. I think our trips triggered an old resentment. We gave out our addresses freely. That may have been a mistake."

Noda grunted. "Revenge slayings."

Miura concurred with a nod. "My future killer is in Tokyo, Brodie-san. I can feel it."

———

A team of six men escorted Akira Miura home.

Once they arrived, two would canvass the neighborhood, then the local shops. Two others would secure the residence. Windows, doors, and other exterior access points would be sealed, then house, garage, and yard scanned for listening, tracking, and incendiary devices. The last pair would work with Miura on safety protocol, including an emergency evacuation plan, after which they would spend the next twelve hours with their charge until two rested operatives replaced them.

However, before the team left Brodie Security, they gathered in the conference room with the Miuras to discuss procedure. Sometime during the proceedings, the son slipped away and cornered Noda and me in my office.

"Thank you for indulging the old man," he said. "The murders have rattled him, but to be frank, we are seeing signs of senility lately, and mild paranoia."

"Has he gone overboard before?" I asked.

"No, but the doctors told us to expect a slow degeneration."

Noda and I traded a glance.

"Noted," I said. "But we'll want to treat the threat seriously until we can prove otherwise."

Yoji Miura remained skeptical. "Your presence will comfort my father, so what could it hurt? But between us, you'll be babysitting."

Noda scowled. "Two men murdered is beyond babysitting."

The head detective's voice was low and menacing. Yoji looked startled until he noticed that Noda's rage was not directed at him but at what might or might not be out there, lying in wait. Even so, when the younger Miura left my office, he gave Noda a wide berth. The detective himself followed a minute later, mumbling about clueless offspring.

Alone, I leaned back in my chair and stared at the ceiling. Deep down, something primal stirred, disturbed by the undertow of Miura Senior's fears. I liked the old veteran a lot. Pulling out his musty suit for the visit. Habitually shaving three years off his age so he could still attract "the ladies."

What I didn't like was his fellow veterans abandoning Tokyo for safer grounds. Nor the triple threat—home invasions, Triads, and old war atrocities. I'd been through a lot in my life. Seen a lot. Had learned the hard way to give any early sign of danger its due.

This could be the world's wildest goose chase, or the beginning of something very nasty.

CHAPTER 3

THERE must have been something in the air because trouble kept coming. First London, then Tokyo.

"Rang 'round and roused an amateur," Graham Whittinghill, the British dealer, said when we reconnected. "Afraid we had a bit of a barney."

My hand gripped the headset tighter. This was not the kind of news I wanted to hear. Graham meant that he and a competing dealer, an amateur in the field of Japanese art, had exchanged some territorial hostilities. At times you need to reach beyond your personal network. Sometimes people you hope you can trust seek to insert themselves into a deal by trying to grab the work first and forcing you to feed one more middleman.

"Happens," I said.

"Deepest apologies. The bugger's turned dodgy. Fed me a load of codswallop."

"Codswallop being crap?"

"Of the grandest order," my British friend said. "I'll give it a sort-out tonight."

We'd met four years ago through a mutual acquaintance and hit it off immediately. Graham was tall and lanky, with dirty-blond hair and a gleam in his eye. My expertise lay with Japanese art, his with Chinese. I needed a trustworthy source because the Chinese art market was a nightmarish maze of top-end counterfeits that could dupe ninety-five percent of the people. Fortunately, the painfully shy Graham was among the remaining five.

I said, "Refresh my memory. Do you know your way around Japanese ink painting at all?"

No one could call Sengai a brilliant brush-meister, but the Zen monk excelled in taking the Japanese love of simplicity to a very human place. His pieces were humorous, playful, and, at their peak, profound. Sengai laughed at life. He commiserated with those of his flock trapped in the workaday grind, but reveled in the bigger picture—that existence is impermanent. Enlightenment had brought him freedom and joy, and his brush danced with the knowledge.

"No, purely Chinese for me, with the singular exception of Chinese themes in Japanese works, which by happy coincidence happens to include depictions of Chinese Buddhist monks in Sengai's oeuvre."

"Really? Why?"

"A dollop of juicy gossip from the far side of the moon. It will hold until you next drop around for a pint. We have a more pressing issue at hand."

"Fair enough. Then let's wrap it up before our rogue dealer sinks the whole venture. Get a peek at any documents, then lock down the owner for a videoconference so I can do an on-screen evaluation."

"Certainly. As I've tainted the undertaking, perhaps we should knock down my commission to half the usual?"

"Wouldn't think of it," I said.

"You are a gentleman, sir, but I'll leave the offer on the table."

"Won't change my mind."

In the extended silence, Graham's appreciation was palpable.

"By the bye," he said a moment later, "since it's come up, should you ever happen across one of Sengai's renderings of a Chinese monk, ring me straight away, any time of the day or night."

"And you mention this because?"

"'You never see one carrot-fly but you see three.' Farmer's wisdom courtesy of my Cornish grandfather."

And that's where we left it—with vermin buzzing and trouble brewing.

The next blow came in low and mean and caught me looking.

CHAPTER 4

WHEN I picked up my six-year-old daughter at the place of an old family friend, I found her fed, bathed, and played out. Once home, Jenny requested a bedtime story. I obliged but she faded by the third page. In Tokyo, "home" meant my father's comfy bungalow, which served double duty as city lodgings during my visits and, occasionally, as a safe house for clients now that Brodie Security held the deed.

Our current trip was designed as a reprieve after the nerve-wrenching ride of Japantown. My plan called for quick stops in Tokyo and Kyoto, where I'd choose some pieces for the shop, then Jenny and I would shift into full vacation mode. I intended to hand over the Miura job to Noda tomorrow or the next day.

A Suntory whiskey at my side, I sank into the family room sofa to map out the details of our visit to Kyoto, but I didn't get far. Intruding on my thoughts time and again were Jun Hamada's final words:

"What's the bottom line?" he'd asked during a last huddle at Brodie Security.

"To catch whoever killed Miura's buddies," I said.

Hamada, our office expert on Chinese crime gangs, hesitated. "May not be possible if we're talking Triads."

"Why not?"

"They're like ants. You only see one or two at first, but if you prod the nest they swarm."

"That doesn't sound good."

His bulbous nose twitched. A hardened ex-cop out of Osaka,

Hamada had been through his share of battles. "You got that more right than you know."

In a distracted state of mind, I carried on late into the night. Hamada's words lingered. I polished off my third whiskey. Smooth though the aged liquor was, it did nothing to kill the sourness building in my gut.

Around midnight, I started entertaining thoughts of sleep. Which is when Inspector Shin'ichi Kato of the Tokyo Metropolitan Police Department rang me on my private cell phone—and elevated Hamada to house psychic.

DAY 2

THE ECHO OF WAR

CHAPTER 5

12:17 A.M.

AT the knock I opened the door to Officer Rie Hoshino, one of Tokyo's rare policewomen.

"Brodie-sama?" she asked in formal Japanese.

"Yes."

"You spoke with Inspector Kato?"

I nodded. "He told me to expect you, though not so soon."

Inspector Kato's protégée wore rouge and eye shadow; both were tastefully applied and kept to a minimum, no doubt to allow her to blend more easily into the boys' club that was the Tokyo MPD. Her uniform was the requisite navy-blue jacket and pants, a sky-blue shirt, and dark tie under a wide, pointed collar. Brass buttons locked down the image, which, with minor variations, echoed that of her male colleagues. Her clear brown eyes were penetrating and her complexion youthful.

"Are you ready?" She gave me a polite smile, her tone all business.

"As ready as I'll ever be. You bring the sitter?"

Hoshino waved and a fresh-faced female recruit stepped into view. "This is Kawakami. Unmarried but the eldest of five children. Will she do?"

Kawakami bowed. "Don't worry about a thing, Brodie-sama. Your daughter will be well looked after. What's her name?"

"Jenny, but she also answers to Yumiko. Her middle name. My cell number's on the table. Call if she wakes up and you can't calm her. She . . . gets frightened sometimes."

With one parent dead, Jenny's radar lit up whenever I stepped too far from her sight. A kid's-eye view of single-parent status could be terrifying.

Kawakami acknowledged my instructions with a second bow and Hoshino glanced at her watch. "If we're good, then please follow me. Time is short."

She led me to a waiting patrol car. "Rear seat, if you don't mind. Protocol."

Once we left the narrow residential lanes, Hoshino's foot hit the pedal. She flicked on the rotating red strobes on the roof of her squad car, and we wove in and around a smattering of slower-moving traffic.

Hoshino caught my eye in the mirror. "You okay back there?"

"Fine. Where'd you pick up the precision driving?"

"My father taught me a few tricks after I insisted his daughter could also handle the road."

"Also?"

"I have two brothers."

"How'd you do?"

"Faster and better."

We rolled on in silence until I said, "Where we headed?"

"Kabukicho."

A chill slid down my spine. Kabukicho wasn't as lawless as rumors made it out to be, but neither was it harmless. Violence in the quarter erupted in cycles, and when a breakout occurred it could be lethal.

"This time of night, that can't be good."

"The inspector wishes to fill you in himself."

"Serious, then?"

Resolute cocoa brown eyes flashed me a look: she wasn't that easy.

I tried a different tact. "Do you like working for Kato?"

The next instant she rocketed the car around a corner with only a whisper of rubber, then met my gaze in the rearview and said yes.

"And police work?"

"I was born to it. Father, grandfather, both brothers joined the force."

"First woman?"

"Yes."

"I wonder—"

"Excuse me a second," she said, and gave a short blast of the siren, sending two doddering taxis scurrying to the side of the road like startled cockroaches.

Hoshino found me in her mirror again. "You were saying?"

"Were you in Kato's unit last fall?"

She swung into another turn, came out of it, and accelerated. "When you and he, uh, worked together? No."

"So you don't know what happened?"

"I didn't say that."

She knew.

We charged into the tunnel that ran under the tracks north of Shinjuku station, turned left, then raced past the terminal station of the Seibu–Shinjuku Line.

The streets came to life.

We had arrived.

CHAPTER 6

WE were on the edge of Tokyo's biggest adult playground.

Overhead, stacked neon signs in kanji characters jutted out from the upper stories of wafer-thin buildings. A river of light in red and blue and green washed over the windshield. Revelers wobbled down both sides of the street, talking in overloud tones, faces flushed with drink.

"A lot of people for a Thursday," I said.

"Getting a jump on the weekend."

Except for a handful of pachinko parlors, movie houses, eateries, and karaoke venues, the district slept through the day. But after nightfall thousands passed through its *izakaya* drinking spots, noodle shops, and pricey Japanese "snack bars" with attractive hostesses attached who would giggle and stroke male egos for the right price. Host bars did the same for females willing to drop some bills.

Our progress slowed to a crawl as we eased deeper into the backstreets, where the sex trade thrived. Love hotels and live shows entered the mix. As did touts for strip joints and no-panty clubs. Hookers hovered in the shadows.

Hoshino finessed the nose of the vehicle into a slender alley. The neon glow faded. Shadows crawled down the backsides of buildings. Up ahead the headlights captured the rear of a second black-and-white. Yellow crime scene tape stretched from one wall to the other with unarguable authority.

When Hoshino cut the engine, darkness swept in.

"Glad to see you're still among the living, Brodie." Inspector Kato extended his hand and we shook.

As I'd stepped from the car, he had emerged out of the night, dipping smoothly under the crime tape.

"What I can't understand is why they still let you carry a badge."

White teeth grinned from a dark face. "Who can?"

We'd met eleven months earlier over the Rikyu affair. At the time I'd been a suspect, not a friend. Kato had walnut-colored skin and wrinkles at the corner of his eyes and mouth. Outwardly, he was a bundle of disarray. No matter how well groomed he began the day, halfway through his shift he would look as though he'd been bodily ejected from an oversize clothes dryer. His attire—tonight a black trench coat and gray suit—was rumpled, and his silver hair resembled a haystack the wind had had its way with. But despite the exterior disorder, he was serenity itself. Nothing ruffled his internal meter. Before following his father into the MPD, the disheveled inspector had trained as a Buddhist monk.

Kato took a stab at deciphering my wardrobe. "Early James Dean?"

I'd thrown on dark jeans, a black T-shirt, and a black leather jacket. My clothing sensibilities would never earn me a call from one of Tokyo's hallowed fashion gurus, but I'd learned long ago that dark colors worked well with my wavy black hair and blue eyes, not to mention my ability to blend in when it came to dark alleys.

"No, lean laundry load."

He nodded. "The single-parent thing. My apologies for dragging you away from your daughter."

I said, "I'm guessing you have a good reason."

His brow crumpled. "Unfortunately, I do."

CHAPTER 7

MOTIONING me to follow, the inspector retraced his steps. I ducked under the crime scene tape, inched past the second car, and nearly stumbled over the reason for his midnight summons.

On the cobblestone lay a pulped bag of bones that had once been human.

The victim's head was pummeled beyond recognition—cheekbones smashed; nose pounded flat; eyes swollen shut. Both lips were split open like overripe fruit, and the front incisors had been knocked out. What wasn't battered and bruised was slathered with a crust of purple-brown blood.

The body belonged to a Japanese male.

It wore a suit.

Beyond that, nothing you could classify as human remained. His own mother wouldn't recognize him.

I inhaled sharply. "You don't see this too often."

"They were thorough," the inspector agreed.

The beating had been relentless, but it hadn't stopped there. Both legs had been broken, as well as the left arm.

The right arm was missing altogether.

I shot a questioning look at Kato for a clue as to why he'd dragged me out here in the middle of the night, but the inspector had grown as still as a stone Buddha.

I cast about for the missing arm. I looked up the alley toward where the MPD had set up a barricade to keep the curious at bay, then down the alley along the other side of the second car and into the shadows and crevices. Nothing.

I moved forward to get a better look, and when I turned back to the body I noticed a strip of duct tape hanging from the underside of the face, a blood-soaked sock clinging to the adhesive. A white sports sock. No brand. No stripes. No design. Generic. A down-and-dirty gag. Simple and unbeatable. Whoever had done this knew a thing or two.

The pair of patrol cars discouraged prying eyes from the back end of the crime scene, but at the front, where the alley spilled into a wider thoroughfare, neither a clutch of patrol boys nor their barrier of cones and yellow tape across the alley mouth could protect the poor soul before me from public humiliation.

Inebriated gawkers feasted. Another moment's entertainment.

The Brodie Security gig took me to some strange places. Places I didn't always want to go. Places an antiques dealer never went. Having spent five years on the edge of South Central Los Angeles and two more in a hazardous section of San Francisco until I could afford better, I was no stranger to violence. But that didn't mean I had to like it. What brought me out here tonight were obligations. They ran deep in Japan. I owed Inspector Kato big-time. And as if that weren't enough, he'd known my father, too.

"Where'd it happen?" I asked.

A beating like this took time, and the alley was too exposed. Add the relatively small blood pool around the corpse and you had a second location.

"Over there," Kato said, nodding to a shaded recess. "It goes in about ten feet. Back end of a liquor store that closed hours ago."

"Do you mind?" I asked.

The detective shook his head. In three steps I was staring down a dirty alcove leading to a rear door. More blood but no arm, no teeth. A pair of battered trashcans tucked up against a wall were all the view had to offer.

I returned to the corpse. "Once they gagged him, they had all the time in the world."

The inspector ran his fingers through his hair but said nothing.

"Find the arm?" I asked.

Kato shook his head.

"Teeth?"

Another shake.

Kato had gone quiet. His gaze was steady. His protégée stood a discreet distance behind him, watching me as intently as her boss did, eyes diving to the pavement when I flicked a look her way.

Something was off.

I said, "So how can I help?"

Kato's attention redoubled. It was open and probing. "One of those minor details we run across from time to time."

"What would that be?"

"We found your *meishi* in the dead man's wallet."

My body went cold. "My business card? Must be a mistake. I don't know this guy."

"You sure?"

Actually, that was a good question. If his own mother couldn't identify him, maybe I couldn't either. And, as far as I knew, my meishi were not passed around like trading cards—much to the detriment of my bank account and what passed for Jenny's college fund. I took a closer look. No spark of recognition had hit me on arrival, and no memory flared now.

"Well?" Kato asked.

"Don't think so," I said.

"We need more than *think*."

I squatted down for a closer inspection. The corpse reeked of fecal matter and decay. Breathing through my mouth, I peered beneath the gore. And came up with more nothing. The face was too damaged.

As I stared, I caught movement in my peripheral vision. A figure separated itself from the cops at the front of the scene and strolled our way. Plainclothes like Kato, but better dressed. By several ranks. Wearing the wide-collared tan Burberry trench coat favored by older Japanese. It was open and showing a prominent paunch.

"The gaijin give you a confirmation yet?" Burberry asked. He had a self-satisfied air and a large square head.

The foreigner bit again. The "outside person." "Gaijin" is a contraction of *gaikokujin*, which translates literally as "outside-country person." The term is observational and a lot less offensive than, say, "alien." However, the shorter form sounds faintly prejudiced, and some long-term foreign residents bristle when they hear it, even though its creation was a simple linguistic shortcut. The Japanese do not consider it offensive and I no longer took offense. I'd moved on. But it could be used in a derogatory manner if given a certain turn. And that is what I heard in Burberry's voice. He would know my name but chose "gaijin," with a disdainful spin, as if I were some lower life-form.

"You got the wallet, right?" I asked Kato.

"Better if you could ID him without it."

A night breeze lifted a fresh wave of foulness to my nostrils. I straightened, exhaling strongly to clear my lungs.

"Be better if you'd invited me for a beer instead of this," I said.

Kato shrugged. "Miura. Yoji Miura."

I felt my heart clutch in my chest. Was this some kind of joke? I scanned Kato's face. Then the new guy's. Did they know Yoji's father had just signed on with Brodie Security? That I'd seen father and son only this afternoon?

Kato's jaw was set. I looked down at the remains. They looked nothing like the man I'd met for the first time earlier today.

And then I saw him.

Yoji Miura jumped out at me. Clarified in an instant like one of those optical illusions you couldn't see a moment before. The body size, the line of the jaw, the slant of his brow. The white shirt, the red silk tie—they were all there. My face collapsed.

Could it really be him?

I extracted a credit card from my wallet, bent down, and with the corner of the plastic pushed back the sleeve of the jacket.

And there it was—one of those goddamn platinum cuff links no one wears anymore.

———

An ageless sorrow pressed in on me. How had this happened? How had I *let* it happen?

Kato watched me with a Zen-like calm.

"I'll take that as a yes," he said, a hint of sympathy riding the soft hump of his voice.

I nodded once. "Met him for the first time this afternoon. Well, yesterday now. His father hired me."

"Impressive," Burberry said. "Twelve hours after he engages your services he's fly food. You must be very good at what you do."

I felt rage swelling up inside me. There was no reason to take that from a stranger. Especially an overdressed one. If the police weren't out in force, I'd flatten the guy's nose in a second. Might still.

I rose to my full height. At six-one and a hundred ninety pounds, I towered over most Japanese, and I towered over this smug bastard. With menace.

Burberry stiffened. "Cage your pet, Kato-kun." He glared at the inspector, then stalked off.

"Who the hell was that?"

"Would have been his case if it hadn't been dumped in my lap along with the two home invasions."

"So he's gloating?"

Kato nodded, adding in a low voice, "And putting in an appearance for show. What did Miura come see you about?"

I glanced around. At Burberry, at Officer Hoshino, at the half dozen other cops within earshot. There were too many ears.

Kato read my hesitation. "The short version now, the longer later."

I frowned.

"I need it, Brodie."

My gut churned. Why hadn't we put some men on Yoji Miura? His father hadn't hinted at any danger to his son, and no one at Brodie Security had considered the possibility.

Now Yoji was dead and shouldn't be.

On my watch.

"His father hired Brodie Security to look into a personal matter," I said, an undercurrent of self-condemnation tingeing my reply.

"What kind of personal matter?"

A public hearing wouldn't do. I settled for vague. "Untoward things were happening to his old army buddies."

Kato said, "Untoward how?"

I stared dejectedly at the mangled remains of my client's son.

"Like this," I said. "And equally permanent."

And suddenly I felt impelled to reach for my mobile. I needed to find out if they'd gotten to my client, too.

CHAPTER 8

B UT Inspector Kato grabbed me before I could make the call. Seated in Hoshino's squad car, I gave him the connection between my client and the home invasions, along with the rest of it.

Staring out the windshield at the milling crowd, he considered my story. "Took their payback out on the son."

"Looks that way."

"Imagine you need to make some calls."

"Do."

He thanked me for coming, and I headed toward a main thorough-fare in search of a taxi, digging out my cell phone as I went.

With the first call I put the men guarding Akira Miura on high alert. With the second I doubled the guard, ordering the next shift in immediately. I told them all why but asked that they let me break the news to Miura Senior. They seemed relieved. The third call set in motion a telephone chain through Brodie Security personnel that would have all the principals and support staff on the case who were not watching Miura in the office by 8 a.m. With my last call I checked on my daughter. She had not stirred.

Small blessings in a storm.

Then I rang back the guard on Miura.

"Get him up and give him some coffee," I said. "I'm coming over."

I wanted a crack at my client before the police.

It wasn't supposed to be this way.

I had never imagined myself manning a desk at Brodie Security. The firm was my father's baby. He had built it from scratch four decades ago, after heading up the MP units policing American military bases around Tokyo.

Once he mustered out, he joined the LAPD, balked at the pecking order, and left to set up on his own, first in Los Angeles—until his shop collapsed due to a lack of connections—then in Tokyo, where the network from his years of service kept him afloat.

At the time, my future mother, an art curator by trade, was working for the American Red Cross in the Japanese capital, a volunteer transplant also from LA. They met, they married, I was born, and I spent seventeen years of my life in Tokyo, the only Caucasian attending the local Japanese public school, where I learned the language, the culture, and so much more.

By the age of twelve, afternoons at Brodie Security were slotted into my routine, as were four weekly sessions with two of the best martial arts masters in Tokyo, courtesy of my father's ever-expanding list of contacts.

For five years I listened to his operatives dissect cases. The conversations were raw and gritty and endlessly fascinating—yakuza blackmailers, philandering millionaires, swift-thinking cat burglars who emptied bank accounts by stealing *hanko*—the carved seals the Japanese used in place of signatures. And on and on.

At the dojos I developed a wicked karate kick and a powerful judo throw. What adolescent boy could ask for more? Then one day my mother took me into the bowels of the Tokyo National Museum, where I caught my first glimpse of Japan's glittering heirlooms, from sixteenth-century samurai armor to profound yet frisky *zenga*, aka Zen paintings, artworks composed of brisk black strokes of ink on a white ground done by enlightened Buddhist monks like Sengai.

What I saw that day woke something inside me attuned to the serene.

Which is when the roller coaster started.

My parents' marriage blew up within the month. My mother and

I were hurled back to her native LA. We landed in an edgy neighborhood bordering South Central, where three times in two days, quick-thinking strikes to my opponent's vulnerable spots stifled the aggressive probing of local gangbangers, who thereafter gave me a wide berth. Some eventually became friends.

Over the next ten years, I enrolled in the local college; refined my martial arts training; watched my mother die of intestinal cancer; moved to San Francisco; worked as a grease monkey under the hoods of other people's cars; stumbled into an apprenticeship with a local art dealer; met and married Mieko Brodie née Kuroda of Tokyo; fathered a beautiful baby girl; opened an antiques shop on my own; and woke up to the news that my new wife had died in a midnight fire while visiting her parents. Jenny was two. Then four years later—last year—my father passed on, punting half of Brodie Security in my direction, though we'd been estranged since the divorce.

It wasn't supposed to be this way.

When the roller coaster slowed, I was a man split between two occupations. Make that three—I was also a single parent. In San Francisco, I bounced between my young daughter and my struggling Japanese antiques dealership on Lombard Street. In Tokyo, I juggled trips to find inspired Japanese art for the shop with my default position as a second-generation PI.

So, at thirty-two, I led a mongrel lifestyle. In the back of my mind, art and detecting had begun to merge. With the first, I introduced works that elevated lives with the same sense of serenity I'd discovered many years before when my mother led me into the dark vaults of that vast Tokyo museum; the second allowed me to help people whose hold on life had dipped downward into disruption or devastation. Both parents were gone, but their ghosts hovered nearby, pulling me in opposite directions.

With a notable difference.

Only one of the pursuits could get me killed.

CHAPTER 9

2:10 A.M.

I GRABBED a cab to Miura's house in Koenji, a youth magnet four stops west of Shinjuku on Japan Rail's Chuo Line. The area around the station belonged to college students, artists, and musicians. Farther afield, old family homes peppered residential neighborhoods, many of the plots purchased long before the war.

I knocked lightly on Miura's door. The wiry Brodie Security operative in charge of the night watch greeted me.

"Did the son's wife call to give her in-laws the news?" I asked.

"No."

"Really? So he knows nothing?"

"No, but he's wondering."

I stepped over the threshold and exchanged my shoes for indoor footwear. Miura welcomed me into his home, worry at the edge of his smile. His place was a standard middle-class Japanese abode with white walls and chunky, building-block rooms.

Once he and his wife were comfortably seated on a brown couch with a coarse wool weave, I broke the news as gently as I could. Miura's eyes went wide with shock. Old soldier that he was, he fought valiantly, muttering "Yoji . . .Yoji" and shaking his head over and over again. His wife rose and alternately hovered over her husband in concern or darted quick glances about the room as if expecting her son to appear at any moment. She was a good fifteen years younger than her spouse, a not-uncommon arrangement in Japan, and while less frail she was far from sturdy.

About the time I thought Miura had his emotions in check, he cradled his face in his hands and fell into a silent, body-racking sob. His wife mumbled something about bringing refreshments and wandered away.

The kitchen was the other way.

I headed to the cooking quarters and opened cabinets until I found their stash. I poured a double shot of Nikka Miyagikyo fifteen-year-old single malt into a coffee mug, trooped back into the den where Miura sat, and coaxed him to drink.

He raised his head from behind moist palms, then reached for the clay vessel and sipped absentmindedly. Tears spilled down his cheeks unchecked.

"Drink it all now," I said. "No sipping."

Miura drained the mug. I splashed more in and he swallowed the second round without prodding. He sputtered, caught his breath, and fell back in his chair, exhausted. Tears still tracked down his face.

Rage tamped any sorrow I was feeling. I'd walked away from Kabukicho fuming. Yoji's death was disturbing on so many levels I didn't know where to begin. My anger had receded during the ride over, but watching my client crumble before my eyes fanned my fury all over again.

I was mad.

Mad at the police for their cavalier dismissal of Miura's claims at the outset. Mad at the fumbling and apologetic Yoji for getting himself killed. But most of all, I was mad at myself for letting someone get to my client's son.

I would find whoever did this.

———

While I waited for Miura Senior to regain control, I considered the disturbing state of his son's body.

During the five years I'd lived near South Central, I'd seen more victims of extreme violence than I could count. Battered survivors. Abused corpses. Locals tortured then shot. So I knew a thing or two about beatings.

I knew four things about this one, and all of them raised alarm bells.

First, the drubbing had been thorough and systematic, not a brainless street mauling. The Triads had wanted something from Yoji.

Second, the number of blows testified to an unnaturally high pain threshold—a level off the charts for a desk jockey. I needed to find out why.

Third, Yoji's continued resistance led to the snapping of limbs. The killers would have leveraged the pain to harvest every last shred of information they needed. All but the toughest folded here.

And fourth and most disturbing, the Triads had signed off with a trademark amputation—an unmistakable communiqué meant to warn away Yoji's confederates and anyone else who might try to follow in his footsteps.

Which meant their message was aimed my way.

CHAPTER 10

IT took nearly half an hour for Miura to recover.

I sat patiently by his side. When my charge wasn't looking, I caught a guard's eye and nodded toward the back of the house. The Brodie op went in search of the wife, returning a moment later with a shake of his head and miming sleep.

"Was it bad?" Miura asked me eventually.

"Yoji was tougher than I would have thought."

Miura absorbed the crumb about his son's last moments with a father's pride. "That's his kendo training. Went twice a week."

Which explained the severity of the beating. Kendo was a rigorous sport revitalized in the eighteenth century after a lengthy period of peace led to the deterioration of samurai fighting skills. The discipline was not without its painful moments, even with near-full-body protective gear, so kendoists developed a healthy endurance to the pounding they took from the stiff bamboo practice swords.

"I wish we'd put some people on him," I said.

Miura's eyes were watery but focused. "It's war, Brodie-san. You can never think of everything."

The old soldier was back. Resigned and philosophic. But back.

"I'm counting on you to find whoever did this," he added.

"I plan to. Tell me what Yoji knew."

"What do you mean?"

"Whoever killed him wanted information. I'm thinking Yoji knew something about China back in the day."

Miura shook his head. "He didn't know a thing."

"Maybe an item you mentioned a long time ago?"

Yoji's father was adamant. "I never told him about the old days. I've done my best to forget them."

I inhaled deeply. According to my brief exchange with Inspector Kato in the squad car, the beatings mimicked those of the home invasions. Yoji was hiding something. The problem was, clients often concealed part of the truth even as they hired you to find the rest of it.

"Maybe an item you discovered on your later trips? Or a secret that has slipped your mind?"

"You're talking spies and covert military actions, Brodie-san. I have no secrets. I served my country as an officer, then returned burdened with a shame of the things I did and saw. We Japanese enjoyed the power of conquerors one moment, then abused it the next."

I studied the man before me. The guilt he carried weighed openly on him now.

Softly I said, "Give me something."

"I've nothing to give."

"It might be small. Less obvious."

"It's the echo of war, is all. China is letting her people out again and the Triads are looking for revenge. *Sho ga nai.*"

It's unavoidable.

I looked away, suppressing my frustration. The jaunty sparkle in the eye of the man who had tottered into Brodie Security dressed to kill in his thirty-year-old suit had faded, but I wouldn't fold so easily. I would not let Yoji's death go unpunished.

"I'll find them," I said.

He smiled weakly. I saw a flash of the old spark. "I know you will. You got notches."

What, I wondered, had Yoji been hiding?

CHAPTER 11

TOKOROZAWA, 4:43 A.M.

I COMMANDEERED one of the two Brodie Security cars parked in front of Miura's home and charged through a tangle of streets out to the suburb of Tokorozawa, twenty miles northwest of Tokyo. Seven centuries ago the area had been the site of a pair of battles that brought down the first shogunate regime. Now it was a peaceful bedroom community noted primarily as the home of the Seibu Lions baseball team.

En route I called to check up on my daughter. Inspector Kato had volunteered to leave the babysitter in place until morning. Officer Kawakami confirmed that Jenny was sleeping soundly.

The navigational system brought me to a halt on a quiet residential street in front of a white clapboard two-story house. Edging a token patch of green lawn was a brick planter with red spider lilies. Around the side of the house a carport accommodated a Lexus.

All typical, all expected.

The unexpected sandbagged me inside.

———

When the front door opened, I found myself face-to-face with my police escort to the murder site: Officer Rie Hoshino, but in civilian apparel.

"Hi," she said, with a flicker of a smile. "Inspector Kato thought you might turn up."

Out of uniform, Hoshino easily overcame the unflattering restraints of the Tokyo MPD's official garb. She wore a subdued navy-blue blouse and skirt, the color bordering on black but still tastefully distant from official mourning wear. The wardrobe change affected her demeanor as well. Gone was the deadpan stare. Under short black hair curling inward, her attentive cocoa-brown eyes were a little brighter, her button nose a little friskier, and the round mature countenance of a Japanese woman in her late twenties a little warmer.

"Didn't see the patrol car out front."

"It's three blocks away, in a public lot."

"Discretion from the MPD?"

"We try."

The second surprise hit when she moved aside to let me in: a child's wheelchair, folded and secured with a bungee cord, rested against the wall behind the door. A cluster of little boy's shoes crowded the entryway where footwear was discarded. The shoes were padded with thick pediatric soles.

I frowned. "How many children?"

"Just the one. A seven-year-old son."

"That's got to be tough."

Hoshino's eyes softened. "He's been partially paralyzed from birth. Down syndrome, too. Dotes on the father."

This case got worse by the hour. "How's the wife taking it?"

Hoshino's forehead wrinkled. "Badly. She won't be comforted."

"Anything useful?"

Hoshino shook her head. "She's in shock. Maybe you could try."

I nodded and Hoshino looked grateful. She motioned for me to follow. I stepped up onto a blond-wood floor with my stockinged feet, abandoning my shoes in the slate-tiled entryway.

A pale yet attractive Japanese woman sat in a heap on a bright-red couch. Roused suddenly, she wore jeans, a rumpled blouse, and no cosmetics. But she had a natural beauty that didn't require much makeup. In her lap was a young boy with a square jaw on a square face, and an engaging smile. His head rested on the woman's chest, and stunted limbs stretched out at unnatural angles. Mrs. Miura rocked him back and forth. Deformity twisted his feet inward.

Worse and worse.

"Miura-san," Hoshino said, "this is Mr. Jim Brodie. If you wouldn't mind, he has a few questions that might help us."

Stroking the child's head with one hand, Yoji's widow gestured me to one of the matching red chairs.

"I'm extremely sorry about what has happened," I said. "I only just met your husband and your father-in-law yesterday. They hired my firm to look into some trouble Miura Senior was having."

She stiffened. "Please do not mention that man in this house."

The boy slid a thumb into his mouth.

"I'm sorry," I said, understanding dawning. Conflict with the in-laws had prevented her from reaching out to them with the news.

I glanced around, waiting a beat for her to settle down. It was a pleasant, livable space. What the Japanese labeled an LDK, a "living-dining-kitchen area." Separated by a counter, the kitchen was set against the far wall, with a petite dining table for four fronting the counter. A family room with the cheerful red couch, paired armchairs, and a wide-screen TV consumed the rest of the space.

"What did they hire you for?" Mrs. Miura asked flatly.

"They were worried about your father-in-law's well-being."

"So typical. I bet there was no discussion about my husband's safety, was there?"

"No, but—"

"I knew it. Just like *that man*. Thinking only of himself. He never wanted us to marry, I can tell you that. Turned his nose up at my family background. After Yoji's first wife died, his father set up an *omiai* with the daughter of an old friend, but Yoji chose me. When our Ken-chan was born, that man shunned his own grandson. Said Ken was proof I was tainted."

Omiai are arranged marriages, a practice still surprisingly common in Japan. Part of the process involved digging through the family history for anything unsavory. *Unsavory* applied to black sheep, less-than-reputable relatives, and anything not *just like us*.

"I'm sorry to hear that," I said, shifting uncomfortably, wondering how much the son could understand.

Lips pulsating, he sucked his thumb at a faster clip. He stared at a spot behind me. The smile was gone. Maybe he understood more than she thought. Or he'd picked up on her rising agitation.

"Listen," I said, "perhaps it's best if we don't talk in front of your child. Is there someone else here who could look after him? Or maybe Officer Hoshino could tend to him in a back room for a few minutes, if she wouldn't mind."

"Oh, don't worry. I gave him a sedative, so he'll doze off in a second. I can't really speak in front of Ken-chan. He's so sensitive, you know."

As I watched I saw the son start, then his eyelids grew heavy. He battled to stay awake, grabbing at his mother, wanting to remain with us. He tried valiantly to resist the pull of the medication, puzzled by his sudden desire to sleep, but his lids drooped and his head lulled against his mother's bosom.

I felt suddenly unclean, as if I'd witnessed something obscene.

Mrs. Miura rose. "Ken-chan demands attention every moment he's not asleep. It's exhausting, I can tell you that."

She left the room and Hoshino turned to me, a growing disquiet pooling in her eyes. "I'm glad you're here. Even with the son gone, this won't be easy."

I took advantage of the widow's absence to get a closer look at our surroundings. There were photos and, surprisingly, there was art. A pair of amateur oil paintings with Yoji's signature graced the far wall. Depictions of a local shrine and a mountain waterfall.

And, on the back wall, a third surprise: hanging on the far side of a tall cabinet was a Sengai ink painting—a Chinese cleric in robes. *Should you ever happen across one of Sengai's renderings of a Chinese monk, ring me straightaway, any time of the day or night.*

I shot up in my seat.

"What?" Hoshino asked.

I shook her off, thinking furiously.

London and now here. Dual sightings are not uncommon in the art world. When a new cache of work surfaced, you often see the same pieces in galleries across the globe for twelve to eighteen months running. After conflicts on the African continent intrude on sacred tribal lands, the same regional statuary, shields, or masks flood dealers' showrooms from Paris to San Francisco. In like manner, multiple sightings of rare Japanese art are reported more frequently than you would expect. Yoji had an affinity for art, so he might covet a Sengai. But two Sengais emerging in close chronological proximity suggested a shared source.

Mrs. Miura returned to the couch, her posture prim. "My Ken-chan has special needs, you know. Yoji was going to take care of us. He was going to take us away from all this."

Hurriedly, I shifted my glance to the nearby coffee table. On it was an array of glossy women's magazines and travel brochures. Cooking and child-rearing in the glossies. Island getaways in the pamphlets. The Seychelles. Tahiti. St. Maarten. Smiling couples frolicked in crystalline blue waters or strolled along pristine white sands.

Mrs. Miura's look trailed mine. "We were planning to treat ourselves to a tiny vacation, if you must know. What can I do for you, Mr. Brodie? As you can see, I have my hands full." A cold formality descended with her words.

"I was wondering if I could look around. Check Yoji's desk, if he has one."

"Look around? Where were you last night? You were only looking after that man. Never mind my Yoji! Never mind us! So typical! Aren't you ashamed of yourself?"

"I've been kicking myself for not—"

"Will your *looking around* feed us? Will it get Ken-chan his medicine and his day care? Yoji was so attentive. Now who's going to take care of us? Who?"

I switched gears, hoping to salvage the visit. "Could you at least tell me where you got the Sengai?"

"Are you insane? You think Yoji's stupid ink painting from China will help? Get out. Get out of my house and don't ever come back!"

Mrs. Miura shifted in her seat, wrapped her arms around herself, and tuned us out. She glared at the far wall as if the world had collapsed on her head and we were the agents of that collapse.

Exiting the house, I took my time examining a collection of photographs in the entry hall. It was all I was going to get.

There was a shot of the three of them on a picnic under cherry blossoms. There was a shot of Yoji among a group of twenty-odd men and women in kendo regalia, helmets tucked under their arms, a mammoth trophy cradled in the team captain's arms. Overhead, a banner in Japanese read NAKAMURA KENDO CLUB. There was a shot of Ken and Yoji at a water park, Ken splashing around happily, Yoji watching with a parent's attentiveness, an empty wheelchair resting at the edge of the pool.

In all the photos Ken-chan had that endearing, joyful smile Down kids often exhibit. He was a happy child. In more than one picture, his parents posed with silly grins on their faces, as if their son had coaxed the smiles from them.

Maybe the wife was right. Maybe it had all collapsed.

Then I glanced again at Yoji in his kendo garb and thought, *Go where the violence is.*

CHAPTER 12

WITH her next breath the widow threw Hoshino out as well. The two of us stood on the stoop.

"That could have gone better," I said in Japanese.

"She's hysterical. A kid to feed and no husband."

"Going to be hard." We commiserated over the family's plight for a moment, then I said, "You have time for coffee?"

Hoshino looked at her watch. "My shift's been pushed back two hours so I could catch some sleep. Not enough time for that now, so yes."

"Strong brew?"

"Jet fuel should power me through. Inspector Kato gave me a message for you, but coffee first."

"Fair enough," I said. "You know, I was thinking, the Miuras could be hurting financially."

"What makes you say that?"

"Yoji liked to treat himself. Platinum cuff links, silk ties, expensive cars. That's a high-end Lexus in the carport."

"Don't forget the tropical vacation."

"Lay the pricey toys and trip over a mortgage, a son with special needs, and a modest salary, what's that get you?"

"Financial headaches?"

I nodded. "Five'll get you ten he spent his way into a hole and borrowed badly."

"You mean the legal loan sharks?"

"Or worse, yeah."

I drank my cappuccino. "And the message?"

We'd settled for chain-store caffeine at the local Doutor coffeehouse in the center of Tokorozawa's awakening *shotengai*, a long narrow lane of stores on the north side of the station that once housed traditional shops like tatami makers and futon sellers but now leaned toward game centers and cell phone purveyors.

"The inspector requested that you pass along any information you think might help with the home invasions."

"Not a problem. Goes both ways, right?"

Hoshino sipped some of her latte. "Unofficially, yes. You're to go through me. He's assigned me to the case."

"Dreams do come true."

She ignored the comment. "He also said, 'Two-way streets are not always toll-free.'"

"Did he expand on that?"

"No."

I nodded, knowing the words were a warning of possible danger down the road.

Her brow wrinkled. "Oh, and he wanted me to apologize for the chief inspector's behavior."

The overstuffed Burberry.

"Appreciate it."

As we spoke, I could see Hoshino weighing the pros and cons of moving beyond official matters. Even if she chose not to, I'd already learned quite a bit about her. She was a fighter, although, like the best of Japan's rising female workforce, she hid it artfully under a soft exterior. She knew when to press, and when to pull back, which was not a gender-specific talent but more vital for the upwardly mobile Japanese woman. What she lacked in experience she made up for with a passionate and forceful feminine doggedness, also sufficiently concealed. I had sensed her tenacity immediately. Hoshino worshipped at the altar of Stubborn, which had long ago been seared into the Brodie gene pool.

"I'll tell him," she said. "He also mentioned you lived in California but didn't say much more than that."

"In San Francisco. I sell Japanese antiques there."

"Why Japanese?"

"I like them. A lot. They are refined and well crafted. The best pieces have a distilled serenity I can't get enough of."

"I've been to California. I did a three-week situational with the LAPD."

"So you speak English?"

"No. I watched and listened and said *thank you* all day long. I saw how American cops handle crime scenes. Muggings. Couple of shootings. A convenience store robbery in progress."

"How'd you end up going? An overseas tour must be a departmental plum."

She hesitated.

I said, "What?"

"I'm one of three chosen 'poster women' for the force. I detest the idea but I had no choice."

"How hard are they trying to equalize things?"

She shrugged. "More women are being hired, but progress is glacial. They'll let the three of us climb a little higher, which I plan to do with or without their help."

"If you don't like it, why not step off the pedestal?"

"Because you take every chance you can get and drive yourself twice as hard and twice as long as the men. And of course you've got to out-think them."

"Is it working?"

"I thought so. Then a few months ago my boss tried to marry me off."

I raised an eyebrow. "Why?"

"I'd uncovered a vital clue in a floundering case. When he called me to his office, I was expecting at least a verbal commendation. He praised my effort then he asked if I would allow him to act as my *na-kodo*."

A nakodo is the matchmaker for an omiai, the same arranged marriage ritual Miura's widow had railed against. It involves a series of meetings between two single people to see if they are compatible.

I was incredulous. "You helped break a case under his command and he wanted to ease you out? Whose ego did you bruise?"

She studied me with a new appreciation. "All of my male coworkers. None of us found anything initially, but one of the witnesses looked nervous so I hung around until his shift ended, then invited him out for a cup of coffee."

"Twice as hard?"

She nodded. "I got him away from his bosses, where he could talk more freely. Then I applied a pinch of pressure and promised I would not implicate him."

"Clever."

"The detectives on the case were overjoyed and treated me to an expensive tempura dinner. In his arrogance my boss never imagined I'd dare say no to his request to play matchmaker. He'd already boasted to 'my future father-in-law,' a high-ranking bureaucrat over at the Police Agency, how good a catch I was and how I'd been properly 'shaped' under his command. My marriage was to be a career move for my boss. When I rejected the offer, they all lost face, so I was transferred to Inspector Kato's section."

"Siberia within the MPD."

Kato's talent was fabled among cops and private badges alike, though rarely acknowledged by his superiors. He was a soft-spoken, second-generation detective who had embarrassed his colleagues by solving too many cases. Ingenious police bureaucrats hammered down the protruding nail by promoting the assistant inspector sideways and giving him his own section staffed with officers tossed in the doghouse. Punishment inside the department became a temporary rotation into Kato's crew. The would-be Zen monk had shrugged it off, and his reputation only grew.

"Inspector Kato's a genius. I'm learning so much from him."

Before I could reply, my cell chirped. I read the display tag. "Excuse me. I have to take this. You're going to want to listen in."

I hit speaker mode. "Hi, Graham."

I'd rung him from Yoji's front porch, but he hadn't picked up.

The dealer's irritation kicked in immediately. "When I grant permission to ring me twenty-four/seven, 'judicious' is the unspoken qualifier."

"Remember that pint of beer you mentioned? Now's the time."

"Surely you jest."

"A second Sengai sighting less than an hour ago."

"Actual Chinese monks?"

"The proverbial robed ones."

Graham was quiet for a long spell. "And I thought the rumors were rubbish."

"What have I found?"

"You sitting?"

"Yeah."

"Strap in, then. You've heard of Yamashita's gold and all the treasure the Japanese looted from Asia during the war years, right?"

"Everyone has."

The legend involves billions in art, gems, and other precious artifacts stolen from China and a dozen more Asian countries. Supposedly, special Japanese military units plundered at will, some led by aristocrats and members of the imperial family. The rumor had it that billions were shipped back to Japan and more billions left for later retrieval in a string of hiding places. To secure the secrets, the conscripted Japanese engineers and others lower down the pecking order were eliminated when they least expected it—a bullet to the head, entombment in the caves with the treasure, or being tossed overboard when they shipped out.

"Well, this concerns the portion of the valuables handed back to Pu Yi. They needed him to appear regal on all fronts."

The Last Emperor again. "You're talking about a lost treasure?"

"Precisely."

"And you know of this how?"

"During a buying trip to Hong Kong about five years ago, someone was shopping Pu Yi's collection, using the lesser pieces as calling cards. The Sengais and some tea bowls. It sounded like a con to me. Might still be. But if it's true, your find makes me think our London piece is another, even without the Chinese monks."

"The timing supports the idea. What kind of treasure are we talking about?"

"Select pieces chosen from a portion of what the Qing rulers and their lot had amassed during its last three hundred years before their collapse began in 1911. Thousands of trunks of the stuff floated around the country during the war years. The Nationalist party escaped with well over three thousand crates to Taiwan, which was said to be, well, if not a fraction of the total, a smallish amount."

"What about the content?"

"A pinch of the imperial Qing collection was funneled back to the Last Emperor's coffers. The Chinese side of the equation consists of imperial jades, porcelains, and scroll paintings from the Forbidden City. Plus the items Pu Yi managed to escape with to Manchuria. On the Japanese side, gifts from Emperor Hirohito and other Japanese admirers. Jewelry for the empress, golden goblets, gems, trinkets, classic samurai swords of the highest caliber, scroll paintings from the palace collection, and more."

"Jesus."

"Yes, an impressive list."

"Anybody give you a price tag?"

"The jungle telegraph put it at forty to eighty million dollars."

I felt my heart rate accelerate. In the art business, every once in a while you get a whiff of a pot of gold. It's always just out of reach and arrives on the tail of the most outrageous rumors. Which is where it usually dies.

But this time the tall tales were backed by two Sengais—and perhaps Yoji's death. But why were the Zen monk's works tangled up in this?

Graham read my thoughts. "For the record, the Sengai pieces were supposedly gifts from a top Japanese diplomat who was an art lover and thought the theme would please Pu Yi."

"Makes a hell of a lot of sense," I said.

"I should warn you that there's an unsavory side. *Tameshigiri* is involved. Did I pronounce it correctly?"

"Yes," I said, feeling something clutch at my throat as I watched the color drain from Hoshino's face.

Graham sighed. "The practice involves testing a Japanese saber on human targets, does it not? Sometimes *live* human targets?"

The term also encompassed testing on inanimate objects, like rolled tatami mats, but that was not where my London friend was heading. I confirmed his query with a one-syllable response that barely escaped my lips. This was creepy stuff.

"I feared as much," Graham said. "Emperor Hirohito sent some classic imperial swords to his 'cousin' Pu Yi as a token of their shared lineage. Under the pretense of a tribute, the Japanese army insisted on showcasing the superiority of this weaponry to the Last Emperor, who of course was all but captive in his elegant mansion."

Hoshino sunk deeper into her seat and I said, "How could anyone know all that?"

"The people shopping the package claimed documentation of the so-called handing-over ceremony accompanies the treasure. Diagrams, notations, photographs. There are decapitations."

A shudder shook my frame. I could find no words but Graham's voice filled the void admirably:

"Here's the hitch on which *everything* hinges, Brodie. Did the Sengai you saw in Tokyo come from China or Japan?"

Are you insane? You think Yoji's stupid ink painting from China will help? Get out. Get out of my house and don't ever come back here again!

"China."

"Then you've sighted the whale, my boy. An actual bloody whale."

CHAPTER 13

BRODIE SECURITY, SHIBUYA, 8:20 A.M.

I COULDN'T shake the image of Yoji's distraught wife rocking her son in her lap. Even though she'd thrown me out. Maybe *because* she'd thrown me out.

With each passing hour my rage only grew. I was furious at myself for dropping the ball, and livid at the unknown assailants who had destroyed Yoji and his family.

So I opened the meeting at Brodie Security by doubling the man-power on the case, even though we couldn't justify charging Miura for more than a fraction of the extra expense. Fireworks erupted and my proposal was gunned down by the staff with a vengeance.

It didn't matter that I owned half the company. The firm was their livelihood. Collectively, they had a vested interest in two things: keeping me alive, because Brodie Security distinguished itself from the crowd with an American president—an indication of overseas expertise—and keeping the company running. A sign of the first had surfaced when the employees corralled Yoji after he showed up on our doorstep in a vaguely threatening manner.

The second flared up with my wanting to increase the footprint of the Miura case. The move would strain Brodie Security's financial un-derpinnings, which remained tenuous at the best of times.

I countered with a detailed rendition of the Kabukicho murder scene, listing the condition of the body in excruciating detail, my face flushed, my words heated.

Noda stepped in with a counterpunch. "*You* work the case."

I'd already lobbed the idea of handing off the Miura file to him, and he'd just lobbed it right back.

Hamada chimed in. "We don't need five or six more people. One extra body would even out the workload."

Hamada smiled as he offered up his comment. Unlike Noda, an abrasive lone wolf, Hamada was a social creature. Ex-cop though he was, he lived to cook and eat, hence a pudgy body expanding by noticeable increments. And the pudgy nose. Most of us had been over to his house for a rooftop barbecue and met his wife and twin teenage sons, who, like their father, had ready smiles.

"But a *live* body," someone at the back called out.

Group laughter broke the tension, and I acquiesced, trapped by my own obsession.

I said, "I know it's been less than a day, but do we have anything? Hamada, any news on the Triads?"

"Feelers out but nothing in yet."

Noda gave me a curious look.

"How about from the police?" I asked.

"Have a sit-down at three this afternoon," another op called out.

"Okay, get what you can but no need to push it since Inspector Kato's going to keep me in the loop."

He nodded. I faced my wild card. "Noda, where are you?"

"Poking around the edges."

Edges. Why should the eternally cryptic detective change his habits for this case?

I turned back to Hamada and asked for his interpretation of the Triad's final gesture.

"Chopping off the arm? 'Stay away.' 'Don't do it again.' 'Keep your mouth shut.' 'We're watching.' Take your pick."

"Maybe all four," Noda said.

"Might be," Hamada conceded.

"So, a pile of speculation but no facts," I said. "All right. I'm done. Anyone else?"

The room was quiet.

"That's it, then," I said. "If I'm missing something, tell me. Be frank. We all know I'm new at this."

Hamada shook his head. "This case is pretty straightforward. You've tagged all the bases."

"*Almost* all the bases," Noda mumbled, sliding me another look.

————

The staff dispersed but Noda hung back.

I wanted the senior detective to explain his last comment, but I addressed another need first. "Got a question for you. Should I have covered the son?"

My guilt over Yoji's death swelled by the minute.

Noda shrugged. "Man called his father nuts."

"Yeah, so?"

"So he had no clue they might come for him."

"The guy's got a seven-year-old with Down syndrome and I'm guessing medical bills that go to the moon."

"At fifty-five?"

"Second marriage. Is there any way we can fast-track this?"

Noda gave me the look again.

"What?" I said.

"You won't like it."

"I will if it'll help."

"No, you won't."

"Spit it out."

He shrugged. "People I know who work with Triads won't talk to me about it. They're afraid. But *you* know someone who will."

My impatience ballooned. When Brodie Security's chief detective grew verbose—and for him, three full sentences was a filibuster—there was usually a zinger attached. But this time I saw none. Noda was mistaken.

"Don't think so, Noda."

The detective's voice was flat when he spewed out a nickname I'd tried to forget. "Tokyo no Tekken."

My blood turned to ice. Damn if he wasn't right. My connections with the underworld and other unsavory types were stronger in LA and San Francisco than they were in Japan. Not out of choice but because in California I'd been forced to live in less-desirable neighborhoods for seven years. But events on these shores had yielded a few affiliations, including the one Noda mentioned.

The only problem was that Tokyo no Tekken was a stone-cold killer.

CHAPTER 14

TOKYO *no Tekken*—TNT for short—translated roughly as "Iron Fist of Tokyo." When people first heard either one, they thought the tag was the overblown nickname of a celebrity boxer or a K-1 fighter. Someone with a colorful or cheesy career, and harmless outside the ring.

But they would be wrong on all counts.

It was the moniker bestowed on a yakuza enforcer who had earned his own file cabinet down at police headquarters. *Yakuza* meaning Japanese mafia, of course. Eleven months ago I'd run head-on into both of his fists and almost didn't live to see the next sunrise. Miraculously I survived, and in a surreal turn of events, TNT ended up in my debt. Between us was an uneasy understanding.

I found his card, a plain white rectangle with eleven digits printed in the center. No name, no address, no affiliation, no logo. Just the numbers. I punched in the string of figures and waited.

The phone rang three times, then three more. On the seventh ring the gruff voice I knew well answered. Involuntarily, my body tensed.

"Yeah?"

"You know who this is?" I said in Japanese.

I spoke long enough to give him a recognizable sound bite so we wouldn't need to exchange names. You never knew who was listening.

A beat later he said, "Yeah."

"Long time."

"Yeah."

"Need to meet."

"How soon?"

"Soon."

He cupped a hand over the receiver and a muffled conversation ensued on the other end. He came back on. "Tomorrow after dark, around eleven. I'll send a car."

"Tonight's no go?"

"I'm in Kyushu. Flying back in the morning."

I rolled my eyes. He probably wanted to sleep in after his return. Yakuza are creatures of the night. They don't rise until three or four in the afternoon most days.

I said, "Then a bar across town in Ueno?"

"No, I'm moving around. Only way I can do it on short notice is you come to me. I'll send a car. House or office?"

"Not necessary. I—"

"House or office?"

He wanted to control the meet from the outset and I wished to avoid just that. But considering the request came from my side, I had little choice.

"House," I said. "I'm off Meiji Street near—"

His laugh was a raw bark. "I see you ain't learned nothing. House it is," he said, and disconnected.

Good thing the yaki enforcer was on my side.

Apparently, he knew where I lived.

CHAPTER 15

'D timed my arrival perfectly.

Yet the moment I strolled into the dojo something felt wrong.

The *kendoka*, as kendo practitioners were called in Japanese, were in full battle gear and prepared for combat. A dozen pairs of fencers faced off, bamboo swords ready at their side, one eye on Nakamura-sensei, the other on their opponent. More than a few heads turned in my direction.

An hour earlier, I'd taken up a post across the street from the Nakamura Kendo Club in a coffee shop. I watched a steady stream of students enter, starting around seven thirty for a special eight-o'clock session, a semiannual contest among the dojo's best fighters.

Passing through the front door at eight twenty, I'd found the entry hall deserted. I slipped into the men's locker room. A straggler was still dressing in the far corner. Around his waist he'd secured a belt of five protective flaps that hung down to cover his lower body to mid-thigh. The belt went over the *hakama*, the pleated trousers of the kendo uniform. Over the happi-coat-shaped *keigo-ki* shirt, he affixed a lacquered chest protector. Last would come a helmet fitted with two padded wings that floated above the shoulders and a throat guard that hung down from the chin.

Sensing my presence, he turned, but I eased behind a row of lockers before he could catch a glimpse of me.

"Who's there?"

Without a sound, I worked my way to the end of the row and slipped behind the endcap.

"Hello?"

The moment passed, he finished dressing, and left.

Once alone, I moved quickly through the room. Name cards were slotted into thin brass frames near the top of each locker. I found Yoji Miura's unit two rows in, secured with a single-dial padlock through the handle. I memorized the location, flipped open the latch of a nearby window, then shifted over a can of air freshener on the sill to hide the open hardware.

Duty done, I headed for the dojo. Nakamura-sensei stood in the center of the far wall, a small but imposing figure with a gaunt face and silver hair. He was dressed in full kendo regalia, sans helmet, and radiated a quiet inner strength that came from decades practicing the Way of the Sword.

The next instant he barked a command in Japanese and the combatants pivoted, gave the ritual thirty-degree bow to him, then turned back to their opponents and offered a shallower bow, eyes locked and alert.

The fighters raised their bamboo swords—*shinai*—straight out in front of them with the tips pointing at their adversaries' throats.

The sensei issued a second order and the bouts commenced.

The crisp smack of bamboo on bamboo echoed throughout the hall. Shaft tapped shaft. Swordsmen probed with staccato movements, seeking weakness and the slightest advantage. Once they found a hole in their rival's defense, they issued a blood-curdling cry of attack and advanced, batting away their partner's shinai and going for one of the four target areas—crown, abdomen, wrist, or throat.

One kendoka immediately made his presence felt. He glided over the floor, his movements fluid and ghostlike. With lightning speed he sluiced forward for the kill, crashing his sword down on the other fencer's head with such force, the recipient staggered and fell.

A referee's white flag went up, awarding a point.

The victor grinned, bowed, and turned his back on his victim.

The fallen combatant didn't rise.

As concerned observers edged toward the prone figure, I heard a voice at my ear say, "That was an outside fighter challenging our dojo. The lesson he learned tonight is, never tangle with the Nakamura Kendo Club."

I hadn't noticed the speaker's approach.

CHAPTER 16

TURNED to find a suited fighter in my blind spot.

"Are you Mr. Brodie?" he asked in Japanese, his helmet tucked under his arm.

The defeated fencer had not stirred. Concerned looks spread. Nakamura-sensei went to attend the stricken man himself.

"Yes," I said, removing my eyes reluctantly from the scene unfolding before me.

I'd called ahead and been granted permission to observe the extra-curricular session. I'd hoped to be left alone, but suspected the Japanese sense of propriety would kick in.

"Sensei is busy, as you can see, so let me guide you to your seat."

"Thank you."

Kendo students not engaged in combat kneeled in formal positions at the edges of the dojo, legs tucked under them, blades at their sides. They lined two sides of the gym. A clutch of observers in street clothes sat along the third side, probably friends and family invited to watch the tournament. My guide led me to a spot between two other men dressed in full kendo regalia.

"This is Tanaka-sensei, seventh *dan*, one of our most dedicated ken-doka, and Kiyama-san, fifth dan. Our head sensei achieved eighth dan three years ago."

"Impressive," I said.

Today the eighth rank is the highest attainable belt—and that is a nearly superhuman feat. Only the legendary Moriji Mochida, who even in his seventies penetrated the defense of challengers decades younger with inexplicable ease, had attained tenth dan.

Tanaka and Kiyama sat like everyone else, with their legs tucked under them. Each pivoted slightly and bowed formerly in my direction, palms flat on the wooden dojo floor in front of their knees. Not sure of the protocol in kendo, I contented myself with bowing deeply from a standing position, then took the indicated seat between them.

My guide left us and Tanaka-sensei said, "We're to answer any questions you might have."

"Thank you," I said again.

"I was told you deal in Japanese art in the States. Is that true?"

To pave the way, I'd given my antiques and martial arts credentials, considering the last my passport to entry. Since Japanese police cadets train in either judo or kendo, if not both, judo is almost a kissing cousin to kendo. Yet Tanaka zeroed in on the art.

"Yes. I sell mostly Japanese, with a smattering of European and other Asian. Scroll paintings, ceramics, prints. Like that."

"Do you carry Japanese swords?"

His eyes lit up as the words left his lips and I saw the familiar fervor of a collector on the prowl.

"Sorry, I only stock *tsuba*."

Tsuba are the decorated sword guards that slide over the tang of the sword, separating the handle from the blade.

I mentioned three dealers I turned to when the rare request for Japanese steel came my way. Tanaka knew them all, and I glimpsed the same recognition in his companion's look.

Which didn't surprise me. Japanese sword collectors are a passionate lot, and the object of their enthusiasm is the strongest man-made blade on earth. The number of sword fanciers is legion. Outside Japan, they encompass businessmen, financiers, Hollywood moguls, martial arts practitioners, military enthusiasts, Japanophiles, anime fans, weapons collectors, policemen, soldiers, knife fanciers, gamers, IT pros, and more. But most worshippers have no interest in any art beyond their beacons of shiny metal. Which was why I didn't carry them.

Tanaka-sensei mentioned a few pieces in his collection and I commented on their rarity.

"So you know swords?" he asked.

"Just enough to get me in trouble."

Tanaka laughed appreciably. "A modest fellow. I like that. I forgot to ask you how you know Miura."

My questioner was a tall, dark-skinned Japanese with narrow eyes and a nose so low as to look almost nonexistent from a distance. Kiyama's skin was almond-colored, his face long and flat.

"Business," I said vaguely.

Tanaka nodded, not wishing to pry. "Miura and the two of us go way back. We were in the same college kendo club. Miura was the same age as me and held a rank one under mine. Kiyama-kun here is three years younger, but is sadly struggling two ranks below, at the fifth dan."

Kiyama reddened noticeably. Tanaka didn't look at all sad about his protégé's inability to rise to a higher position.

I said, "Thirty years of kendo? Did Miura keep it up?"

"We all did. Yoji was a busy man. Too busy, I always told him. But even with the work handicap, he managed to capture sixth dan."

Tanaka-sensei's eyes shifted briefly to Kiyama in another subtle dig.

An ambulance crew rushed though the doors of the dojo, toting a portable gurney. They swiftly examined the stricken fighter, shifted him to the emergency stretcher in one practiced movement, and whisked him away.

Neither Tanaka nor Kiyama paid any attention to the departing warrior.

———

Tanaka took the conversation in a different direction.

"Do you mind if we talk swords?"

He spoke softly so only the three of us could hear.

"Not at all."

Kiyama smiled but said nothing, content to let his superior by rank and age speak for the both of them. A wallflower kendoka.

"You must run across some Japanese swords in America from time to time because, well, of the confiscation programs after the war. Many American soldiers took them home as souvenirs."

"People bring them into my shop on occasion."

Tanaka's eyes brightened. "I thought so. I've given up on finding *koto* by Masamune or Muramasa, but I have most of the *shinto*, *shin-shinto*, *gunto*, and *gendaito* slots in my collection filled. My *shin-shinto* section could be stronger, though."

Tanaka had just rattled off the full gamut of sword types, from oldest to newest. The names translate as "old swords," "new swords," "new-new swords," "military swords," and "contemporary swords." Tanaka sought old swords from two of Japan's most famous swordsmiths.

"I might be able to fill in a gap or two of the newer blades, if you're patient," I said.

"You wouldn't happen to have a koto from Masamune or Muramasa in a back room, would you?"

Kiyama and I laughed. Tanaka was only asking about every sword collector's Holy Grail.

"Believe me," I said. "I wish I did."

When peace took hold in the samurai world at the beginning of the 1600s, the koto gave way to the new sword. What was "new" was its shape, which became more elegant and a shade less practical, since the weapon inched toward ceremonial. However, as cutting tools they were still deadly, and they came back into use decades later when the shogun reinstated kendo to bolster his depleted fighting force. The new sword in turn fell to the new-new sword, many of the influential smiths inspired technically and spiritually by their koto predecessors.

"Is there even the slightest chance such a koto might come your way?"

"None whatsoever," I said. "But if one did, is there any chance you could afford it?"

The price for a signed koto blade ranges from four thousand to three hundred thousand dollars, depending on the swordsmith, rarity, condition, and quality. Common specimens of a lower grade are available, but as soon as a collector reaches for anything with a cherished pedigree, the fees jump to fifty grand, a hundred, and beyond. For a weapon forged by either of the two Big Ms, the sky's the limit, if and when they come on the market. That said, the bottom line was this: old blades fashioned before the seventeenth century are prized above all others.

"None whatsoever," he replied in turn, and we all laughed again.

"Perhaps I might impose on you to let me know the next time someone walks into your shop with anything significant."

Trading in swords wasn't my favorite endeavor but I still needed to put food on the table.

"I could do that," I said.

The combatants returned to the dojo floor and took their positions for the second round.

Tanaka singled out a pair. "Keep your eyes on Arato and Motoyoshi. The two best fencers in the dojo. Motoyoshi's sharp but doesn't have the killer instinct. Arato's got the reflexes of a cobra." Tanaka leaned toward me with a grin. "And a wicked final stroke."

I nodded. Arato was the dueler who had defeated the visiting swordsman.

Tanaka's voice dropped another notch. "Speaking of battle, I have two swords with test-cutting inscriptions." He gave me a knowing smile.

My breath caught in my throat. The implication was unsettling. To prove the sharpness of a blade, test cuttings were conducted. Which meant tameshigiri—the same technique of slicing up the human body that Graham had mentioned with great hesitation in relation to the Last Emperor and the Japanese army.

The testing involved human cadavers or criminals sentenced to death. Warriors with good connections could have their newly acquired blades tested by authorities in the field, while other samurai were forced to sneak out late at night and chop down an unsuspecting peasant or a townsman out carousing. When an official test cutting was performed, the result—perhaps "one body cut through the torso"—was inscribed on the haft, along with the name of the samurai who performed the test, say, a well-known fencing instructor or even an official executioner.

"You're sure they're actual test-cutting inscriptions and not forgeries?"

"Yes. You come across anything like that?"

Inwardly, I cringed. Living bones are soft, and a skilled swordsman could cut through them with little or no damage to his weapon. So well known was this fact that there's a tale—true or not, it's hard to tell—of a thief who remarked to his executioner that, had he known he would be put to death with a sword, he would have eaten some stones just to damage the blade.

"No, sorry," I lied.

Actually, I had. But my policy was to politely refuse swords inscribed with test-cutting testimonials.

"Too bad. I have swords with proven two- and three-body cuts, but I need a four. I'd pay well."

"You interested in test cutting too?" I asked Kiyama.

He shook his head. *Good. Normalcy prevails in some quarters*, I thought.

Out on the floor the second round of bouts began. Kendoka leapt into action. Arato and Motoyoshi exchanged sharp slaps of their shinai, advancing and retreating in equal measure. Motoyoshi resisted a head feint, then deflected a fresh charge from Arato and attacked in turn without success. Behind their grilled masks, the eyes of each fencer burned with determination.

For five minutes, strikes were given and parlayed, then I saw Motoyoshi's stance weaken. He'd run out of steam. Arato sensed it in the same instant. Quick as a snake, he darted in, flicking Motoyoshi's weapon aside with a fierce slap, then pressed in for a strike to the crown of the head. The referee awarded a point.

Tanaka said, "That's the best scrimmage I've seen all year!"

There was a commotion on the floor and Kiyama leaned forward.

"What's happening?" I asked.

Tanaka frowned. "The judges have gathered."

Kendo has a philosophy. In seeking to perfect your fighting technique you are also seeking to perfect yourself, improving day by day, weeding out personal inadequacies and developing humility, courtesy, awareness, and largeness of spirit.

In addition, matches are often judged with an eye on the long game. Can you keep your composure under pressure? Are you able to stay aware, collected, dignified? The ideal state of readiness for the winning warrior of old, so the theory went, was a blend of spiritual detachment and attuned fighting skills. Many believed that if a warrior's mental attitude was flawed, he would eventually be cut down in battle.

The judge raised his red flag, indicating a penalty for Arato and a default win for Motoyoshi.

Tanaka was disgusted. "You see that! They're signaling Arato attacked with 'improper spirit.' He gave in to the quick temptation for a score. But you know what? In a real battle, the blade would have cleaved the skull in two and his opponent would be dead."

Never tangle with the Nakamura Kendo Club.

Which, unfortunately, was what I was about to do.

CHAPTER 17

A S I watched the front of the dojo from my window seat in an *aka-chochin* across the street, my cell phone vibrated.

On the other end of the line, Brodie Security's computer whiz said, "Found what I could."

An *aka-chochin* is a classic "red lantern"–style Japanese pub-slash-eatery in which the after-work crowd can unwind. The menu usually offers yakitori, grilled fish, and other snacks, along with a wide range of alcoholic fortification.

"You get the birthday for the son?" I asked, cupping my hand over the mouthpiece so my voice wouldn't disturb nearby customers.

"Everyone's. You'll have five in all. Plus anniversaries, home and office addresses, mobiles and landlines, national health insurance policies, credit cards, passports, cars, driver's licenses."

"It'll take the whole night to run all those numbers."

"I only hope it's in there."

My order arrived. Yakitori, a whole grilled Pacific saury, and a beer.

"Thanks, Mari. Anything easy to remember?"

"No. All random."

"Why should we be so lucky? You have a guess?"

"I like any of the birthdays. Or his wedding anniversary."

"I'll try those first, then."

Mari hesitated before she said, "Be careful, okay?"

Seconds after we disconnected, Mari's text came through. On my cell I now had the most likely numbers in Yoji Miura's life that he might tap for a locker combination. If I couldn't find the sequence on Mari's list, I wouldn't get into the locker.

Which I desperately wanted to do.

Lockers are private out-of-the-way spaces. A poor man's safety deposit box. People are known to put things in them they don't want others to see. A spouse, child, or coworker cannot accidentally stumble on a secret in a school or gym locker.

I dug into the fish and had some beer. My phone buzzed a second time, and when I answered a voice with an English accent said, "This a bad time?"

"I have a minute. What's up?"

"You're whispering. Tell me there's a pretty lass next to you in bed and you dearly wish not to wake her."

"Not this time, Graham. Sorry to disappoint."

"Then it's the other, right?"

"The other?"

"One of your exploits. You have an admirable facility for attracting the unsavory. I live vicariously through your escapades, Brodie."

My British dealer friend was a notorious wallflower. Like Kiyama, the quiet kendoka I'd just met. The guy hadn't spoken a word the whole time I was in the dojo. Graham Whittinghill suffered from the same affliction. Suffocatingly modest, self-deprecating, and shy. At art gatherings he accomplished what needed doing, but outside of work he dropped the conversational ball every time. It was a wonder he'd found a wife.

"I promise to work on it. What's up?"

"A shocker, I'm afraid. The Sengai's been nicked."

"*What?*"

A few patrons looked around and I bobbed my head in a half nod of apology, then lowered my voice. "Is this connected to the treasure?"

"Could be. I don't know."

"We still talking about the rogue dealer you mentioned?"

Graham sighed. "He's an uncouth lad, our Jamie Kendricks."

"It's a shame. I wanted to see the piece."

"Well, the owner emailed me a photo earlier in the day. I'll send it to your mobile as soon as we're off."

"Please," I said.

At the dojo, the interior lights went out. "Listen, I have to go."

"Right. My apologies for the ongoing madness."

We disconnected and a moment later my phone hummed with an incoming photograph. The Sengai was brilliant.

The work was of the quality artists dream of painting, dealers dream of finding, and collectors dream of owning. It was all I could have hoped for and the best effort by the playful monk to come on the market in years.

Which reinforced the lost treasure theory. A Japanese diplomat would present nothing less than a top-notch piece to the Manchurian emperor. Even a bought-and-paid-for emperor.

Unfortunately, it was in the wind and pointing toward much more on the horizon.

But where? And what?

At ten minutes after eleven the kendo sensei exited the dojo, followed by his second-in-command. Both were in street clothes. The sensei waited patiently while his assistant locked up, then they bowed to each other and headed in opposite directions. Tanaka and Kiyama had gone home twenty minutes earlier.

I paid my bill, left the shop, and strolled across the road, then slipped into a narrow passage between the club and the futon shop next door. With less than twenty inches between the buildings, I was forced to turn sideways to inch by pipes and cantilevered air-conditioning units.

The window was still unlocked. I hoisted myself up, raised the windowpane, and let myself down with barely a sound. Pulling out an LED penlight four times more powerful than most flashlights, I headed toward Yoji's locker.

I thumbed up Mari's list on my phone, and with the slim LED tube between my lips turned the dial of the combination lock, starting with the son's birthday. It didn't work.

Was Yoji a romantic? I tried his wife's birthday. Still no go. I fed in their anniversary date. Nothing. A loyal son? I keyed in both his parents' birth dates and their anniversary, all numbers he should also know. The lock didn't budge. Then I gave the far-too-obvious a spin—Yoji's own birthday—and the shackle fell open.

Christ, Yoji, could you be more simple-minded? Or naive? Or were you a little more self-involved than you let on, with your neckties and fancy accessories?

The kendo lockers were tall to accommodate the swords. Yoji's uniform sat neatly folded on the shelf above the slot for street shoes, with the helmet on top. The undergarments were absent, no doubt taken home to be washed.

Three swords were propped in the corners, two well used, a third recently purchased, its white bindings still sparkling. A broken shinai, battered and yellow with age, rested behind them. Little more than the handle and a portion of the blade remained. I guessed it had sentimental value. Maybe a souvenir from a hard-fought battle. A cluster of temple charms hung from its hilt.

On the walls of the locker were snapshots. Of his wife and son. Of his parents. Of an attractive woman I imagined to be a sister or a cousin. And center stage on the back wall was a print of a proud Yoji holding up a kendo trophy.

I removed all the photographs and slipped them into my shirt pocket, buttoning the flap. I dropped the temple charms into my pants pocket. When I did so, something inside the shaft of the sword fragment rattled. I brought it out and shook it. The rattle grew louder. I slid off the rubber-ringed sword guard encircling the end of the fractured blade and a key fell into my palm. I pocketed it, then poked around between the layers of clothing but found nothing else of interest.

I closed the locker and refastened the lock. The next instant I heard a click and the lights flickered on overhead. I looked down the aisle. A solitary man in a kendo helmet and a nylon mask underneath to hide his face blocked my path back to the window.

His sword was up and pointed at my head.

"Over here, pretty boy," a voice said behind me.

I glanced the other way and saw two more men in the same guise.

I didn't recognize the voice.

But I did recognize the damage their bamboo swords could do.

CHAPTER 18

Go where the violence is.

The first time I poke into Yoji's life, out it comes. Not a good sign.

"Find what you were looking for?" the biggest of the pair said.

"No."

At a glance I saw that none of the three had Tanaka's flat nose or Kiyama's longish face, shapes I could make out despite the headgear. These were guys I didn't know.

"A guest who behaves dishonorably after we show him hospitality needs to learn respect," he said.

The other two nodded.

"I apologize," I said. "I'm on my way out now."

"Did Nakamura-sensei treat you with disrespect?"

"No, of course not."

"Did *anyone* in our club behave improperly?"

"I'm looking for the person who killed Miura."

"Miura's connection to this dojo is none of your business."

"Was he popular?"

"None of your business."

"Enemies?"

"You repay Nakamura-sensei's kindness by violating the sanctity of his dojo and prying into our business?"

Our business. "If I'd asked to take a look inside the locker, would Nakamura-sensei have let me?"

"Not without clearing it with Mrs. Miura."

"And she would have said no," I answered before I realized what I was saying.

The speaker glanced at the solitary figure at the other end of the aisle, who seemed to be the leader.

"We're in agreement there," the headman said. "I'm thinking we should comfort a grieving widow."

His voice was deep and steady and there was an unmistakable finality in its tone. A heavy silence crept over the proceedings. Any hope I had of escaping with an apology had vanished.

I heard shuffling, followed by a battle cry as the largest of the pair charged. His bamboo shinai rose and started on a downward arc. Trapped in a corridor of lockers and unable to evade the strike, I brought up my arm and took a stinging blow on the thickest part of the bone near the elbow.

Without protection a bamboo sword can cause internal bleeding, break small bones, or knock you unconscious, someone had once told me.

My attacker galloped by with the kendo follow-through he'd been taught. As I'd seen executed a couple hundred times in the bouts earlier tonight. At the end of the aisle, he stopped, pivoted, and positioned himself a half step behind the leader, who approved the foray with a curt nod.

These guys thought this was a game. They'd spent hundreds of hours practicing *kata* and *waza* routines, learning to target head, wrists, sides, and throat with deadly precision and demonic speed.

My arm throbbed. I looked at the spot where I'd been struck. It was starting to swell.

I looked at my opponents.

There was no sign they would be letting up anytime soon.

CHAPTER 19

T HE leader gave the first swordsman the go-ahead nod and his follower readied himself to come at me again. Then the headman
signaled the kendoka to my rear.

A two-man attack.

Still confined by walls of lockers, I prepared as best as I could. I
spread my feet. I slid my right foot back for a better balance. I lifted my
arms slightly. I shook out my hands and stretched my fingers. The first
man yelled and sprang forward. His blade went up. Then behind me
came a second high-decibel cry.

The only advantage I had against these guys was *street*. They were
indoor duelists who had decided to take their training out for a spin.
I'd had more than my share of scrimmages in the real world. After that
though, the rest was downhill—they outnumbered me and their swords
gave them four feet of extra reach.

The first man raced in, feet gliding smoothly over the floor, the tip of
his weapon hypnotically bobbing left and right. As soon as he committed to a path, I faked in the opposite direction. It didn't deter him. He
landed a jarring blow. I caught it once more with my forearm. Too late
did I realize he'd cleverly targeted the same spot. The pain was magni-
fied. A third crack to the same area and I wouldn't be able to lift my arm.

Then, as before, he started to glide by.

I rammed him with my shoulder. His body crashed into the lockers.
They clattered and swayed. As his mouth opened in surprise, I stomped
on his instep with my shoe. Kendo is practiced barefoot in the dojo. Do
that in real life and you'll pay.

He howled and fell, dropping his sword.

From behind, the second man delivered a bone-crunching strike to my right shoulder. A wave of excruciating pain rolled through me and I collapsed to my knees, grabbing my collarbone with one hand and yanking the weapon from the felled swordsman with the other.

I staggered up as the first fighter began to crawl away. When he'd moved beyond my reach, he dragged himself upright. Unable to support his weight on both feet, he hobbled over to the far wall and leaned back against it. He was out of commission. *One down*, I thought. Unfortunately, he was the weakest of the three.

I turned toward the remaining two kendoka.

The second man gauged my mood through narrowed eyes, then rushed in, not giving me a chance to regroup. In the narrow valley of metal, I pushed the captured sword out and turned it sideways. With this strategy, I figured I could jam the lane and stop any incoming strike.

I was right—and then painfully wrong.

He lunged. I parried his first swing, running forward to meet him. Our blades slid down each other, and locked at the hilts. *Good*, I thought, until my opponent deftly rolled his wrists around the block and brought the edge of his blade down on the crown of my head with a resounding crack.

Son of a bitch. Swallowing the pain, I shot my knee into his stomach and he doubled over. I grabbed his helmeted head and flung it against the lockers, then plowed the heel of my hand into his solar plexus. He crumbled up, gasping for air.

Number Two wouldn't be getting up anytime soon.

I turned to the third man. "Four hits. I'm hurting. You've made your point. Let's call it a night and leave it at that."

He didn't bother answering. He simply raised his sword.

CHAPTER 20

THE leader would be the toughest.

"All right, scumbag, take your shot," I said in Japanese, projecting confidence and cockiness. I wanted to puncture his quiet self-assurance. A play that I'd successfully run many times before.

My gambit yielded a flicker of a smile. I glimpsed no pride. Nothing egotistical or maniacal. Nothing gloating or superior. Simple acceptance of my ploy for what it was.

Then he surged forward. I whipped up my sword. My final opponent feinted a body attack, pulled up when I countered, then neatly swatted my blade away and delivered a sharp shot to the side of my head, immediately backpedaling out of range. I'd been ready to tackle him as he slipped past, but having witnessed the fate of his friends he neatly avoided the trap.

He'd nailed me just above my right ear. My head was ringing and my eyes spun. I looked over at him. His sword was in the ready position, the tip pointed at a spot between my eyes. His lips spread in a grin under the black mask. Arrogant bastard. But he had reason to be.

My own weapon poised to attack, I stepped forward, probing the space between us. Our blades touched a few inches below the tips. He tapped mine. I'd seen this maneuver in the day's matches. An initial feeling-out. I tapped back. His smile grew. Then his wrists firmed. I steeled myself. He tapped twice more, then slapped my weapon with such force that my wrists turned sideways, taking my shinai with them, and he rolled inside and connected with a second blistering blow to my right shoulder and again pulled back.

My shoulder burned, but I gritted my teeth and took advantage of his retreat to swoop in, my sword up and threatening. But the muscles in my twice-battered shoulder rebelled and I couldn't fully lift my weapon. Screw it. I stormed in. I might have to take another pummeling to get inside the arc of his blade, but as soon as I did I could do some damage with my hands.

But he outthought me. Once more he backpedaled rapidly. He turned fluidly around the end of an aisle then down another lane of lockers. His shinai hovered overhead, ready to descend.

I stalked him, only a few paces behind, picking up speed and confidence as I went. His eyes tracked my progress, then suddenly his sword dropped briskly, pointed right at my throat. I stopped on a dime. Six inches from the end of his weapon. *Jesus.* He didn't thrust, which he could have, but was more than willing to let me skewer myself on his sword tip if I couldn't manage to stop in time. Contact would have crushed my throat and I would have choked to death in seconds.

This guy possessed a whole other level of skill.

I needed a new plan. But before I could devise one, he was on the move again. His sword rose and twisted in a quick half circle. I shifted mine to counter. My shoulder resisted, and his shinai hammered my other shoulder. I grunted in pain and backed up a few feet, both shoulders throbbing, my blade drooping. He pounced, slamming my weapon aside with lightning speed then pounding my rib cage with a scorching blow. I winced. I saw white light behind my eyes. I heard myself wheeze. The bamboo shaft was deadweight in my hand. I let it drop. When he drove at me the next time, I pivoted, turned my hips, and sent a sharp side kick at his approaching figure, wondering if my reach was long enough.

I never found out.

He drew up short, his weapon hovering, and when my foot snapped harmlessly at a target that didn't materialize, he brought the edge of the shinai down hard on my fully extended leg, then swung it around and up and connected with a bone-rattling follow-up to my skull.

My knees buckled. My forehead crashed into the lockers and I hit the ground.

Just before I blacked out, I heard my first conquest say, "Do you think he got the message?"

In the leader's voice I heard a sneer. "He more than got. He knows next time we won't be so lenient."

CHAPTER 21

I SLIPPED in and out of consciousness, a patchwork of impressions floating through my head. Hands hauled me up and dragged me half a block away, then dumped me unceremoniously in a back alley like yesterday's sushi.

Like Yoji.

Had I stumbled onto his killers? Was I about to lose my life?

I wasn't going to wait to find out. I roused myself and crawled several feet on my belly before everything went dark again.

———

Sometime later my hearing returned. Then my sight. I couldn't stand, so I edged forward on my stomach.

Maybe I could find a place to hide. Between buildings. Under some shrubbery.

My progress was measured in inches.

I heard sirens. A patrol car rounded a corner up ahead, tires squealing. Headlights washed over me. Brakes hissed. Concerned voices approached.

Overhead, a policeman spoke. He sounded young. "Thought the caller was hallucinating when we got the report of a gaijin B and E, but here he is."

The cop made it sound like I was a wild bear in from the wilderness.

I relaxed. Even ignorant help was better than no help at all.

"Defiling Nakamura-sensei's place," a second cop said. Older this time. Gravitas behind his words. "I studied with Sensei at the academy."

Squinting into the darkness back the way I'd come, I could just make out three heads watching from the shadows.

"Do me a favor—" I croaked before my voice deserted me.

"Right, dirtbag. Anything for you," the older cop said. He slammed his boot into my stomach.

His partner looked around hurriedly but said nothing.

"—call Shin'ichi Kato," I wheezed.

The junior cop looked at his partner. "You hear that?"

"No. And don't care." He kicked me again.

The younger one cocked his head at me. "Isn't that the inspector over at—"

"Could be all seven of the lucky gods, for all I care. Tonight, his luck's run out."

"He looks pretty badly beaten."

"Of course he is. The kendo boys are going to lay into thieving scum. What I'd do if I didn't wear the uniform."

More blows came in. I curled up into a ball.

"That's enough, Kondo-san."

"Stop using my name, idiot," Kondo said, punctuating every word with another kick.

"He passed out."

"Not yet, he hasn't."

More jolts with the boot followed until I faded into black once more.

Then the yakuza came to visit.

DAY 3

HANDCUFFED

CHAPTER 22

S IR, you can't be in here."

"Outta my way," a gruff voice snarled, and the attending nurse yelped and scooted off.

The familiar voice drew me out of a medically enhanced sleep. I heard a chair being dragged in my direction, then a heavy body dropped into it. The chair groaned under what sounded like considerable weight.

I took a mental swipe at the cobwebs of my drug-induced oblivion. I tried to open my eyes and failed.

"Goddamn meds," I mumbled.

I heard a glass being dragged from the side table. The next instant water landed on my face.

"That help?" the voice said.

Oddly, it did. The cobwebs dissolved and the weight pinning my eyelids lifted. I found myself looking into a hard stony face with cold brown eyes. Impassive. Brutal. Callous. Anchored by a broad boxlike jaw. Below that, massive arms were crossed over a massive chest.

"Long time," I said.

In the chair sat Tokyo no Tekken. The yaki enforcer topped out at six-four, two hundred and forty pounds. Big for an American, gargantuan for a Japanese. This was the man who'd thrown the water on me. And he was on my side.

At least for the moment.

Everything about the strongman was memorable. Girth, scowl, fists.

His eyes traced a chain that ran from a handcuff around the bedrail to its companion at my wrist. "Popular as usual, I see."

I wiped the water from my face. "Misunderstanding," I said.

"Welcome to the club." He nodded at my injuries. "Who did this?"

I shook my head. "Don't know exactly."

"You got an idea?"

"Always have an idea."

"How many were there?"

"Enough."

The yaki stared at the wraps around my head and chest. At the feed in my arm.

"Three or more," he said.

"Three it was."

TNT hooked a finger in the collar of my hospital gown and lifted the flimsy cloth, exposing a large welt that blackened most of my collarbone.

"What they use?"

"Shinai."

A spark of interest flared in his eyes. "Kendo swords? Those bamboo play sticks can crack bones."

"They tell me I got a fractured rib somewhere, but it could have been worse."

"You see faces?"

I shook my head incrementally. I knew there'd be pain if I moved it more. "Nylon masks under kendo helmets. No faces. No names."

"Not for long," he said. "Give me an address."

"Leave it alone."

"You sure?"

The yaki owed me big-time, but the offer sprang in equal measure because of his very nature. He was one of the few men I knew who was born to fight. Fully unleashed, he was a killing machine. In his earlier days he'd been a rising boxer on the Asian heavyweight circuit, but because he was born into the "undesirables," or *burakumin*, an outcaste group originally despised for handling such "impure" jobs as undertaker or tanner but now just despised, his career had been short-circuited while he was still too young to know any better. I could let him loose on the dojo and he'd crack heads until he found the men who'd assaulted me, but I wanted Yoji's killers alive.

"Yeah, I'm sure."

The light in his eyes dimmed. "Staff here see us talking, they know enough to give us time. But hospital security is gonna swing around soon enough, so you got something to ask?"

"I need to know about the Triads. Whatever you can tell me."

"*Whatever* covers a lot of ground."

"Won't know what I need until I hear it."

TNT shook his head. It was large and square and both ears were cauliflowered. "That ain't gonna happen."

"Okay, related to the home invasions."

He studied me. The silence between us lengthened. His eyes were flinty black dots now. There was a darkness in them you couldn't penetrate and didn't want to look at too closely. After his fists, they were his most unnerving attribute.

"All you need to know about the Triads is you wanna stay away from them."

I shrugged. "Can't do that. I'm working on a murder case that probably involves them."

"Which one?"

"Two days ago. A salaryman named Miura."

"Kabukicho killing. What's he mean to you?"

"His father is my client."

"Was the son?"

"No."

"Then drop it."

"Can't."

The yaki stared at me. "You got a soft heart, Brodie. Gonna get you killed one day."

I said nothing.

Eyeballing me for another beat, the oversize enforcer said, "Can't give you details of the business without the boss's say-so."

"Don't need close up and personal."

"Good. 'Cause you ain't gonna get it."

I said, "Find me a line on the Triads who did the home invasions or Kabukicho."

He blinked once. "Can't help ya."

"Why not?"

"All the big Chinese gangs here are connected. Some with us."

"What's that mean?"

"Means killing Japanese families is not smart business. We don't like it. They don't do it."

"Chinese gangs did it before."

"That was then. Some Triads were stomped on. It stopped."

Over the last three decades, Triads have become increasingly entwined with the Japanese mafia groups. The Chinese gangs' weapon of choice was any long blade. Long, glittering, chopping instruments were preferred. Machetes, cleavers, large knives. But they weren't particular. Steel in all forms worked for them. There was something repulsive to most people about sharpened blades—and something terrifying.

"So the Triads didn't do it?'

He scowled. "Not ours. Probably no other gangs neither."

I pursed my lips. "No one will know it came from you."

"You're dunking your head in the wrong shithole."

"You didn't see Kabukicho."

He scoffed. "Know more about it than the cops."

"How can you be so sure it's not Triads?"

"Because if they did it, they'd want you to know."

"Me?"

He gave me an impatient look. "You been banged up the head bad, Brodie. Not *you*. Whoever they wanted to know. Your client for one."

He had a point.

"Problem is that leaves me with nothing."

"Tell me what you saw."

I told him about the beating. Yoji's face. His legs and arm broken, the other one hacked off. The gag. All of it.

The yaki cracked his fingers. "You know what they were after?"

"No."

He frowned. "How many hacks?"

"I don't know. Five, six, ten. A lot."

TNT scowled. He looked away, thinking. He looked back at me. "Okay, maybe you got Triads. Maybe. Ones they send to do the killings are dumber than rice cakes. When they cap a guy, they never do him quick. And they're sloppy with the chops. Always a lot of blood. Part is for show to put in the scare. The other part is 'cause they're garden-slug dumb."

"So you can get me something, then?"

The big man was annoyed. "I'll ask around, but it still don't mean it's them."

"Never hurts to cover all the bases."

His eyes became slits. "You don't listen good, Brodie. You stick your nose in Triad business, they might just take it off. For practice."

DAY 4

BESIEGED

CHAPTER 23

WHILE I slept, the ax was falling.

A nurse had put me under again. I tossed and turned, and yet I woke the next day rested and feeling much less like a whipping post.

Rie Hoshino arrived after lunch. During my comatose hours on either side of TNT's visit, a number of people had dropped by, including Noda and Hamada, our go-to man on the Triads. The pair left a note saying that they would return when I was awake but in the meantime would press on with the case, a counterintuitive but correct move in our little world. The family friend with whom I'd left Jenny as I headed blithely off to the kendo club two days ago also paid a visit.

Hoshino was back in uniform. A look of concern battled the professional demeanor the Tokyo MPD expected her to maintain. The job won out.

"Are you all right?" she asked a little too formally for my taste.

"Battered and bruised but recovering with the speed of the ever agile."

The quip earned a disapproving headshake. "What happened last night? The owner lodged a complaint against you for breaking into his dojo."

Nakamura-sensei. I wondered if he'd led the attack or directed it from afar. Calling fighters back to the dojo after someone spotted me.

"Three men attacked me with bamboo swords."

"*Three?*" she said, the facade cracking.

"Two of them are regretting their decision. The third one is off gloating somewhere."

I gave her a condensed version of the confrontation, after which she said, "My God. People have *died* from unchecked blows of a shinai without body gear."

"Well, none died last night."

Which is when she dropped the first bombshell. "But did they consider the fallout? Criminal charges are pending."

"You're joking? After beating me senseless?"

She studied me with the skepticism of her profession. "First, you broke in. Second, you took a swing at the policemen on the scene."

"I didn't swing at any uniform. I was bleeding out in some alley, unconscious most of the time. What I do remember is being kicked *after* the cops arrived."

"Is that true?"

"Yes."

"Don't play games with me, Brodie. I'm no pushover, and I don't care if you are Kato's friend."

"Which is as it should be. Off the record, I climbed into an open window to search Yoji's locker."

"How did the window *get* open?"

That made it official: she wasn't an easy mark.

"I unlatched it earlier."

Hoshino had taken notes as I related the events. Now she set down another line.

I eyed her notebook sourly. "Since you're keeping score, the cop who drop-kicked me into unconsciousness was named Kondo. He trained with Nakamura."

She added a final notation and snapped her book shut, a knitted brow joining a seemingly permanent grimace. "Brodie, you're on the hook for a B and E."

"I told you in confidence. Anyone else asks, I'll plead the fifth."

"Wrong country, wrong answer."

I was silent.

Hoshino's face softened a notch. "Inspector Kato suspects that the report is missing some details."

"Glad to hear it. Yoji studied at the dojo for years. Maybe he made enemies. Maybe he griped about his father's 'delusions' regarding the home invasions and someone took advantage of the information to kill Yoji and make it look like Triads."

Hoshino considered the idea. "Or maybe it *was* Triads."

"Maybe."

"Or it's about the Sengai and the treasure and cutting Yoji out of the deal."

"Also possible."

"So, more motives, more suspects, fewer answers."

"The floodgates have opened."

Hoshino produced a small steel key and released the metalwear around my wrist.

I rubbed the chafed skin. "Be nice if you led with that."

She shook her head. "I needed to hear your side. And there's a catch. You'll have to hand over your passport. A compromise Kato made until the kendo mishap is cleared up."

"Come on. Jenny starts school in San Francisco right after the Kyoto trip."

"Not anymore."

"That's some compromise."

Hoshino dangled the handcuffs in front of me. "It's better than recuperating in a jail cell. Which, by the way, could still happen. In a flash."

I blew out a loud breath in frustration. "The MPD's looking at this all wrong. I struck a nerve. Unraveling *that* is what's next."

Against the strongly worded objection of the doctor in attendance, I checked myself out of the hospital and accepted Hoshino's offer of a ride home. In the car, she was polite but distant.

I turned stiffly in my seat. "Have you got some makeup with you?"

"Of course. But I don't use much on the job."

As at our first meeting, Hoshino's cosmetic touches were understated yet expert. She wasn't interested in impressing anyone with her feminine wiles. But neither was she working at being one of the boys.

"It's not for you," I said. "I'm in need of a makeover after I wash up."

"What about your precious 'unraveling'?"

I smiled. "Beauty before head-bashing."

CHAPTER 24

UNDER the hot downpour of a much-welcomed shower, my injuries throbbed anew but I gritted my teeth and let the spray massage the soreness. Welts and bruises had bloomed wherever the swords had connected. The good news was, all the moving parts still moved.

I emerged a new man. After toweling dry, I swallowed some of the prescribed meds, then slapped on adhesive pads. As I was brushing the grime from my teeth, my cell phone buzzed. I rinsed hurriedly and answered with a garbled hello.

"Heard you got out," Noda said. "What the hell happened last night?"

I relayed the story again, and with Hoshino out of earshot mentioned my haul: the key, the temple charms, and the photos. He was most interested in the key.

"What kind of key?"

"Common house key."

He exhaled impatiently. "No such thing. Bring it in," he said, and disconnected.

I slid into a clean pair of jeans and a black T-shirt, then headed downstairs. Hoshino had settled on the couch in the family room.

She looked up. "Feel better?"

"Much."

"Good. After you pick up your daughter, you should come back here and rest like the doctor advised."

"Can't do that. Every day on my back makes it that much easier for Yoji's killers to slip away."

"You overrate your stamina."

"You don't know that yet."

One of the MPD's finest reddened noticeably.

Into the silence I said, "I'm ready to go as soon as you perform your magic."

She put out her hand. "Passport first."

"You know what I said about feeling better? I take it back."

She frowned. "I don't want to take your passport, but I have no choice, so please don't make this harder."

In the face of a nearly flawless argument, I retrieved the travel document in question.

"Thank you," Hoshino said, slipping the blue booklet into her purse. Then she fished out a petite compact and covered the bruises on my forehead, spillover from the two head strikes. A critical eyebrow rose as she inspected her work. "That ought to fool your intended audience, if no one else."

"I hope so," I said. "Otherwise I'm in deep trouble."

Hoshino laughed. "Time to go."

She'd agreed to take me to Jenny. A minute from our destination her official cell went off.

Peering at the display, her brow furrowed. "Sorry, I have to take this."

Instead of pushing the intercom function, she coasted to a stop at the side of the road and removed the phone from its cradle. I gazed out the passenger window, offering her the illusion of privacy.

Hoshino listened—and turned a shade of pale evident even in her reflection.

"I understand. He's not to come," she repeated with a meaningful glance in my direction. She kept her ear to the phone for another moment, hung up, and dropped a second bombshell:

"There's been a new killing. Somebody named Doi. Another man from Miura's old unit."

CHAPTER 25

THE second I strolled into the vast kitchen, Jenny ran up and buried her face in my stomach. Coming up for air, she launched happily into a tale about her stay. About the sweets she'd eaten, the anime figurines she'd received as gifts, and the neighborhood girls she'd played with. Next, she pressed me about joining the soccer club at school, which started next week in San Francisco.

"Did you sign the papers yet, Daddy? Coach Nancy says I need them before I can kick the ball."

Jenny had light brown skin, straight black hair, and a gap-toothed smile. At six years old, with her front baby teeth gone and the new ones not yet arrived, she was at an in-between stage I found disarming and utterly captivating.

"Sorry, I haven't had time to read them," I said. "But I will."

Enrolling her on the soccer team was no simple matter. The school had presented me with a four-page "rule book" and a two-page release form. Joining involved supplying your child with the proper equipment, drinks, and a snack for every game, as well as volunteering for various duties throughout the season. As a single father with two businesses barely scraping by, I had little free time and a burgeoning respect for soccer moms.

"The season's starting soon," my daughter said.

"I know, I know."

I was in way over my head.

Mariko, family friend and babysitter, stepped up to say hello. She was the seventy-one-year-old private cook for a wealthy local family, old friends of my father's, which is how we originally met. She moved freely between her employer's mansion and the cottage out back where she and her butler-husband lived. After one glance at my face, Mariko's smile faded and she turned away, finding work in a far corner of the kitchen, but not before a look of concern flashed across her features.

Jenny tugged at my arm. "And when can we do the stuff together like you promised?"

"Tomorrow," I said hastily, an answer I'd regret for a long time to come.

The third bombshell fell at Miura's. The last man standing under his command was in residence.

"Happened yesterday while you were, uh, indisposed," the Brodie Security man on duty told me in a low voice meant only for my ears. "There's a memo on your desk. Both Doi-san and Inoki-san came here."

"*Both?*" I asked.

He nodded. "I figured Miura-san could use the company, and to have them all under one roof seemed a good idea. Then Doi-san insisted on sneaking back to his place after nightfall to pick up a change of clothes and feed his goldfish. He wouldn't be talked out of it. Wouldn't let me send someone. And since he wasn't a client, I could only advise."

I shook my head sadly. I'd seen this type of brain slip before. There was probably a medical term for the condition. If not, there ought to be. Simply put, hiding out made people stupid. Their thinking regressed, and after they lived with a looming threat for a time, it seemed— suddenly—less alarming. They believed they could handle it. Or they rationalized the situation and figured things weren't as dangerous as they originally thought. Or their grasp on the fragility of their own mortality lessened and they felt, if not invincible, then at least incredulous that someone would actually want to harm them.

In the next stage, often inflamed by cabin fever, a new and false reality settled in, and under the cover of night they ventured out to one of their old haunts—a friend's, a lover's, a familiar restaurant, a favorite drinking spot, even their own home—and the hunters pounced. End of story.

"Tried to talk him out of it," the Brodie Security op was saying, "but he was a stubborn old guy. Kept babbling about his goldfish."

I'd never met the man, but Doi's old army buddies were inconsolable and, in the face of fresh confirmation that they were in the crosshairs, frightened to death.

"Don't suppose you had a chance to talk to him."

"Sat down with both men. Empty wells."

In the next room, Miura and Inoki stared at a quiz show on the tube. I said hello and commiserated over their loss. Their heads bobbed in thanks, then swiveled back to the television.

Civil conversation had dropped off a ledge.

Eventually, Miura said, "Glad Inoki didn't leave. I'll pay the additional fees if there are any."

I cast a look at the guard. He gave me a head shake. I said, "As long as you're both under this roof, there'll be no extra charge."

His eyes moist, Inoki turned to his friend. "Thanks for taking me in. I have nowhere else to go. My son's place is small and his wife was complaining. Just like the old Korean saying: 'After three days, fish and houseguests begin to smell.'"

Still in his eighties, Inoki must have been the baby of the group. He was thin, wiry, and energetic. His arms and elbows flew about when he spoke. The eternal excitable boy.

Miura patted his friend's shoulder. "Stay as long as you like. We've got plenty of room."

"Thank you."

"Any thoughts about who's behind this?" I asked Inoki.

His face collapsed into a nest of wrinkled anguish. "What else could it be but our return visits to the village?"

They nodded in unison and an instant later they drifted away into the fatalistic backwater that Japanese escape to when avoidance seems the safest course.

I called them back. "Your lives are on the line. Give me something."

They gave me bleak looks and no answers.

"So that's it?" I said.

Inoki's shoulders sunk. "Everyone from the old days is dead. All we came up with was Wu. He *might* know something. Because he's Chinese. Or was."

"Who's Wu?" I asked.

Miura's look was dismissive. "A traveling doctor from a nearby village in China. Not Anli-dong, but close. There were rumors he settled in Japan for a few years after the war, then returned home. Or maybe stayed. I also heard he'd passed away four or five years back. So forget it."

I shook my head. "Wish I could. Unfortunately, people are after you. Unless you plan to hide for the rest of your life, someone like this Wu could be your only hope. Clearly, these guys aren't going to stop."

CHAPTER 26

BACK at Brodie Security, I fell into my seat and ran my fingers through my hair in frustration.

People were being murdered and we had nothing. Or nearly nothing.

I'd had no time to gather my thoughts since my B&E at the kendo club. Everything in the immediate aftermath—my beating, the forced overnights at the hospital, TNT, the threat of pending criminal charges, Doi's murder—had swallowed up the hours. And I'd left my daughter in Mariko's charge for the third day running.

So where was I? What had the drop-by at the Nakamura dojo yielded? They'd been on me from the moment I'd walked in. Veiled looks, a chaperoned seat, my reception in the locker room—all of these suggested I'd struck a nerve.

But what kind of nerve?

Mari arrived with a cup of steaming green tea.

"Thanks," I said, looking up into a face spilling over with concern.

"Are you okay, Brodie-san?" she asked.

Behind her, Mari's apprehension was echoed on the faces of a half dozen staff members crowding the doorway.

"I'm fine," I said. "Besides, you *know* I've seen worse."

My last comment raised faint smiles and vague nods. Everyone wandered back to their desks, mollified if not convinced, no doubt thinking of Japantown and Soga, the men we faced back then.

Noda and Hamada wandered in and shut the door behind them. They both looked me over but said nothing.

"Caught out," I said.

Hamada chuckled. "Goes with the job."

Noda said, "You weren't headed to a moon-viewing party. Got the key?"

I dumped my haul on the desk—key, temple charms, photos. My attackers hadn't considered that I might have walked off with some of Yoji's keepsakes. Or they didn't care.

Noda snapped up the key. Hamada grabbed the charms.

I looked at Noda pointedly. "How's the edge-digging going?"

"Slowly."

Brodie Security's grand communicator. The chief detective was squinting at a serial number punched on the key head.

I turned to Hamada. "Anything on the Triad angle?"

He nodded happily. "Meeting tonight. Looks promising."

"Good. We need something."

Hamada raised the cluster of charms by their drawstrings and let them twirl lazily in the air. "He's bought everything the suckers buy. Prayers for job promotion, longevity, family health, safe driving. Amulets to ward off evil spirits. Protection from injury. Superstitious guy. Didn't save him, though."

"Maybe he bought them because he was into something dangerous," I said. "What if we talk to one of the monks?"

Hamada tossed the bundle back on the desk. "People purchase charms like lottery tickets. On the other hand, sometimes they unburden themselves to a temple monk they trust. Couldn't hurt to make the rounds."

Noda said, "What do you hear from Inspector Kato?"

"Got to get on that," I said.

Noda scowled. "Sooner would help."

"Give the kid a break. He got bashed up pretty bad."

Noda snorted. "Cover-up's not working."

Shit. That was for Jenny's eyes only. I'd been so distracted I'd forgotten to remove it. I snagged some Kleenex and began rubbing. No wonder the staff had looked so anxious.

Without missing a beat Noda added, "If you're done playing dress-up, we need to get a handle on this thing quick. Only two of those old soldiers left."

DAY 5

PURSUED

ITCHING to hear what the police knew, I'd rung Hoshino late yesterday from Brodie Security. With my afternoon promised to Jenny, we
agreed to meet first thing in the morning at Chatei Hatou, an elegant
European-style coffeehouse tucked away down a side street in Shibuya.

"This is one of my hideaways," Hoshino confided once we commandeered a wooden table in the back under the watchful eye of towering
European cabinetry. "Only a couple of blocks from the stationhouse
but far enough away so none of my coworkers will wander in. The
master is the king of pour-over."

As Hoshino explained it, the owner had risen above barista to "master brewer." His attention to detail extended to the quality of the water,
the roasting of the beans, their aging when called for, and the shape and
texture of the drip cone.

"Naturally, he does a separate pour for each cup," Hoshino said in
a whisper, wonder edging into her voice. "It's a five-minute routine.
Sometimes more."

I chose the house pour-over cappuccino, Hoshino a Venetian coffee,
then I asked about the progress on the Kabukicho murder.

"Why don't you start?" the MPD's caffeine connoisseur suggested.
She wore street clothes again today. A beige blouse and white slacks.
And, like the last time I saw her out of uniform, there was an appealing
buoyancy. Her eyes sparkled.

"Sure. We're working a number of angles, but leads are scarce. Miura
Senior's been no help at all. Even after the Doi murder, he had nothing
to offer. But Noda is looking into several things, including one of my

'acquisitions' from the B and E. Hamada met his Triad connection last night and should be checking in shortly. You?"

Hoshino took a moment to digest my report. "So, no results as yet?"

"We're working on a new approach to the dojo, and I've got another feeler out but, no, nothing concrete."

The other feeler was TNT. I decided to wait before mentioning the exchange to Hoshino. Inside access to Tokyo no Tekken wasn't the kind of connection you trotted out to impress a woman you had an interest in. Especially one with a badge.

Hoshino's next comment proved my instincts prophetic. "You may have noticed that I did not ask about your 'acquisitions.'"

"I did."

"Let's keep it that way."

"Done."

"Thank you. On our end, Yoji Miura's dental charts matched, and Mrs. Miura came down and ID'ed her husband's body. They cleaned him up some but we're not morticians. She became hysterical again. Kept asking who was going to take care of her family. We sent her home with a trauma specialist."

I nodded. "Breaks my heart. Anything unexpected?"

"Detectives found a potential witness who saw two Chinese near the scene."

I sat up a little straighter. "How near?"

"Coming out the back end of the alley about the right time at a 'fast walk.' He'd been to a couple of bars that night, so his memory's fuzzy. What he remembers are bad haircuts and cheap clothes like you see in China. He looked at mug shots, but the results were inconclusive."

"Too bad. Did he think they were Triads?"

Hoshino pushed out her lips. "He doesn't know what Chinese gangs look like. A lot of people don't."

I swallowed my disappointment. "Is that it?"

"No. The killers used a meat cleaver to hack off the arm. The impressions the labs took suggest a blade about eight inches long, four inches high, and weighing approximately two pounds. The kind of chopping implement found in a butcher's shop or a Chinese restaurant. They're running comparisons from Japanese, Chinese, and German cutlery manufacturers, and cross checking the chop marks against the home invasions."

I tiptoed in with my next question. "Was . . . Yoji alive when . . . ?"

Despite her determination to present a professional front, Hoshino blanched. "The ME thinks Yoji was not only alive but conscious when they took the arm. Because of the *way* they cut it off."

I hung my head, seeing red.

"The ME described the instrument as 'unusually blunt,'" she added, with a shiver.

Meaning prolonged hacking and unimaginable pain.

It was several moments before either of us spoke.

Hoshino broke the silence first. "Can I ask you something?"

"Sure."

"What do you think of Inspector Kato?"

Not the question I expected. I wondered if the brutality of the attack had shaken her. Or if the lack of progress had undermined her confidence in her boss.

"They don't come much better. It'd be nice if that's what you thought."

"I do."

"Why are you asking, then?"

She looked down and blushed, a modest gesture I took to immediately. "I know the office scuttlebutt, but I have my own impressions and I wanted confirmation from an outside source."

"Stay with Kato as long as you can," I said. "They'll be moving you out eventually."

She nodded to herself, then surprised me with her next comment. "If we are going to be working together, maybe you should call me Rie. I like the American custom of using first names."

"I can do that."

"But in front of others, it's still Hoshino."

"Of course."

I knew Japanese businessmen who'd worked in the same office for decades, gone out drinking together more times than they could count, and still called each other by their surnames. So entrenched is the practice that when Japanese coworkers are asked a colleague's first name, they are often unable to recall it.

"And yours?"

"Jim."

Her eyes glistened. "That's a nice name. It's solid but has a soft beginning."

"Thanks. I think."

"But *Brodie* suits you better. It sounds stronger. Streamlined and bold."

"I answer to both."

"Would you mind one more question?"

"Shoot."

"Has there been anyone else since your wife died?"

I paused. "I was expecting small-caliber but you're firing mortars."

She laughed. It was natural, infectious, and womanly rather than girlish. "You're a grown man. You can handle it. Has there?"

I shrugged. "Casual dating. A couple that might have turned serious."

"Japanese?"

I admired her tenacity. The lady wasn't going for subtle. She was wondering if I was one of those men who fixates on Asian women.

"One American lawyer from Boston, one Japanese woman I met at Brodie Security."

"What happened?"

"The lawyer was too focused on herself and wanted me to send my daughter away for schooling."

While she took a moment to absorb this new information, our coffee arrived.

I drank my cappuccino, Rie sipped her Venetian. Her manner was ladylike, confident, and anything but cloyingly cute. *There is something substantial here*, I thought.

Eventually Rie said, "I'm sorry. Asking questions is part of my job. I guess it's become a habit. So you don't, um, prefer Japanese women?"

I smiled at her persistence, also part of her job. "I'm an equal opportunity dater. I like women who, if things work out, might be a good role model for my daughter, if I ever go that route again. And since we're being so up front about these things, what kind of men do you date?"

"Well, first of all, I do *not* date anyone inside the department."

"I wouldn't think so. Unless you're partial to career suicide."

"Precisely."

"How about men you're on a first-name basis with?"

"Sometimes."

The antique clock on the wall struck the half hour. It was later than I thought.

"This has been fun, but I've got to run."

"I need to get to the office, too."

"Before I go, can I ask if you passed on my message about the London dealer to Kato?"

"The one who might have stolen the Sengai? Yes. The inspector gave Jamie Kendricks's name to the passport authorities."

"Great. I'm out of time, but let's do this again. Maybe over dinner next time. I'd ask you along today if you weren't working."

"It's my day off."

"But you just said—" I slapped myself in the forehead in a mock reprimand. "Look what country I'm in. Of course you're working on your day off. But I was thinking more of—"

"A date?"

"Yes."

"We're in the middle of a big case. My biggest."

"So learn to juggle."

She shook her head. "Work comes first. Besides, I prefer one distraction at a time."

"So I'm a distraction?"

"A *potential* distraction."

That sounded promising.

CHAPTER 28

WOULD she or wouldn't she?

Rie had left me dangling, saying she had urgent business back at the stationhouse but it should only take a few minutes. If nothing else required her attention, she'd meet us at the ticket window.

However, tide and impatient daughters wait for no one. As soon as my taxi pulled up to Mariko's, Jenny rocketed out the front door, struggling under the weight of a large daypack.

"Guess what," she said as she dove into the taxi and crawled over my lap to the far window. "Obaa-san took me to the Ueno Zoo. I saw pandas from China and bitsy-witsy hippos from Africa!"

"You mean the pygmy hippos?"

"Yeah, those."

"That's great."

Mariko, the "grandmother" in question, shuffled up to the door in a pale-green workaday kimono, one of many in her wardrobe.

I said, "Thanks for watching Jenny again. Any trouble?"

"Of course not," she said in her accented English. "And no needing thank me. I watch her like I watch you when you even smaller."

"Don't remind me."

She smiled. "I make you picnic lunches for the boat."

"Thank you."

"Let's go, Daddy," Jenny called, her head craning out the window.

Mariko glanced at her charge fondly. "She waiting on you long time. Play with your only daughter and make a great day for her."

I said I would, waved, and we were off. I'd planned to take the train to economize, but I gave in to Jenny's unvoiced eagerness to ride by cab. As we drove through the streets of Tokyo, she bobbed up and down at her window, offering a running commentary on the sights as they whizzed by, then popped her head in to ask about the soccer papers, forcing me to admit I hadn't performed my paternal duty on that front.

"Daddy, do it soon, okay? School starts any day now."

"I know, I know. Tonight."

I hadn't the heart to tell her she might not be going.

"And after soccer comes pooling. The doctor papers are for both."

"Swimming," I said.

Along with her best friend, Jenny had started lessons at the local public pool from the age of four, and the pair rose to the top of their class, winning a string of trophies over the next two years. I encouraged any new outside interest and thought soccer a great idea, except for my attendant duties. A new sport meant one less parental worry—among a seemingly bottomless basketful.

———

Rie watched our taxi roll to a stop and greeted us with a smile and some snacks. Trust a demon driver raised in Tokyo to beat us across town.

I'd planned a cruise down the Sumida River, Tokyo's main waterway. As our ferry inched away from the dock and headed lazily toward Tokyo Bay, we had a clear view of the Asahi Brewery Headquarters and the Tokyo Skytree.

Jenny gawked at both. Rie explained to her that the funny golden carrot atop the Asahi building was really a sculpture of a flame shooting sideways by a famous artist called Philippe Starck, and that the needle-shaped Skytree was, at two thousand feet, Japan's tallest structure, with an observation platform so high you could see the curvature of the earth.

My phone rang. A scrolling message tag informed me that Noda was on the other end. I stepped toward the front of the boat, out of earshot of Rie and Jenny.

"Ask the girl about her Chinese connections," Brodie Security's chief detective said.

No greeting. No small talk.

"The girl?"

"The woman cop. She's there, isn't she?"

"Is there anything you don't know?"

"Sure. Whether her connections are any good."

"How'd you find out?"

"Poking around *all* the edges."

Before I could request an update on the more promising edges, the dial tone was buzzing in my ear.

Jenny ran up and tugged my arm. "Daddy, you said no work today."

Over the PA system, our guide began her narration: "*We are passing under the first of thirteen bridges spanning the Sumida River between here and Hamarikyu, our first port of call. Hamarikyu, now a public garden, was once a shogun family villa . . .*"

"Well, others are doing the work, but I have to stay in touch in case they need to tell me something. That's fair, isn't it?"

She puffed out her lips in a pout as she considered my question, then turned to Rie. "Do you do that too?"

We stood on the bow, which acted as a viewing platform. Now we headed downstairs into the seating area, an elegant indoor picnic setting with deep leather booths, spacious wooden tables, and gleaming brass fittings around wide windows with expansive views of the river and the city beyond.

"Yes. I'm on call even on my off days, just in case," Rie said, as we all slid onto the cushioned benches of a booth.

"In case of what?"

Oops. Afraid of spooking Jenny, Rie glanced my way, her eyes wide.

"In case her boss needs her," I said. "Police stuff."

Jenny nodded. "Okay, Daddy. I guess that's just the way the world spins."

Rie looked at me with questions in her eyes and Jenny jumped in, breathless, to explain that the phrase was our private take on how the world worked. Good things and bad things came and went and you had to live your life the best way you could, letting both wash over you. You could enjoy the good, but shouldn't cling to it, just as you shouldn't let the bad drag you down, because before you knew it the good would come around again.

"That's a very sensible philosophy," Rie told Jenny. "I like it."

"Thank you. It's Daddy's and mine."

Jenny smiled proudly and Rie smiled back. Without missing a beat, my daughter hit me up for ice cream money. I doled out some bills. Remembering an earlier lesson in manners, she asked Rie what she'd like, then me, then off she rushed.

"So much energy," Rie said, watching Jenny's mad dash for the food counter.

"Too much, sometimes. Listen, you don't by any chance have any good Chinese connections, do you?"

She looked startled. "Yes, I do. How'd you know?"

"Noda. Best not to ask any more."

She shrugged. "I did a home stay in Hong Kong my senior year in high school."

"Can't imagine that would be of much use."

"It was a prominent family. The father owned a five-star restaurant and a chain of supermarkets. The family loved sushi and made me teach them the names of all the fish in Japanese. We're still close. Their son is about my age. He went into international finance and came to Tokyo. He's a rising star here."

"Hmmm." How the hell had Noda unearthed this tidbit?

Rie smiled. "Would you like me to contact him?"

I said yes and told her what I wanted. I talked fast because Jenny would be rejoining us any second. When I finished, I added that I was surprised she hadn't tapped the source herself.

Rie's answer was firm. "I don't involve friends in my work. It can get tricky. But if we go through you instead of the department, I don't mind."

"Makes sense. One more thing. Could you ask him if any of his acquaintances know a doctor called Wu?"

"Do you have a full name?"

"No. He was in Manchuria around the time Miura was. If he's still alive, he might be able to give us background."

Rie frowned. "That's awful vague."

"That's all I've got. But Triads are the priority."

Jenny returned holding a cardboard box with rings punched out to keep the cones upright. She set the carton down, grabbed a double chocolate tower, and began licking furiously.

I said, "You'd think you hadn't had ice cream for years."

Rie laughed and Jenny said, "I haven't! Not since two days ago!" Her tongue had turned dark brown. "Can we go to the front of the boat again? I like the view there."

"Sure."

I passed a cone to Rie and we headed up to the bow. Above a row of cushioned benches, the front was open. The wind buffeted our faces and felt good on my skin.

Jenny delighted in gazing at everything on the river. She followed the progress of a fishing boat heading home with drying nets glistening in the sun. She repeated the name of every bridge as it was announced, and since each one had a distinct color she memorized the shade and recited the whole string of colors with every new sighting. As we passed the sumo stadium in the Ryogoku District, she made me promise to take her to a tournament.

Rie and I fell into small talk. When my phone rang a second time, I made apologies and dug it out of my pocket. Noda had sent me an email with an attachment. My reaction must have shown because Rie said softly, "What is it?"

"I'm not sure."

I'd yet to open the attachment, but the subject line had startled me: *Get somewhere safe, now!* I tapped open the attachment.

In the rectangular frame of my smartphone was a headshot of a bloodied Hamada. His usual good cheer was nowhere in sight. His gaze was unfocused and lifeless. The bulbous nose was ice-blue.

I zoomed out and nearly dropped the phone.

Affixed to his brow with a six-inch ice pick was a passport-size photograph of me.

And his head wasn't attached to anything.

CHAPTER 29

THERE were three of them and they came on fast.

They had boarded from the stern, maybe steering a speedboat alongside the ferry's blind side and affixing a portable nautical ladder to the hull.

A crewmember moving calmly but swiftly toward the rear alerted me first. By that time the second intruder was on deck. An argument began.

None of the passengers in the cabin noticed. Those on the stern benches watched the exchange grow heated. A moment earlier they had been enjoying the riverside scenery. The next instant, strangers appeared and a tempest unfolded before them.

Even now, no one in the cabin seats had noticed. Except the serving staff.

Then, without fanfare, the two intruders flung the crewman overboard. At the same time the head of a third man appeared at the rail.

The first man scanned the cabin. His eyes locked onto mine, then the scanning stopped, and he said something out of the side of his mouth to his companions.

From a distance they looked Japanese but didn't. They moved forward. A bit closer and they looked Chinese but didn't. Though my visual sense seemed scrambled, my survival instincts kicked in, as clear as ever.

Looking upstream and down, I said hurriedly to Rie, "Can you swim?"

"Yes. Why?"

She hadn't seen them yet. She'd be of more use with Jenny.

"Forgive me. Take good care of my daughter."

Only the beginnings of a puzzled expression had formed before I lifted her 110-pound frame over the rail and released her.

Her arms flailed wildly as she tumbled head over heels and landed on her stomach.

I swept Jenny up next, saying, "The world's spinning, Jen. Time for a swim. Take a deep breath." I waited a beat as she inhaled. "Good. Head for the shore."

Before she could respond, I dropped her feet-first over the edge. My heart clutched in my chest the way it had the first time a doctor had administered a vaccination shot and—too young to understand—Jenny had cried out in pain.

But now, as then, it had to be done.

She took the drop like the fish her swimming trophies had led me to believe she was. Recalling her work on the springboard, Jenny instinctively spread her arms for balance and pointed her toes downward.

I watched her hit the water feet-first.

For the moment, my daughter was safe.

I ran.

CHAPTER 30

IN the fraction of a second before I acted, I'd considered alternate scenarios. Rie and I stay and fight. The three of us jump overboard.

But neither would work.

The first exposed Jenny to a high-risk situation, especially with Rie's skills unproven. The second opened the possibility of being attacked in the river. The three men could—conceivably—follow us over the side. And they had a boat, which meant at least one more person. If any of them caught up with Jenny in the water, it was a moment's work to drag her under and drown her. Or signal the boat to run her down. Being a good swimmer would mean nothing.

I saw only one option. Stay and fight *alone*.

Maybe Rie could have covered my back. Maybe she couldn't. There'd been no time to find out. Whether she could or not, if I'd asked she'd have insisted she was capable, or she'd want to wave her badge. I had no time to explain the photo of Hamada's head. And since it was likely that the new arrivals had chopped up Hamada, who was a former Osaka policeman, flashing her credentials would only get her knifed or shot.

Further, Rie hadn't been attuned to the newcomers' arrival, which suggested her experience was still limited and didn't yet extend much beyond her police training. So I'd sent her into the water to watch my daughter.

There would be hell to pay later. I could see the fury in her eyes as I released her over the side—fury and shock and hurt and bitter disappointment. Regret tugged at my conscience.

But that wasn't the worst of it.

In that instant, the thing budding between us had withered and died.

I watched them advance toward the bow.

They were fifteen yards away, and closing. People were staring now. The three men moved in unison, swiftly and without words. In a wedge formation. One in front, two in back. They zeroed in on me. Murmurs went up. Part-time serving staff roamed the lower deck, but minimum wage didn't buy help in this situation. The intruders pushed an old woman aside and she shrieked.

A knife came out.

On the front deck there was a long cushioned bench for passengers. It traced both sides of the bow and came to a point in the middle. A low wall topped with a shimmering brass rail contributed back support. A gunwale stretched about ten inches beyond the rail, providing a slim walkway around the perimeter of the vessel.

The gunwale was my only option, so I took it. Springing over the rail, I circled around to the starboard side of the boat.

The three boarders caught my move mid-cabin and ran to the nearest window to cut me off. Luckily for me the big square Plexiglas panes were battened down with decorative brass bolts.

Safe for the moment, I paused to see what my pursuers would do next. They clawed at the plastic, which did them no good. They ran their hands around the window frame, looking for an instant-release latch. They found none. After a quick consultation, they split up. One man headed toward the bow. Two headed back to the stern.

In a moment I would be trapped.

So I went up, a delaying tactic at best.

I'd discarded the idea of joining Jenny and Rie in the river. The ferry was moving relentlessly toward Tokyo Bay, but at a leisurely pace. The men wanted me, so the more distance I put between them and my involuntary castaways, the better.

I clambered onto the roof. It was long and white and peppered with a row of skylights running down the middle. When I peered through them, I saw bewildered passengers gazing up at me. I edged toward the front of the boat, where I expected a single assailant.

His head came over the edge. Our eyes locked. He grinned and pulled himself up. I surged forward, gauging the distance. His chest appeared, then his waist. I kept going. He noticed my approach, knew he couldn't raise himself upright in time, and began backpedaling down the side.

But it was too late.

I veered just before contact so I wouldn't run over the side and straight into the water. I struck him with a roundhouse kick, swinging my hips and leg toward the bow.

I hit the center of his chest with the outer padding of my right foot. His rib cage collapsed and his grip broke. He flew back, limbs spreading wide like some human starfish. The thrust of my kick sent his body up and out, then gravity took over as his momentum slowed and he tumbled backward into the Sumida River.

I heard shouts from his mates at the stern. The first was on the roof, the second right behind him.

And they both wielded blades—a knife and a cleaver.

The guide's disembodied voice reached my ears. *"Up ahead is the Kiyosu Bridge. Raging fires devastated the area in the aftermath of the great earthquake of 1923 . . ."*

A shadow blanketed me. The bridge loomed. Glancing over my shoulder, I saw the support structure, with its I-beams and industrial-size bolts. Had I wanted, I could *count* the bolts. I was that close.

Before I knew it the bridge was overhead, only eighteen inches away. I jumped up and seized an I-beam.

My shoes now hovered above the ferry's roof. The plan called for a simple gymnastic maneuver: wrap my legs around the beam, scamper away upside-down to the end, then climb up the side of the bridge. Enough of the structure was exposed to accomplish the feat. But when I snatched a look at my attackers, I saw they were too close. Sticking to the plan would get me a blade in my back.

From ten yards away, the closest man lunged at me with the cleaver raised over his head. I swung away, brought my knees to my chest, then pushed forward. With the boat's help my feet slammed into his chest a beat before he could bring the steel down.

He flipped over on his back and banged his head hard. The collision propelled me abruptly backward again as his friend sidestepped the fallen body and raced in. My momentum shifted forward. The third man aimed his knife, but the combination of the boat's speed and my forward motion upset his timing and he ran past me before the arc of his attack could be completed.

The timing was tricky.

But now my last opponent was behind me.

I performed a quick hand shuffle to reverse my position. Right hand to left side of the beam, left to right side.

He pivoted and made ready to come at me again. We faced off. Then he looked beyond me. It didn't take a genius to see that the end of the roof was fast approaching, so he sheathed the weapon and took a running leap, flinging himself into the air and latching on to my waist as the last of the roof sluiced away underfoot.

We both hung over water.

His hands were wrapped around me. His eyes wandered longingly toward the sheathed knife, but he couldn't snatch the blade without surrendering his grip, so the gutless dickweed turned his head sideways and bit me. I winced and jerked away, then swung my hipbone back and smacked him in the nose.

Call it an improvised headbutt. Same idea, different part of the body.

I hadn't been able to get much force behind the move. The blow would smart but the impact was not enough to discourage an experienced fighter, so I pulled my hip away once more and kneed him in the groin. His hands went instinctively to his crotch and he plummeted into the swirling river thirty feet below.

Hooking my heels over the lower flange of the I-beam, I inched forward along the bottom of the bridge until I reached the end, then worked my way up the side, grappling with the open structure for holds. A minute later, I tumbled over the guardrail onto the pedestrian walk, startling a young couple strolling hand in hand.

They jumped back. Other people stared.

I ignored them all. I was stiff and sore and felt the aches from the beating at the kendo club pulse anew with my extracurricular exertions.

I'd pay for the rooftop skirmish too, but for the moment I was free of pursuers—with my head still attached.

I needed to find Jenny. Had she made it to shore?

CHAPTER 31

"YOU'VE destroyed my career," Rie said.

The first words out of her mouth left me speechless. I could think of a dozen retorts after her forced dunking, but that wasn't one them.

She trembled with rage and despair. "In one thoughtless, uncaring moment you've crushed everything I've worked to accomplish. I will *not* be part of the third generation in my family to join the police force. I will *not* be the first woman. I will *not* get my detective's shield."

Rie and Jenny had reached the riverbank two minutes after I'd flung them into the water. Safety was only forty yards away. Once ashore, Rie had hailed a taxi and directed the driver to follow the river access road until they caught up with the ferry.

As I'd trotted toward the west end of the bridge in search of them, they surprised me by leaping from the cab. Jenny ran into my arms and Rie started in. *Before* I could thank her. Only later did I learn from Jenny that Rie had apologized in advance for what she would say when they met up with me again on the bridge, which explained my daughter's uncharacteristic calm during the confrontation.

I said, "Maybe I saved your life. Did you ever think of that?'

"That's arrogant and chauvinistic. I can handle myself. I have training. Did *you* think of that?"

"Yes, I did, but kendo is useless against men with knives and meat cleavers when you have no weapon at hand. Look where it got Yoji."

"I studied kendo *and* judo."

Twice as hard.

"You didn't mention judo."

"There is no law that says I must tell you everything about myself. But I *am* a police officer."

"How could I know about the judo?" I said, purposely ignoring the "police officer" bit. It hadn't helped Hamada.

"How do you think this is going to look?"

"Like you rescued Jenny?" I said lamely.

Her eyes flared. "They'll say a civilian couldn't rely on me in a confrontation. I'll be a laughingstock. There's going to be horrible nicknames. 'Take-a-dive Hoshino.' 'Wet-behind-the-ears Hoshino.' It'll be endless."

"I put myself on the firing line."

"Because you had no confidence in me."

I looked skyward in frustration. Problem was, Rie was right about the fallout. But I'd opted for what I believed was the safest solution in the few seconds I'd had. We were both right and, in our insistence, both wrong.

"It's not that," I said. "I'm a parent. My daughter comes first. Before me and before you. I'm sorry, but that's the way it is. It was an on-the-spot decision. I thought it the best way to salvage the situation with the least amount of danger to both of you."

"So, again, in your eyes I was of no use. Did it even occur to you that I could help you hold them off? That two would be better than one against their number?"

This only got worse.

"Yes. That's what I'm trying to tell you. But it gave me less flexibility. There were three of them. In a face-off that would have left one man free to grab Jenny and then use her as leverage against us. I would never expose my daughter to that kind of danger. Even if it meant bruising your ego."

Rie deflated. "It's not my ego you punctured. It's my livelihood. But no matter. My career's over."

She looked at Jenny, then me. Then she shrugged. She saw the inevitability of a parent's reaction even if she wasn't one herself.

"Why?" Jenny asked. "You saved me from the river."

Rie brought herself under control. "No, Jenny-chan, you did that all by yourself. The problem is hard to explain. It's like kids teasing you in school. As soon as the first cop on the scene realizes I'm a police officer, I'm dead. By tomorrow, the word will have spread."

Then she told me how she'd called in the incident herself once she found me again. It was only a matter of moments before the police arrived, and with them her ruin.

An idea occurred to me. "Walk away," I said.

"What?"

"Walk away."

"I can't do that. I have responsi—"

"Yes, you do. To yourself first, then your family, then the MPD. In that order. So leave us."

"I can't—"

"You can and you should. Go now. While there's still time."

I looked around. I saw two squad cars about half a mile away, coming fast along the access road, lights flashing, sirens silent. Farther back, on the river, a patrol boat motored toward us. Too bad the speedboat was long gone.

"But people know I know you."

"Across town in Shibuya and Shinjuku. Not here."

"But if they make the connection—"

"—then we can worry about it."

Rie hesitated, torn between duty and self-preservation. "I have to explain things."

"No you don't. I'm capable of handling the police."

"But when they ask for me, you'll—"

"—I know nothing about you. You happened to be out sightseeing or shopping on your day off, so you called it in. Clean yourself up and come back if you want, but they'll only want you as a witness later since you were off-duty. Am I wrong?"

"I'm not sure, but—"

"—I'll say there was a woman with us but she left. I'll say she was Japanese-American, with an American passport, and didn't want to get involved. They'll never know. Even if they bother to look into the fake name I'll give them, it won't lead to you. I'll just refuse to give them the woman's real identity because she doesn't wish to get involved. End of story."

Jenny started to speak. I gave her a swift look that said this was *not* the kind of lying we always discussed, and I'd explain later.

"But—" Rie said.

"Go. Hurry. There's no other way."

Rie opened her mouth to speak, paused, closed it, and nodded glumly. "You should have trusted me, Brodie" was all she said before she turned her back on us and walked off. At the end of the bridge, she melted into the crowd, returning twenty-five minutes later dried and groomed and wearing a different blouse and pants, no doubt procured from one of the many shops a few blocks over.

In the interim, the police had arrived. Six squad cars and fifteen policemen had gathered, many of the cops arriving on bicycle, a common practice in Tokyo. The tally was courtesy of my very attentive daughter.

Rie identified herself. After the officer-in-charge took down her name and badge number, he passed her off to an underling, who listened to her report with growing disinterest. At the conclusion, both men mumbled perfunctory thanks and dismissed her with the usual platitudes about getting in touch should they have any further questions.

Would my plan work? Maybe.

In her brief reappearance on the bridge, Rie smiled once at Jenny. She made no eye contact with me.

When she walked away for the second time, she didn't look back.

You should have trusted me, Brodie.

DAY 6

BLACK WIND

CHAPTER 32

J ENNY and I couldn't go home.

For us there was only one safe place in all of Tokyo. We slept on a pair of futon in Brodie Security's back room, with five men on more bedding in the office space between our bunks and the front door.

Jenny's radar was up. I could see her wondering if I—her one remaining parent—was in danger. She was nervous and confused. She hadn't seen the Triads when they boarded the boat. She'd spotted me on top of the ferry, but with buildings and trees interrupting her view from the taxi, she wasn't entirely clear on the chain of events. Since my falling-out with Rie had unfolded before her eyes, Jenny's focus hovered around the quarrel on the bridge, an unexpected silver lining. The police interviewed me out of earshot of my daughter, so I was able to smooth Jenny's ruffled feathers with a white lie about our sleepover at the office and a short exchange about Rie, which ended on a good note.

"Is she really mad at us, Daddy?" Jenny had asked, her eyes beginning to droop.

"Only at me."

"Can we play with her another day?"

"That's a very good question. Truthfully, I don't know, but I hope so."

"I still love you, Daddy."

"And I you. Are you sure you're okay with all that happened today?"

"Oh, yes. I'll tell you why later, okay? I'm sleepy now."

Jenny had always been like that. She either announced she was going to bed or simply trundled off into her room without a word.

I said another time was okay, speculating on what "later" would bring, and my daughter was asleep the next instant. If only Rie would come around so easily.

———

At 7:04 a.m., Jenny and I headed for the airport.

Under the pretext of getting her back in time for school while I was stranded in Tokyo for business, I put my daughter on the first plane out of Haneda Airport. I wanted her away from Japan fast. The flight flew to Singapore, where, after a two-hour layover, she would board a plane to San Francisco. Two capable Brodie Security operatives would deliver my daughter to Lieutenant Frank Renna of the SFPD, a good friend. Jenny would stay with him and his family until things calmed down on these shores.

Renna and I had been through this two months ago with Japantown. It was hard to believe that a similar scenario was playing out again.

Right up until the time she passed through security, Jenny had babbled on alternately about her great swimming test in the Sumida River and her upcoming soccer adventures. Despite her cheerful demeanor—due, in part, to my signing her soccer papers—I wasn't entirely convinced she'd come through the incident unscathed, so I'd asked Renna and his wife to keep an eye out for any signs of anxiety.

I left the airport hoping Miura's case was a domestic affair confined to the Japanese archipelago.

———

With Jenny safely tucked away, I returned to matters at hand.

At 9:08, I walked back through the doors of Brodie Security.

At 9:12, everyone involved in the Miura case gathered in the conference room.

By 9:21, we had planned our next moves and rallied everyone for in-house damage control, which included procedures for my safety going forward.

Minutes after we wrapped up, Rie rang with news.

"I am making this call under protest," she began. "What you did yesterday was inexcusable."

All the warmth of our meeting in the coffeehouse and the first moments on the boat was smothered by a rigid formality. When I tried to jump the chasm, she cut me off:

"I don't wish to discuss the ferry incident further. However, after yesterday's attack, new information is essential for the case, so I am moving forward with your request, which I cleared first with Inspector Kato. Your involvement is acceptable but your role is unofficial. These are conditions you must agree to without question or modification."

Jesus. The doghouse to end all doghouses.

"Are you there, Brodie?"

I said yes.

"Do you agree?"

I said yes again.

"Good. My home-stay friend came through. We need to go to Yokohama Chinatown."

I was impressed. At Brodie Security, we'd dug up nothing but dead ends. We'd found no helpful notes in Hamada's desk, and the homicide detectives found nothing on his body, which had turned up six hours later at a construction site. When I'd checked in with TNT, the yaki leg breaker had nothing to add. Even Noda had shuffled into the office in defeat.

So the Chinatown lead was welcome. Especially since C-town was notoriously impenetrable.

"And?" I said.

"My friend has found something through the family associations. Do you know what they are?"

"Yes."

Informal family groups function as anchors for resident and incoming Chinese. The loose-knit alliance finds lodging and employment for the newly arrived, supplies low-interest loans for anyone wishing to start their own business, and even arranges funerals. The associations revolve around common family surnames and crossed all social barriers. You have bankers and dishwashers with the same surname, so they all belong. You also have loan sharks and gangs. If you aren't careful, a harmless inquiry could bring the Triads or Tongs to your front door. In this case that could be ruinous.

"Did you get guarantees?"

"Of course."

"Do they know of the possible Triad involvement?"

"What do you take me for?"

Right. I retreated to the procedural. "So what's the next step?"

"My friend's name is Danny Chang. He said there's an old Chinese activist from the mainland we should talk to."

Few people today are aware that Yokohama Chinatown had harbored Chinese rebels in the past, and some famous ones at that. Chiang Kai-shek, aka Jiang Jieshi, a leader of the Nationalists in China and later their ruler-in-exile in Taiwan, had used Yokohama as his base at one time. As did his mentor, Sun Yat-sen, or Sun Yixian. You could pick up a lot when you rooted around in Asian history, but Rie's lead was still a long shot.

I said, "Why did he think an old rebel could help?"

"Because he's one of the most respected members of the Chang family association."

"And you trust your friend with this?"

"Yes. But go carefully. With Chinese, there are *always* others. I know nothing about them."

When I punched in the telephone number Rie had supplied, I was greeted with a series of tonal shifts. The signal sounded like it was being rerouted over ancient landlines rather than flying between cell towers, meaning the path would be that much harder to trace. I counted five pitch changes.

"Yeah, what want?" a voice finally said in choppy Japanese.

"Danny Chang sent me."

"You man named Brodie?"

"Yes."

"You want ask about home invasions?"

"And the others. Yes."

"Why you want know?"

"Because the victims were friends of my client. I think the killings have a connection to a murder in Kabukicho, but I don't know what it is. Or why they are doing what they are doing. Or who."

"What kind friends?"

"I can't say."

"Good-bye, Mr. Brodie-san."

"Wait. What do you need?"

"What friends?"

Right. Again, I had my client's confidentiality to consider. This time weighed against our lack of progress. Would this lead anywhere? Hard to know. It continued to feel like a long shot, but on the other hand, it *was* a Chinese connection.

"Old army friends," I said. "From World War Two."

"Hold."

A hand covered the mouthpiece on his end, and I waited out a muffled conversation of staccato questions and answers in a rhythm that was not Japanese.

The voice came back on. "Why you find these killings?"

Single-minded fellow. No thank-you for waiting, no apology, just rapid-fire questions.

"Hello? Why you find these killings?"

"I went to Kabukicho and noticed the similarities. Yesterday, one of my friends was killed. His head arrived at my office by messenger with my picture nailed to his forehead. Minutes later some men with meat axes attacked me on a ferry."

There was another huddle behind the shielded receiver. "Okay. Maybe we help you. I introduce you my uncle."

"Good."

"Rie come, you come. That's all. No more others. Nobody follow, nobody watch. If others come, we kill them, we kill you."

"Maybe Rie should stay behind."

"We kill just you. Rie friend to us."

"She's a friend to me."

"Maybe she not always choose friends wisely."

Now there's something Rie would agree to. Doing so in front of these guys could get me slaughtered.

I said, "She chose Danny Chang."

"No funny funny. No follow. We kill."

"Okay. Tell me where."

"You know Chinatown?"

"Not well."

"Okay. You go Sakuragicho Station and jump taxi. You tell driver Silver Dragon Restaurant and pass through Good Neighbor Gate. That Zenrin Mon in Japanese. Maybe driver no want do because always crowded, but you pay extra him. We watching."

"Fine. Then what?"

"You go restaurant three o'clock. You tell name Hozumi Higuchi. You order Full Lucky Dragon Course. They bring tea. You sip three times. Both you sip three times. You spill tea and say, 'Oh my pant ruined.' That final signal. Then you wait. Do not change way of doing instruction. Do not do clever anything. Okay?"

"On my pants? I'll dress down. No designer."

"What?"

"Never mind."

"I say no funny funny. We kill. Kill easy as make funny funny, okay?"

"Okay."

The line went dead.

I did not like the guys we were hunting and I'd developed an immediate dislike for the Chinatown guys, too, even if Rie could vouch for them.

I called the resourceful lady herself and told her we had a date with a man who threatened four times to kill me. She was thrilled.

CHAPTER 33

NODA didn't like the arrangements any more than I did.

"What do you know about Chinatown?" I asked.

"Old school, new school."

"Which are what?"

"Old is gambling, prostitution, extortion, illegals, drugs, fake Guccis, turf wars with machetes."

Some of that I knew. In Chinatown, feuds flared and faded with each wave of immigrants wanting to stake out territory. New blood fought old, region fought region. Gangs from Shanghai, Fujian, Beijing, Hong Kong, Taiwan, and places deeper in the Chinese mainland few of us had heard of gave the public periodic bodies and lurid headlines.

"And new?"

"Hacking, credit cards, identity theft, software piracy."

"Guns?"

"Not for public consumption. Police don't like to be shot at."

Japan, like Britain, had a strict no-gun law and enforced it rigorously. What Noda meant was that if too many bullet-riddled bodies surfaced, the police would tear Chinatown apart brick by brick, disrupting all operations, legal and otherwise. Everyone would suffer.

"So, besides all the legit people in the family association, we'll have some boys flying under the radar. The guys I talked to are cautious. If they've seen even half of what we have, that's exactly how they should be. So, maybe this is not a goose chase."

"Still don't like it. Chinese can be tricky."

"We don't have much choice."

Noda scowled. "A ninety-eight-year-old virgin has more options."

———

Noda drove us as far as Sakuragicho Station, grumbling most of the way.

With Inspector Kato's blessing, we swung by and picked up Rie at Shibuya HQ, then dropped down to Ebisu and caught the Shuto Expressway No. 3 heading south. When we hit the onetime swampy wetlands of Shinagawa, we cut over to the Shuto No. 2 exchange and scooted along the shore toward Yokohama.

Rie sat beside me in the backseat. Over her shoulder the waters of Tokyo Bay sparkled. Up ahead, the chemical plants of Kawasaki spewed yellow-gray fumes.

After her initial greeting she fell silent.

I said, "Any more information since we last talked?"

"No."

"Any comments at your office about yesterday?"

"No."

"No insults or innuendos?"

"Could we not talk about that now?"

A muscle in Noda's right shoulder pulsed.

I nodded and we drove the rest of the way to Yokohama in silence. Which was for the best.

With the upcoming meet, I needed to get my mental house in order. I might have lost my chance with Rie, but I didn't want to lose my life as well.

CHAPTER 34

A S soon as I stepped outside, I felt eyes crawling over me. I went around to Noda's side of the car and leaned on the sill.

"They're here," I said.

"Yeah."

Rie said, "How do you know?"

Noda shot her a look. "Feel 'em."

"Oh."

"Where?" I said. "I got end of the lane. Either the blue Mazda or the gray Subaru. Maybe both."

Noda nodded. "Subaru, Mazda, and a cab or two."

"That many?"

"Probably have a fleet en route."

"Makes sense. Should be in good hands." I glanced at Rie.

"They're my friends," she said.

Noda frowned. "Still don't like it."

"Can't be helped," I said. "Come on, Rie, let's go meet your Danny Chang."

"Watch yourself," Noda said.

I nodded and we headed toward the line of taxis.

Noda made a show of waving and drove off as arranged. We slid into the first car in line and the driver asked, "Where to?"

"The Silver Dragon Restaurant in Chinatown. Through the Zenrin Mon."

"The gate's a bottleneck this time of the day."

A bottleneck. Figured. Give our watchers time to get a close look at anyone following.

"An extra thousand?"

"Done."

Yokohama is the black sheep of the Greater Tokyo area. It is something less than Japanese, and something more.

Until the 1850s, it had been an impoverished fishing village on the sandy shores of Tokyo Bay. Sixty families harvested rice and sea cucumbers, which they exported to China at a hefty premium.

Then the American gunboats arrived.

The ships' overwhelming firepower forced the ruling samurai to open the country's doors to trade. The West's advanced weaponry also mooted all the shogunate's efforts to revive kendo and samurai sword-fighting skills.

His arm twisted, the shogun turned the sleepy backwater village of Yokohama into a fenced ghetto.

But despite a studied neglect from the authorities, the outpost flourished. Trading houses from Europe, America, and China grew rich, and Japanese merchants brave enough to risk contact with the oversize barbarians also prospered. Yokohama evolved into a hybrid sea-front town where the adventurous native tasted—for the first time—ice cream, beer, meat, and bread.

The Chinese entered the picture quietly. They dropped anchor with the big Western trading houses out of Hong Kong and nearby Canton, working as servants, carpenters, longshoremen, and compradors, the trading-house foremen of legend who wore long, well-oiled queues and soon learned to read Japanese because of the related Chinese writing system.

Over time, the Chinese eased out many of the aging trading firms they had begun with, until they were in turn passed over by Japanese who had become accustomed to Western ways.

Today, Yokohama herself has been all but dismissed by nearby Tokyo, becoming, in part, a suburban bedroom town for Tokyoites priced out of choicer city center locations. Even so, Yokohama and its residents retain a large measure of their pioneering spirit and port-town pride.

The taxi driver said, "Chinatown straight ahead. That's the gate."

"I see it."

"I could still take a side street. It's bumper-to-bumper up there."

"Through the gate, please."

He shrugged and our cab slowed to a crawl behind a line of cars. On the sidewalks affluent Chinese from Beijing and Shanghai studied shops with a critical eye. Young women strutted by in the latest designer fashions, while day laborers from the mainland cut through the crowds in stained undershirts, with burlap sacks hoisted on their shoulders.

We rolled under the gate, a double-roofed tower on vermilion pillars. The crush of bodies grew thicker. A clatter of Mandarin and Cantonese rose up all around us like a flock of chatty birds. From Chinese restaurants and bakeries, the smells of sweet cakes and shrimp and stir-fry filled the air.

Two blocks down our driver turned right, pulled to a stop in front of a Chinese herbalist's window with a sign touting fresh deer-horn shavings, and pointed across the street. "Silver Dragon Restaurant there."

I forked over the fare and Rie said thank you.

As I paid I glanced discreetly around. Nothing. The feeling of eyes-on was gone.

That didn't mean much.

We were deep inside their territory now.

CHAPTER 35

WE pushed through sparkling glass doors. Outside, the restaurant flashed a black marble facade, red pillars, and a miniature potted peach tree in a large olive-green vase. Inside, there was more black marble on the floors and walls, and olive green on the tables.

Chinese chic.

I mentioned the name Hozumi Higuchi to a young hostess in an emerald-green silk dress with a high collar and ocher embroidery. No eyebrows were raised and no raving gang members emerged from the shadows with machetes.

She consulted a reservation book, then led us up a flight of stairs to a private room with undulating dragons slithering along the upper edges of three walls and floor-to-ceiling mirrors along the fourth. An oversize lazy Susan sat in the center of a round banquet table for twelve.

"Will the others be arriving shortly?" our escort asked, in stilted but grammatically correct Japanese.

"We're all here," I said.

She cocked a head at the table. "Two peoples?"

I nodded. "We have big appetites."

The hostess checked her reservation pad, shrugged, and left.

An instant after we were shut in, a door at the back of the room opened to admit an older woman bearing menus and two cups of tea on a black lacquer tray. She set a cup of tea in front of each of us, bowed, and retreated.

I spread the menu. "I'm feeling plucky today. What say we splurge on the Full Lucky Dragon Course? My treat?"

The Full Lucky Dragon Course selected by the anonymous voice on the phone sat in a lowly corner of an attenuated list of special courses. It offered your blasé egg-drop mishmash, a beef dish, and dessert. The Silver, Gold, and Platinum courses rose in position and opulence, featuring shark-fin soup for openers, followed by Peking duck and a parade of delicacies from abalone to lobster to braised sea cucumber.

Rie studied the menu. "You have a reason for your selection?"

"Yeah. I wanted to tell you in the car, but you requested silence."

She narrowed her eyes at me. "On *non*business matters."

"Ah," I said. "We're to order the Full Lucky Dragon, sip our tea three times, then I'm to spoil my wardrobe. Now you know as much as I do."

"Thank you."

"Sure."

Doghouse.

When a waiter in a starched white shirt and olive-green vest pranced in, I ordered the lowly course as instructed and got a frown of disapproval.

Nobody in this place was clued in to our special invite. "Last time," I said, "we tried Platinum and the duck was off."

"I'm sorry, sir."

"Think nothing of it."

"Yes, sir."

No funny funny. He collected the menus and departed.

We lifted our teacups and drank. I spilled a few drops on my pants and said, "My best Levi's will never be the same."

Then our unseen hosts rolled out the first of their surprises.

CHAPTER 36

ONE of the floor-to-ceiling mirrored panels swung away from the wall and a Chinese man rushed into the room. He had a faint knife wound under his left ear and one eyelid hung lower than another, like a broken insect wing.

"My name Lester Chang. Same Chang like Danny Chang. You come quick, mister. You too, miss. No talk-talk."

We followed him through the hidden door and into a dark hall lined with peeling sheets of bare plywood, then down narrow steps. The smells of stale stir-fry saturated the air.

At the foot of the stairs, a cook in a greasy apron and two inches of ash drooping from his cigarette stepped from the kitchen and handed our guide a steaming cup of tea. The cook said something in Chinese and Lester Chang listened and frowned.

Rie looked at Lester. "What did he say?"

"He say, no Brodie people follow, no other people follow."

An electric pulse seemed to roll down Rie's back. "Of course not."

"We must be very sure." Lester thrust the ceramic teacup at me. "Drink this."

"What is it?"

"Medicine."

"What *kind* of medicine?"

"Kind of medicine you no drink you die. You already drink drug."

Rie started. "But Danny Chang said—"

"He say you be safe if all okay. All okay. Mister fellow drink, be more okay. Tea also have very expensive ginseng. No charge, heh-heh." He winked at Rie.

Ginseng is taken as an all-around tonic to improve blood circulation, liver functions, and what is vaguely referred to as "manly stamina." Even as the corners of my mouth rose at the thought, a pool of anger welled up in the pit of my chest. I'd noticed the separate cups of tea instead of the usual communal pot, but thought nothing of it at the time. Stupid. Only mine was tainted. These guys were devious.

I drank.

Our newfound Chinese friend said to me, "Raise your hands," and when I did he searched me from head to toe, roughly yanking my shirt free from my pants, feeling for weapons and wires. "Okay, you no carry."

Then he bowed deeply to Rie. "I must do same, miss. But be not worried."

She nodded, and his fingertips glided sparingly over her swells and curves, light and respectful and unobtrusively grazing all the potential hiding places with the touch of a highly skilled technician who knew his job. His hands never lingered. Good thing, otherwise he'd have more than poison to worry about.

"Now your shoes, miss." He examined Rie's shoes and handed them back.

"You also, mister."

I slipped out of my black-on-black Reeboks. Our guide reached inside and felt around, then examined the bottoms thoroughly. With a frown, he gestured for me to slip them back on. He watched me closely through narrowed eyes as I did so, sulking and grumbling to himself.

He'd found nothing and was unhappy in the extreme.

Not a good sign.

CHAPTER 37

WE slipped out the back of the restaurant into a shaded alley and headed west at a fast clip, our escort anxiously glancing ahead and behind and into each crevice between buildings.

Open doorways lined the passage. In industrial kitchens, foot-high flames danced from rows of Frisbee-size gas burners, while hatless cooks shuffled husky woks—sometimes one in each hand. Cleavers lay around like fallen leaves. On chopping boards. On counters. More hung on the walls with other utensils. All were within easy reach.

"Don't bump walls," our guide said, nodding at hardened rivers of congealed grease trickling from kitchen vents. "Dirty yellow dripping catch you, it never let go. Like Chinese ghost."

The alleyway bisected a narrow road of grocers and hole-in-the-wall Chinese grills for locals. Lester Chang motioned us into the shadows. He covered the last ten yards alone and coughed into his fist.

Rie whispered in my ear. "Our feet are still on the ground, but we've left Japan."

"No argument here."

A man hawking bamboo steamers from a rickety wooden table on the far side of the street began brushing his wares with languorous sweeps of a feather duster as he cast bored looks around, in search of potential customers.

When the merchant scratched his ear, Chang said, "Okay, we go now," and the three of us shot across the street past the first manned checkpoint, and into the next leg of the alley, turning twice into progressively narrower passageways until we came to the rear of an antiques shop.

Entering on Chang's heels, we paused to let our eyes adjust to the gloom. The ornaments of Old Yokohama spilled from every shelf: leather valises from Austria, Russian samovars, Dutch delftware, Chinese medicine chests.

Chang grunted at the proprietress, an eighty-year-old woman bundled up in a shapeless gray dress sitting behind a classic cash register with brass fittings and a marble panel across the front.

She turned her head away as we passed. Survival instincts.

Lester led us to a side room, where he rolled aside a French bureau on casters to reveal a waist-high service door.

He pulled the panel aside and knocked twice. Inches away, a matching door in the neighboring building swung open. Stooping, we shuffled through and swept by the large stainless-steel sinks of a fishmonger's kitchen, the smell robustly piscine. At the far side of the shop, we stepped directly out the door and into the rear of a waiting delivery van.

Wooden pallets ran across the floor of the van. Underfoot, water sprinkled with glistening fish scales rippled when we boarded. Three wooden vegetable crates upended and covered with stained dish towels made up the seating. Rie and I sat side by side along the length of the van directly behind the driver. Lester took the crate across from us.

He was still frowning.

Unseen hands slammed the doors shut and the van shot forward. All the windows were darkened. No one could see in. We couldn't see out. The vehicle took a circuitous route, often over uneven roads. Water sluiced under the pallets. Fish scales winked in the dim cabin light.

At various points along the route, the driver flicked his lights on and off. Checkpoints. Two minutes after the fifth such exchange, we entered a murky enclosure. We parked. The driver rolled down his window. There was a mumbled exchange in Chinese.

The van doors swung open with a creak. The sound ricocheted in the darkness of an unlit warehouse. Our heels hit cement with a crack. More echoes. Overhead, a skeletal network of iron beams hovered in a cavernous gloom. Along each wall, a man stood guard, gun drawn but hanging loosely at his side.

Right. No one would get past them without a fight.

The driver tossed two uncovered crates of fish into the van, his alibi for the return trip. Without a word, Lester scurried through a darkened doorway. We trailed after him and then down a blackened stairwell to a basement. He lifted a steel plate in the floor and we descended a metal ladder into the sewers.

We found ourselves in cool cement piping eight feet in diameter. Straddling the stream of waste in the pipe's curved belly, we scuttled forward as if we had chains around our ankles. When another ladder appeared, we climbed upward into a second warehouse. More men with guns. This time tucked in their belts. A commercial cab idled near the door. There would be hundreds of similar cabs on the streets of Yokohama at this time of the day.

Lester pointed at a hose curled on the floor. "We wash shoes, ride car."

Rie and I hosed off our footwear then slid into the waiting taxi. Our guide stepped in after us. The automatic door swung shut, and the car rolled out into traffic.

"Cautious bunch," I said to Rie.

Lester gave me a grumpy look. "You speak more loud. Please repeat what you say for my ears."

I did.

He frowned. "Uncle is Chang family Ti Zang."

"What is Ti Zang?"

"Ti Zang is Ti Zang. He knows good answers because he lost his everything."

"Rie?"

"I don't know. Sounds holy."

Our escort gave us a toothy snarl. "Yes, yes. Holy Ti Zang. We do everything to protect holy family Ti Zang. Everything."

I stared. "What kind of everything?"

He put a dirty finger in his right ear and scratched. "Many years ago we meet men like you talk of. Enter houses, kill families. Very strong fighters. First time they kill our four guards and contact like you. Second time, we ready ten men. Their men are two. They kill four. We get one."

"And the contact?"

"Very dead. He first target. We learn disappearing is better than fighting. Their fight is strong."

I nodded, gloomy thoughts rising.

He grinned. "But our disappearing is stronger."

The taxi came to a stop in a blue-collar neighborhood. The homes had stucco falling off in chunks. Roofs were patched with corrugated steel.

Lester Chang pointed at a modest steel sign ringed with rust at the edges. "Danny Chang is there."

The sign announced the entrance to Yokohama's Chinese cemetery.

CHAPTER 38

WE trekked down a shady path and found Danny Chang leaning against the cemetery gate at the base of a hill. He wore white summer slacks and a beige linen jacket over a black T-shirt. He pulled a cigarette from a pack of Dunhill Lights.

"Hello, Rie," he said, the cigarette balancing between his lips.

"Hello, Danny. Thank you for making time to see us."

"It's always an honor to be of assistance."

On the other side of the gate, crumbling slate steps led uphill to a stony butte. Single-family bungalows and shoddy apartment complexes crowded the foot of the hill. A pair of snarling stone lions flanked the gate. Tradition had it they were Buddhist guardians of sacred grounds.

Chang's eyes were proud but approachable. "You must be Brodie. I apologize for the ride. Our association has lost many men. Men who are loyal but not fighters."

I said, "So we heard. You have an interesting group."

Danny shrugged, volunteering nothing.

I said, "Our escort said some curious things."

Danny raised an eyebrow. "Such as?"

"That the association would do anything to protect your uncle."

"True enough."

"He called him 'the Chang family Ti Zang.'"

The skin around Danny's eyes crinkled with the dry amusement of a hundred generations. "It is a fitting title, I think."

"What is he? A monk?"

"No. Ti Zang is the protector of children and suffering souls. He speaks for those who have no voice."

I said, "A religious leader? A pilgrim?"

"Not a leader like you mean. Maybe a pilgrim of life. Like a living Buddha. He is nothing and everything and he is holy."

"I see."

Danny's skin crinkled again. "I think you do."

Rie stiffened. "Danny, your men poisoned us."

"Just Brodie." He flicked his cigarette butt at a patch of weeds and shoved his hands in his pants. "There is much at stake."

Rie's expression was stern. "Some of your men look, well, shady."

"The family association pulls together, but people have different talents, Rie. And we have to let them do their jobs the way they know how. The Changs gain only widows when we grow careless."

"But poison?"

"After you talk to Uncle, you'll see why we're so careful. Of course, had your friend here pulled anything, he'd be dead."

"Danny!"

"Sorry, Rie, those are the rules around Uncle. Over the years some people have come after him, and others sent small armies."

I said, "So what was in the antidote? Our guide looked distinctly unhappy when I drank it."

Danny grinned. "Lester? I can imagine."

Rie said, "Why?"

"We don't know Mr. Brodie. Only you."

"And Lester Chang's role?"

Danny cleared his throat behind a tight fist. "Should things have gone sour, he was granted certain concessions in return for performing the rather tricky task of disposal."

"What kind of concessions?"

"Nothing really."

Rie said, "We are not moving from this spot, Danny Chang, until you answer my question."

Danny lit another Dunhill, inhaled deeply, and stared at Rie, exhaling smoke with a sigh. "Lester was pouting, wasn't he? Always does when things go well." He took another long pull of his cigarette. "In exchange for disposing of a traitor's body, he has harvest rights."

"What do you mean?"

"Body organs."

"Danny!"

He gave another shrug. "Big black market. Transplants, elixirs, delicacies for connoisseurs. What can I say, Rie? Compromises must be made."

"You could have started by putting a little more faith in us."

"Procedure was set long ago. Besides, it's a time-honored Chinese tradition."

"What tradition is that?" Rie demanded with constabulary disapproval.

Danny grinned. "Waste not, want not."

"Go ahead and laugh, but your Lester Chang looked like he might take matters into his own hands."

Rie's eyes flung daggers, and I wondered if she was taking out some of her frustration with me on Danny.

His grin vanished and he grew deadly serious. "The Chang Family Association is honorable when it gives its word. So are the Changs, and all are Changs today. Now, shall we stop arguing over procedure and go see Uncle? He will be waiting."

CHAPTER 39

W E called them Black Wind. No one meet them and live. Except me."

"I've never heard of them."

Uncle Chang turned world-weary brown eyes in my direction. He had a full head of silver hair and a triangular face with dark sacks under the eyes. "You say some men attack you?"

"Yes."

"How?"

I told him about Hamada's severed head with my picture, and the raid on the ferry. Then I backtracked to the home invasions and Yoji's murder. I skipped over the death of the third man in Miura's troop since I had almost no information on it. Last, I mentioned that the meat cleaver used to hack off Hamada's head looked to be the same instrument employed to remove Yoji's arm, according to the latest police update. This was courtesy of Rie on the ride over, in a very terse report.

Old Chang absorbed my disclosures without expression, his eyes probing in a manner older than the ages.

———

His look had been cryptic from the start.

Danny had led us up the set of decaying stairs to a hilltop crowded with Chinese tombstones.

Behind a brick temple with vermilion doors, I saw the mausoleum, home to the "patient dead." Years ago, a coffin ship would transport the deceased back to the motherland. The custom ground to a halt when

Mao closed China. The caskets of homesick expats piled up. I wondered if they still waited.

"This is Uncle Chang," Danny had said.

The mysterious man we'd come to meet sat on a cemetery bench. He wore a gray knit shirt and a threadbare navy blazer with a rolled Chinese newspaper stuffed into a side pocket. He'd plunged right in with the Black Wind.

Now he asked, "The killers came at night?"

"All except the ferry attack."

"With chopping weapons?"

"Mostly."

Uncle Chang closed his eyes and placed his hands on his knees. His breathing slowed. I sent a questioning look at Danny, but his gaze was fixed on the family Ti Zang.

A minute passed. Then another. Chang opened his eyes, reached for a pack of Guangdong cigarettes on the bench next to his leg, and lit up.

"What you think, Brodie-san?" he asked, exhaling the question with a blast of blue-gray smoke.

"Everyone thinks they're Triads."

"What *you* think?"

From a distance they looked Japanese but didn't. A bit closer and they looked Chinese but didn't.

"I want to believe we're dealing with Triads because it gives us a clear target, but I'm not convinced. And one of my sources insists it's not Triads."

Chang nodded in appreciation. "You found clever source."

"So you know who they are?"

"I know who they *aren't*," he said, his gaze shifting to a middle-aged Chinese couple emerging at the head of the stairway.

They bowed to Uncle Chang and headed toward the graveyard. The man, in a worn yellow windbreaker and a sagging undershirt, carried a watering can. The woman cradled a bouquet of flowers wrapped in newsprint. A pale blue summer dress hung on her thin frame.

"Many of my friends rest their bones on this hilltop," Uncle Chang told me.

I nodded.

"We inhabit this country for a safe life," he continued, "but we never forget our homeland. China is like tired mother who takes bad lovers and has no time for her children. We can return to her only after time passes and her latest lover has gone away. Ming Dynasty, Qing Dynasty, Nationalists, Japanese Imperial army, Communists, Mao's Cultural Revolution, capitalistic Communists—they are all bad lovers. We Chinese worship our country, but we are unlucky in our governments."

"I'd say so."

Chang's eyes followed the couple as they wove through the tombstones. "This is fine spot for visit to my friends, don't you think?"

"Yes," I said carefully, "pleasant."

Chang exhaled a thin stream of smoke. "Good. You are serious man. Your ears are open to listen. So I tell you story."

"I would be honored."

"It is not pleasant story."

"I've seen my share of unpleasant in the last few days."

"Then I pray your recent troubles have prepared you."

CHAPTER 40

I WAS born in a village so small the mapmakers turned their faces away.

"Like my father, I became a traditional herb doctor. Fourth generation in our family. We traveled over countryside filled with Chinese farmers working Chinese soil and grazing Chinese pigs and sheep and cows. We owned horse for pulling our cart. This was great good fortune. Other peoples have only donkeys. Most have no animal and when they plow their field they are donkey.

"Father and I visit sick peoples all over northern Manchuria, getting our payment sometimes in coin but mostly in chickens and goats and rice and sorghum. Sometimes people have no money or food to pay so we give them some chickens and goats and grain off our cart. My father was generous man, and honest. You would know this because our house was modest and my father had no concubines. Also, he was clever man. His cleverness save my life.

"In our house we have no rich decoration like other doctors. No Western furnitures, no velvet curtains, no Chinese carpets from big city. 'Don't breed envy in others,' my father say. His money went in 'garden-bank,' a steel box set in our backyard under large gray stone.

"'After big good luck follow big unluck,' my father teach us. 'Safety first, then luxury, but only small luxury.' I listen well to my father's speakings. At seventeen I marry. My fifteen-year-old wife pick out one silk dress so she can feel her beauty. Her selection is green with lucky dragon-scale pattern and she is delicate and lovely in it. We bury our money in garden-bank. We are happy, and the wise gods fill our needs.

One day, just like my father tell us, unluckiness arrive in our village, and it is unstoppable.

"With money from garden-bank I escape to Japan. Now I live in Yokohama in small China."

Not entirely convinced the conversation was headed in a useful direction, I said, "So there or here you met the people who might have committed the home invasions?"

Uncle Chang shot a plume of cigarette smoke skyward. "I know style of groups who attack me over many years, so I show where you find answer."

"Fair enough. Do you know an Akira Miura by any chance, from the old days back in China?" I pointed Miura out in a photograph I'd liberated from his home.

Chang squinted at the picture. "He look like lead army man in next big town."

"If you know him, maybe you know a Wu? He was a doctor like you."

Uncle Chang grew still. Danny turned pale. The next instant two armed men emerged from behind the mausoleum, guns leveled our way.

Rie shot me a fearful glance.

The gunmen inched closer.

"What is it, Danny?" Rie whispered.

Uncle Chang said, "I am doctor you seek. I am Wu."

CHAPTER 41

HEARING one coincidence too many, I'd played a hunch.
Now a pair of thugs stood four yards away. Close enough to put a hole in me without effort. Far enough away so that I couldn't get at them. I'd promised to come alone, and stuck to my word. Wu's people hadn't committed to anything.

Lester, our sour-faced escort, no doubt also a Wu, might get his wish after all.

———

Before I could stop her, Rie exploded. "So is anything you told me true, Danny?"

"Rie," he said. "You have to understand. I—"

Uncle Wu jumped in. "All is true. Name change is for safety only."

Rie shifted her wrath to the newly minted Wu. "Are there any other 'true' things for safety only?"

One of the gunnies panned his weapon in Rie's direction.

Wu flushed. "Chang Family Association is Wu Family Association. We spread no more safety lies."

Rie rolled her eyes. "And you, Danny *Chang*. My so-called friend. If this is really the Wu Family Association, what are you doing here?"

Danny cast a nervous glance at the triggermen. "Keep your voice down. They don't understand Japanese and if they think you're a threat . . ."

Rie's eyes flared. "What? They'll *shoot* me?"

"Rie, please. These guys—"

"Are what? Never mind. Just call them off."

"Only Lester can do that."

"I know I asked for your help, but why'd they let you in this far, Danny?"

Rie's longtime Hong Kong friend pursed his lips. "My, um, mother's maiden name is Wu."

Rie closed her eyes. Her face reddened. First me, then Danny had dented her professional pride.

"Hear me out," he said. "Around Uncle, danger is the byword. He has worked for years to help his people back home. He sends supplies. And literature. He speaks for those who have no voice. The party doesn't like it. They send men. Some of them are killers."

I laid a reassuring hand on Rie's arm. "You really can't blame them for being cautious. It was Brodie Security they were worried about, not you."

"Exactly," Danny said.

"Well, then," Rie said, her professional calm reemerging, "we have questions. Lots of questions."

"I understand. Let me have a quick word with Uncle." After a hurried exchange in Chinese, Danny turned back to us. "Uncle is old-school. He wants to explain in his own way. Is that acceptable?"

We agreed. Not that we had much choice.

Danny punched a number in his cell phone, conducted a second rapid-fire exchange in Chinese, then disconnected. A phone on the lead shooter's hip buzzed. Flashing a warning look in my direction, he scanned a text message, then slipped the gun centered on my chest into the back of his waistband. Both men disappeared once more behind the mausoleum.

Wu's gaze swept from the tombstones to us.

His brow had darkened.

CHAPTER 42

NOBODY know why seven Yang family members wake up dead," the Wu patriarch began in a subdued voice, "but whole village was terrified."

My thoughts ran immediately to the home invasions.

"Very very big unluck. Old Yang was village head for years. Japanese army announce plague kill Yangs so everything must be burned. All of village gather to watch towering orange flames eat three generations of Yangs.

"But death visited our village even earlier. Every month traveling vendors come for big market day. Summer cottons and fine silks are colors of yellow and green and red. Good-luck charms from famous temples glitter in morning sun. In bamboo cages there are fatted brown ducks and rabbits. You can find turtle eggs and dried jellyfish and fresh-picked mushrooms. Spirit-mediums wearing dark turbans of mountain peoples talk with ghost-spirits of departed loved ones.

"One market day Japanese platoon marched into our village and kill first two peoples they find. The soldiers send five bullets to Hatless Yu, who repair carts and dig irrigation ditches. They stab their bayonets into Great-Grandmother Sweet-Fists Liu. She would ball up her hands into fat red fists and when she open them village children always find sweets inside.

"With these twin deaths Japanese army tame my village. We are near big highway into North Manchuria. Our rich farmland yields many kilos of rice and sorghum and vegetable. Japanese take all for their troop. The army reach their hands everywhere. Crops, livestock, and store supplies disappear. They raid homes and grab mini gold bars and every valuable. Our village become poor overnight.

"The soldiers were short and mean-eyed. We hear other Chinese call them *wogou*, 'dwarf bandits,' and we now understand why. But they are worse than their name. They take over village office. They take over farm policy bureau. They take over police station. Into our schoolhouse come Japanese teachers. They force Chinese teachers to wash floors on their hands and knees and kick them in front of Chinese children to prove Chinese learning has no worth.

"Number Two man in village before unlucky Village Head Yang wake up dead is Xeng Shinyin. Xeng has only one child. Her oval face and wide lemon-shape eyes are famous in our region. She is Once in Thousand Moons Treasure. Xeng push her to study most polite Japanese phrases in new schoolbooks, and when we have arrival of important dwarf bandit she sing Japanese song at welcome ceremony. Two weeks later traditional matchmaker arrive from faraway big city. A month following, a grand marriage is celebrated. They carry Xeng's daughter away to new Japanese husband's house in big city. It is the finest ceremony in our village history, with famous Chinese musicians and wedding sedan of most expensive red silks. Two months later when Yang family wake up dead, Number Two Xeng become Number One Xeng.

"Our tiny village rejoice about big marriage. It must bring big good luck, we believe. But we are wrong. Dwarf bandits take even more and soon we have only gruel. We crush boiled leaves into it for flavor and nourishment. We get thinner and thinner and my patients catch many diseases. I am busy all day and many nights. Only New Village Head Xeng grow fat. He take two concubines and build big house with high walls and many fruit trees.

"Big bad luck had found us. And on fourth harvest Black Wind found me."

CHAPTER 43

BLACK Wind men walk light and quiet. With them come Chinese collaborators who can speak dwarf-bandit language.

"Black Wind group pay respect to Japanese village head then charge into my home without bows or manners. Knowing I am traveling doctor, they show me a list of villages and ask me to guide them. In their faces I see dark clouds so I decline, saying my hands overflowing with sick peoples. One patient is there. The leader shoot him and ask me to introduce other sick peoples. Also my wife and child. I agree to lead them.

"We travel at night dressed in straw rain-capes and wide hats of Chinese peasant-farmers. In daytime we sleep in forests or hills. I listen to their stories. From years of travels I grew ears to absorb language because Chinese dialects are many. Two years before Black Wind come I already absorb dwarf-bandit tongue.

"That is how I find Japanese soldiers have only disdain in their hearts for us. We are dogs to them. Beneath hate and envy. How can you be jealous of dog? How can dog speak their language? They believe it impossible even though they have two Chinese traitors with them. But I never talk dwarf-bandit words to dwarf bandits. Too dangerous. My captors address me in simple Chinese and I answer in Chinese they can understand. Chinese traitors do not speak to me at all. I am dog to dwarf bandits but I am bug to them.

"My captors are nine. Seven dwarf bandits and two Chinese. All of them are vicious men. They carry special poisons. One poison is no-taste, slow-action poison. They drop it in village wells before morning water is taken. Around midnight, the horrible screamings begin. Men and women shriek and moan. Stronger men sometimes run into streets, clawing at their throats until blood flows. Then they collapse squealing and thrashing in middle of muddy village road, dying like slaughtered pigs. I am doctor. I want to run and help. But I am always bound to tree. Watching from woods, my captors laugh and laugh.

"Like this we visit one or two villages every week. Nightly, they tie me to tree and they watch dying with great happiness. Sometimes, when village is small, my captors do killing by hand. I can always tell when those days approach because joy dances in their eyes, and when they return I can see sleepy satisfaction on their faces.

"Strapped to tree, I watch their shadows move in moonlight from house to house. They circle first and kill village dogs, then enter each hut of mud bricks and straw and kill all family members.

"In two minutes, one Black Wind fighter destroy lifeblood of family maybe fifty generations old. In ten minutes, five families. In fifteen minutes, nine men butcher whole sleeping village.

"One morning, after their hand murdering, I am fixing rice porridge with pickled plums from dwarf-bandit homeland. Suddenly village gong is pounding loudly in craziness.

"A Black Wind man say, 'We miss one,' and they all laugh."

"The gong sounds twice more and then old man comes running down dirt road right by our hiding place. His feet are bare. He is howling at heaven. My captors creep to edge of trees. The old man runs away, still yelling to skies, 'The devil has risen! The devil has risen! They are all dead!'

"I have nicknames for my captors like Snake Eyes, Crazy Fingers, Silent Knife. There is baby-face soldier I call Young One. He say, 'That was good' and they all snicker. Then strange conversation start.

"'Someone was sloppy.'

"'He must be punished.'

"'Severely.'

"'We need to train harder.'

"'Punishment is must action.'

"'No,' says Snake Eyes, their leader, 'reward is. Our guardian is teaching us new good thing. From tomorrow we leave one alive.'

"'But why?' Young One asked.

"'Because this new thing help our work. Rebel guerilla groups from these parts are killing our soldiers. They snipe them at night, then run into hills and villages to hide. Our job is to return powerful message: you kill soldiers, we kill your families. Our guardian is showing us a stronger way to spread message.'

"And so they do as Snake Eyes command and his devil wisdom is powerful. Soon Chinese people think Japanese demons ride Black Wind sent by angry gods. They see nothing. They hear nothing. But whole villages wake up dead.

"I am only Chinese who know real truth. Then one day I understand bigger truth. Black Wind kill unlucky Yang family. Not plague. It happened *after* Xeng's daughter marry big dwarf bandit. Next I see biggest truth. To keep their secret, Black Wind must kill me too.

"Five weeks later we arrive at big waterway. Bodies float down it like fat gray balloons. Men, women, children, Old Honored Ones also. Dwarf soldiers make their Chinese servants throw bodies in water. To put Chinese bodies inside ground is much trouble. Inside river is easier.

"That day I guide men to last village. Talk is softer that night. I cannot hear their words. Next morning they send me to wash laundry by river.

"When Young One walk toward me, he is jumpy. He never smile at me, but on this morning he give me big grin. Other men are all older and better at hiding feelings. They flatter me, give me good food and sweets, even though I am dog in their eyes. Young One never hide his disgust for Chinese. But on this morning he is stretching his lips wide, giving me a smile warped like old cartwheel too long in sun.

"The hairs on my neck tell me why he is coming. I smile and go back to washing. I watch him from my eye corner. When his gun comes out and his aim is ready, I let myself fall in river. He fire three times but only one bullet hit me. A body is passing and I fall on top of it. It is slimy and cold and fat with bad air. My body slides over to far side. I can see V-shaped bites on corpse where river snakes feasted. The water is fast and pink with blood. Some of it is mine. Strips of flayed gray flesh float on surface around me. The smell is like thousand sewers and my stomach insides pour out, lumpy and bitter, but I lay still. Body smells and my stomach stink gather round me. I can hear Young One chuckling. His sound is close.

"I cling to underbelly of dead body. I keep my eyes mostly closed. I hide my breathing. Fat carcasses with balloon bellies are everywhere around me, washed ashore or snagged by reeds. A teenage boy corpse is beached on a sandbar. Crabs scuttle over him. Greedy little pincers nip his young flesh. I know my new blood might draw river snakes, so I must escape water soon.

"Young One calls to me in his baby Chinese. 'Wu, I am sorry. You know me. I like games. This is bad game. Big mistake. Come back. I fix you sweet bean cake. Come back.'

"His voice is near. When I no answer, he fire gun and I feel a bullet enter Thousand Sewer Body. I make my body jump. He fires again. I jump again. I hear Young One laugh. 'Now, you really dead, Wu. One more mongrel gone.'"

Abruptly, Wu fumbled for a cigarette. His hands trembled. It was a long moment before he could pull one out.

"You poor, poor man," Rie said.

Wu blew smoke out with a deep sigh. "You are kind to consider this old man, Miss Rie. Retelling is like reliving."

"What terrible, terrible things you saw."

Wu blinked. "Yes, very big unlucky. But what come after haunts me more."

CHAPTER 44

AFTER safety is certain," Wu said, "I leave river. I collapse onshore and wake up in farming village I know. I am conscious long enough to teach my rescuers how to bandage wound, then I wedge bullet from hip and pass into blackness.

"For ten days I live in deep fever. I dream of my wife and child. Their smiling faces beg me to return. I tell them soon soon. Once I am home again I will run my hand over my son's smooth cheeks and enjoy my wife in her lucky dragon dress. We will feast with duck eggs to celebrate our reunion.

"When my fever flies and my strength rebounds, I travel to my village. In two weeks, I reach home. Every night I dream of my family, and every morning I wake with smiling face.

"My escape is miracle number one. Our reunion will be miracle number two. For one lifetime, that is enough. After I reach home, I vow to live a quiet respectful life.

"When I appear at village entrance, the children run off screaming. In the marketplace no one looks at me.

"My mind is greatly confused. First I think I did not survive and have turned into ghost-spirit. But I pinch my arm and feel pain. Next I think they know my shame. But learning Black Wind secret is impossible. Then I think Snake Eye's men spread lies about me. But they planned to kill me, so this cannot be.

"Suddenly, I read in villagers' avoiding looks most horrible truth of all and I run.

"But of course I am too late. Only ash is left of my home. Wild dandelions already sprout from the cinders. My neighbors tell me my family woke up dead one day after my leaving.

"The pain in my spirit has no bottom. A big storm rises in my head. I will never more feel my son's smooth cheeks, never more see my wife in her dragon dress. These are heart-cracking matters."

No doubt, I thought as I watched Wu reach yet again for the comfort of his cigarettes. For hundreds of years, including much of the twentieth century, China had been rocked by endless political turmoil and civil wars. Wu was tripped up by the Japanese, but the number of tragic stories offered up by his countrymen and -women involving vicious politics and wholesale slaughter between warring Chinese factions amazes me to this day.

"But you were home, so you were safe at least," Rie said.

"It is true I had some small good luck."

Mining the undercurrent in Wu's voice, I understood his comment was a token gesture of politeness for Rie's sake, and nothing more.

We were headed down still darker roads.

———

"My head storm show me monstrous vision.

"Row and row of people I see standing in deep valley. They have white-powdered faces and white mourning clothes. Their mouths are opening and closing, making big *O* shapes like ten thousand hungry goldfish. They speak angry words I cannot hear. There are children and parents and Old Honorable Ones. Many are my old patients. I wake up screaming.

"I am in dark room with candles burning all around me. Old Green Tooth Meng flies to my side, saying 'Finally, finally, fever is broken.' It is first night of my consciousness but sixth night of my head storm. I am with my village again, but ghost-spirits have followed me home.

"At first light Green Tooth Meng's son wheels me to village temple in a donkey cart. I am too weak for walking. I burn spirit money and incense for ghost-spirits in my dream, but when I close my eyes they appear immediately. I burn double spirit money and pray to Goddess of Mercy.

"But no matter what I try, they haunt my every night with same open-closing mouths. Same white faces. Same white clothes. I pray more. I burn mountains of money. Still they come.

"On my fifth dreaming night, ghost-spirits no longer show angry faces. On sixth night they beckon me. When I go to them they part, a white sea of bodies, their goldfish mouths opening and closing, opening and closing. They are calm, showing me same suffering I can feel in my own cracking heart. Up close I see their clothes are not white suits of mourning but everyday wear of farmers, housewives, butchers, and peddlers. They are trapped between life and death. I see ghost-fathers and ghost-mothers and ghost-children with big questioning eyes. I see ghost-women with ghost-babies in their bellies who have bigger questions.

"The ghost-spirits speak every village name I visit with Black Wind. They are unsleeping souls of murdered villagers. They call me. They see I keep their secret. This is my . . . my . . . *ming yun*. Danny, what is *ming yun* in Japanese?"

"*Shukumei*," said Danny. *Fate*.

"Yes, shukumei. I know they are my fate because I feel them alive in my heart. They live next to heavy sadness for my family. After wartimes end I tell their story but find no open ears. For many years I try. Communist Party people do not like my story. They tell me to stop talking about old war business.

"But ghost-spirits press me so I continue. One night my house burn down. I make lucky escape. In its way of killing new Chinese government is same as old. I know they come again if they see me alive. My time in motherland is done.

"So I take money in my garden-bank and travel across land for many days. I sneak into Hong Kong, then into dwarf bandit land. Here I can voice ghost-spirit story because Japanese people share much war suffering with Chinese people. But I find old Japanese soldiers have same problem. No one wants hear their nightmares.

"We Chinese know how to eat bitterness. Our own rulers kill more of us than any foreign power ever did. We endure. We are patient. But I cannot live forever. I try many years. I help many in motherland but I have no success for ghost-spirits. When I see no more ways, you are sent to me, Mr. Brodie-san. This meaning is clear. So I give you what you seek, but from you I need two promises."

I couldn't imagine what I could offer Wu, even though after all he had been through I felt bound to help if a way could be found. I said as much.

"That is heartful answer," he said. "First, you must do nothing to make more killing of Wus."

He didn't want his people compromised. "Fine," I said. "No names. What else?"

"You must . . . expose what I reveal today in your most big public way. This is what ghost-spirits beg of me."

I glanced at Danny, then Rie. Both looked back expectantly.

"Again," I said, "there is nothing I would like better than to help, but I don't see how."

"Danny say you climb out of big trouble in this land. Are his words true?"

"Yes."

"Your power is this climbing. You climb up and tell ghost-spirit story. Not angry telling. Not revenge telling. Compassion telling. In revenge the world darkens. You must make new light when you speak."

I took a deep breath. I gazed up at the summer sky. Night had come and the stars were shining. The air was thick with heat, and the firmament was blue and cloudless. Below us, the homes of carpenters and truck drivers and laborers fanned out over an undulating landscape. People stepped off buses. Others headed home with plump vinyl shopping bags of groceries for the evening meal. *You must make new light when you speak.* Whatever I did, would it make a difference? People would still take their buses. They would still carry home their evening groceries.

Drawing heavily on a fresh cigarette, old Wu watched me with an ageless patience.

Maybe one night, around a dinner table, a family would see a news item. It might excite them. Even startle them. They would discuss it. Perhaps the scene would repeat itself in households around the world.

Not in all of them, but enough of them. Maybe only one in ten. Or one in fifty. Still, ripples of understanding would spread through the collective consciousness and the understanding of past events would deepen. A small awakening might be born.

Life would move on, corrected. Perhaps only minutely, but corrected nonetheless. Life might become a little better in some quarters for some people. And possibly, those ripples would affect the thinking of decision makers dispatching men to do undesirable deeds that could be better accomplished in other ways.

This was what Wu desired.

This was what the ghost-spirits required of him.

He was their last hope.

And I, it appeared, was his.

He speaks for those who have no voice.

"Okay," I said. "I'll find a way."

Wu smiled. "Thank you. The people you must seek for your trouble are Chinese spies."

"Not Triads?"

Wu shook his head. "Triads not do your killings."

"How do you know?"

Wu's smile turned enigmatic. "I know."

"Where can I find spies who would help?"

"You know many peoples in this land. Seek for them among many you know."

"Why a spy?"

"Because that is where your answer is."

Great. A verbal Möbius strip. Endlessly twisting and circling.

Rie looked as unhappy as I felt. "A spy? Are you sure?"

Wu's nicotine-stained finger jabbed the air. "Chinese spies often imitate Triad butchers to hide their own doings. You find right spy, you find right answer. This I guarantee. *Then* you tell world about ghost-spirits. Wu is waiting."

DAY 7

THE END OF "ONCE"

CHAPTER 45

SLEEP did not come easily after Chinatown.

When I finally dropped off, ghost-spirits in white apparel appeared, silently mouthing words, their lips forming perfect *O*s. I woke with a start and, unable to get back to sleep, replayed Wu's story, then a brief exchange with Rie on the train back to Tokyo.

"You know," she'd said, "*you* can follow-up on Wu's idea, but the MPD can't pursue such vague insinuations without risking a diplomatic incident."

"You have a point," I said.

"Do you think Inspector Kato knew?"

Two-way streets are not toll-free. The good inspector suspected I might prove useful.

"He knew," I said.

My talk with Jenny early the next morning lifted my mood considerably. She'd jumped into the new school year with fervor. Classes didn't start for another three days, but she was already kicking the soccer ball around with her new teammates, discreetly shadowed by one of the Brodie Security men.

Jenny bubbled over with enthusiasm when she mentioned her two goals in practice yesterday, which impressed me. Or maybe that was just a proud father's point of view. Questions about my return were uncharacteristically absent due to her excitement, and I hung up, relieved that things were going well on one front, if nowhere else.

———

I called Hiroshi "Tommy-gun" Tomita's cell phone and the *Tokyo Seikei Shimbun* reporter answered on the first ring.

In Japanese I said, "Can you talk?"

"Buzz me back in two," he said, and disconnected.

Tomita was a hard-nosed Japanese journalist in his forties whose scoops regularly blasted corrupt pols, shady developers, and other scurvy lowlifes off their feet. Hence the nickname. Last time, I'd rung him on the paper's landline and he'd scolded me for my carelessness, telling me incoming calls were monitored. The big Japanese newspapers, with a nudge from the powers-that-be, kept their newshounds on tight leashes. Having learned my lesson, I reached out to him on his mobile, knowing I would need to wait for him to find a quiet corner away from prying ears.

In two minutes I hit the redial button and he answered swiftly.

"Hey, Brodie. How's Jenny-chan?"

"Good. She came for a short while this trip. Yours?"

"Did you know that two teenage boys can pack away more kilos of rice a month than a full-size sumo wrestler? And then there's the meat and the fish and the noodles. We buy Cup Ramen by the truckload. I don't cash my paycheck anymore. I just donate it to the local grocer."

"Heard that can happen."

"At least you have a girl. They eat less."

"Time will tell. Can you meet?"

"Business?"

"Yes."

"Got two deadlines, so it'll have to be later, around midnight. Will that work?"

"Fine."

"I owe you a beer for the Japantown exclusive, but sounds like I'd better save it for a different night."

"Yep."

"I hear ya. Take a stroll in Golden Gai around witching hour. I'll find you this time."

"Again? Are charades really necessary?"

For our previous get-together we'd met in a public park in Ikebukuro, on the north end of central Tokyo. He came in disguise with a watcher at each point of the compass.

Tommy snorted. "You joking? After the last meet I know to treat you like there's explosives strapped to your backside."

"That was then."

"Can you say differently this time?"

I considered the question. During our previous get-together, three guys with guns had tried to run me down, but Tomita's cohorts had sounded a warning that allowed me to get away—but only by seconds. This time there was Yoji's murder in Kabukicho, Hamada's head delivered to our doorstep, and the rooftop showdown on the ferry.

I caved. "Truthfully, no."

"Damn right you can't. I have *good* friends who are telling me to stop taking your calls."

That was a new one. For all its size—thirteen million people in central Tokyo, thirty-four in the greater metropolitan area—Japan's capital was a vast collective of overlapping networks. News traveled the grapevine with lightning speed and if it hit your network, you knew soon after.

Still, I was pissed. "You can't be serious."

He cackled like the hard-core scribe he was. "*They* are. But the way I look at it, you only live once."

"I don't know how to take that."

The cackle rose a notch. "Simple. To some people you're radioactive. To me you're an old friend and a good source."

"Just what I'm saying. How about we meet at an out-of-the-way place I know?"

Tomita snorted. "No, I'll choose. I take risks but I'm not suicidal. If possible I'd like to live to the *end* of 'once.'"

CHAPTER 46

SOMETHING new was in the air. It peeked from its hiding place during Tommy-gun's call and pranced into view during my next conversation.

"Japan is a nice country," Kazuo Takahashi said. "We are a good people. Our government strays too much, though."

I'd rung my Kyoto art-dealer friend a couple days before to postpone my buying trip to the old capital, asking him at the same time to let me know if he heard anything about a new Sengai coming on the market. This time I'd called to confirm that the postponement was permanent for the foreseeable future.

The murders I kept to myself.

"Last night a Chinese elder told me the same thing about his country," I said.

"I imagine it is true." Takahashi's tone was subdued. "We Japanese have much to offer, even if we have our secrets."

Since Takahashi was intelligent enough to know he was preaching to the converted, I replied with a standard two-word rejoinder in Japanese—and waited.

His tone turned morose. "We have culture, art, achievement. We have history. But in our past we also have a violent, militaristic side born of our samurai roots. You ran across remnants of that in Japantown. We took our medicine and cleaned up the mess. Now you've got another case, and it involves the war, does it not?"

A vast collective of overlapping networks. "Yes. How'd you know?"

His pause was long. "Certain circles in the Japanese art world now pay attention to your activities, and word trickles out."

"I see. Do any of those circles include you?"

"No, but they like to keep me informed. It's nothing insidious. If anything, it suggests your stature has risen. You've become 'eminently watchable,' as one colleague put it recently."

"I don't know how to take that," I said for the second time today.

"Nor do I. But back to the main: Japan has her secrets, as you well know. Many are open secrets. We Japanese are aware of them, are ashamed of them, and don't speak of them often, if ever. Our embarrassing moments remain, for the most part, confined to these shores. The language barrier and our shame constitute an effective blockade."

"Maybe it's time to let those secrets out," I said, "so the skeletons, or ghosts, can finally be put to rest."

"A very Western concept."

"A very human one."

The Japanese prefer to bury their shame rather than face it. Some of the younger generation were adopting a more open attitude, but the older generation still preferred deep-sixing a problem, mistake or not, and bearing the guilt. To them this was heroic. It epitomized the traditional spirit of *gaman*—forbearance. Made them feel admirable. Like martyrs. But to people caught in the middle—like Miura—holding their tongues led to a slow acidic burn of the soul.

"Your suggestion is not without merit," Takahashi said.

Even given this last admission, no further progress was made.

Maybe at another time, in another place.

After all, the laments of Miura the ex–Japanese soldier, Wu the old Chinese activist, and Takahashi the traditional Kyoto art dealer carried a common thread.

Something new was indeed in the air.

And for me it had an unnerving edge.

CHAPTER 47

WAS strolling through the Gai's narrow streets a few minutes before midnight, an eye peeled for Tommy-gun Tomita, newshound.

The Golden Gai is a cozy hive of some two hundred bars wedged into twenty thousand square feet. For decades, progress has chipped away at the edges of this ramshackle collection of watering holes, but the core remains. Some places are members-only. Others cater to groups: artists, writers, directors, or fans of this, that, and the next big thing. And, as with everything Tokyo, old shops fade away and new ones emerge.

I wandered leisurely up and down the Gai's lanes, letting myself be seen. There was a good chance I wouldn't recognize Tommy-gun. He had the ability to transform himself—wigs, makeup, postures, gestures, the whole works. His personal form of job security.

But this time he came undisguised. There were no embellishments on his wiry five-seven frame. He wore jeans, an olive-brown sport coat, and a pale-blue dress shirt, sans tie. Black glasses hovered desperately over a flat nose, the bottom of the frames resting on his cheeks. His dark hair was in fashionable disarray, his one concession to style.

From twenty yards away, over the heads of a couple dozen revelers, I caught sight of him walking toward me. We locked eyes but he showed no sign of recognition.

I knew what that meant.

I walked on, ignoring his approach.

Behind Tomita a watchful figure lingered. Tomita glanced at the screen of his smartphone, then looked over my shoulder, saw something, then his whole body relaxed and he smiled at me.

When he was close, I said, "The man behind you in the gray suit and green tie yours too?"

He nodded, the next instant latching on to my arm and steering me down a linking alleyway, then right into a passageway five feet wide, then into a crevice where our shoulders brushed the walls. After a last right, we made a quick dash through a slim wooden doorway and up a flight of dark-tiled stairs to a small room with a bar, five stools, and a solitary table by a window with tattered shoji, overlooking the last swatch through which we'd just threaded our way. We took the table. Tommy waved at the proprietor and called out our order, suggesting familiarity.

"You're at it again," he said softly in Japanese.

"At what?"

"The dicey stuff."

"How could you possibly know that?"

"Made some inquiries. Heard some rumors."

"How is *that* possible?"

"First, because I'm good at what I do, and second, because after the Rikyu incident and Japantown, you draw notice. You're a minor celeb on these shores. Surely someone's told you by now?"

I grimaced. "That kind of fame I don't need."

"You dive into dicey, that's what you get."

"I'm only carrying on where my father left off."

Tomita shook his head. "Closer to the edge."

"Isn't that what you do?"

"Well, yes, but I can only lose my job. You could lose your head."

The passing reference to Hamada sent a shock wave through my system. "You heard."

"Yes. Sorry. Didn't know him personally but was told he was a good man, and good at what he did."

"Very true."

We were quiet for a spell, giving the man—the father of twins, long-time Brodie Security op—a moment of his own.

My client's son was bad enough, but Hamada was part of the collective family my father had gathered together. The loss hung over the entire office. The single consolation was the heavy life insurance my father had insisted on carrying for employees. When I stepped into the role as part-time bicoastal owner-operator, the advisory service the lawyers attached to the transitional phase urged me to quietly drop the policy. The savings would turn Brodie Security from a marginal enterprise into a hugely profitable business I could sell for a substantial gain if I "chose to divest." The premium was that large. I refused—and divested myself of the advisory service instead.

Eventually I said, "How informed are your sources?"

"I know something about Triads. That's why I've got ears and eyes at the front and back and across the street upstairs." He placed a prepaid cell phone on the table. "You know the drill. One ring, we run. This time down the back steps, out the back door, to the right. *Not* the stairs we came up. The hidden ones behind the bar."

He pointed to an egress with a framed reproduction of the *New York Times* front-page announcing the attack on Pearl Harbor. I looked around for the first time. War memorabilia hung on wood-paneled walls. World War Two helmets, Japanese and German. Old rifles. Bayonets. A Japanese movie poster for *Gone with the Wind*.

In some corners of Tokyo, stray copies of the film had circulated surreptitiously, screening endlessly in wartime bomb shelters to help the people pass the long hours underground. As the Japanese authorities fought the American government, Hollywood entertainment captured the hearts of the populace.

I said, "Is this a right-wing bar?"

Except for the movie poster, everything in sight was vintage war memorabilia. Was this my friend's way of telling me he'd connected some dots?

Tommy raised a hand. "I'm not done yet. Then first left, second right. Then into a taxi idling on the corner. The taxi will only wait thirty seconds after the first man arrives. For safety reasons. You need to remember that in case we get separated. Only thirty seconds. If you don't make it, you're on your own. Now I'm done."

An uneasy silence settled over our corner of the room. The last time we met his preparations for an on-site escape route had me convinced he was paranoid. I no longer thought that. His paranoia had saved my life.

"Got it."

"Good."

Tommy-gun searched my face for more answers. He wasn't going to get them. The owner trotted over with two mugs of beer, a plate of dried squid, and a small cup of mixed nuts.

After he left, I said, "What are we doing here?"

"Did the owner a favor once."

The five barstools were filled with regulars. They huddled together, deep in a heated discussion involving General Yamamoto, the commander-in-chief of the Japanese fleet during World War II. They ignored us.

"But right-wing?" I said in a low voice. "The customers might string you up."

Tommy shrugged. "The owner was going for vintage forties but he attracted a dash of the reactionary right. That's why the pointed greeting. They see I'm a friend of the proprietor, they'll tune us out. The real threat is out there. This is the last place anyone will look. So tell me what I can do for you."

"Bottom line, I need a spook. And not just any spook. A Chinese one."

"Did you check craigslist Tokyo?"

I ignored the brush-off. "A source says I'll find answers if I can plug in high enough up the food chain. Can you help?"

Tommy frowned into his beer. "I tell you I can, you suddenly know a lot more about me than I want you to know, cowboy."

"'Cowboy?'"

"What's in it for me?"

"I don't call you a samurai swashbuckler."

"And?"

"A story dating back to the war."

"No thanks. What else you got?"

"That's it."

"Brodie, war stories are a dime a dozen. You know that. Even after old soldiers stopped coming out of South Pacific jungles."

I *did* know that. But I'd promised Wu. I hadn't had the heart to tell the old doctor just how tough the uphill climb for publicity would be.

"This one's worth more," I said.

"Mine's bigger than yours."

I eyed Tommy. I needed to avoid mentioning the home invasions. It would start him sniffing down my side of the tracks. Which could prove dangerous for both of us.

"Can't do it," I said.

"Can't help you, then."

"Why you playing hardball?"

"Because my connection's top of the heap. Think *kaiseki* at Kitcho in Arashiyama. I don't like to tap into this one except under extreme circumstances."

Kaiseki is Japanese haute cuisine, an epicurean extravaganza of the finest foods in season, served in a string of courses on elegant ceramic tableware and impeccably arranged as only the Japanese can manage. Kitcho is the birthplace of modern kaiseki, and Arashiyama a breathtakingly picturesque rural district on the outskirts of Kyoto. In short, as high-end as you could get. Tommy was saying that access to his source, just like a meal at Kitcho, was going to cost me.

I studied my reporter friend. He was resourceful and trustworthy, but when he smelled a story, out came negotiation skills that would make a hardened salesman weep.

"Connecting with him," he added, "can be dangerous."

"All right. The war story and—*only* on my say-so when the time is right—one about the home invasions."

"I *knew* there was more."

"But you can't jump early and you can't go digging yourself. You'll get us killed. I need a promise on that."

Tommy sat back, his eyes glazing over in lust. "Okay, I know a guy."

"Like that, is it?"

The shine in his eyes gave way to dark pools. "I wasn't joking. With this guy you'll be stepping into an alternate universe."

"Don't go melodramatic on me, Tommy."

My journalist friend put his hands on the table and stared at them for an extended moment. "We've known each other for a long time, right?"

"Yes."

"I'd like to keep it that way. You're absolutely *sure* you need to talk to a Chinese spy?"

"It's vital."

"Okay, then I need your word on two things. First, no matter what happens next time I call, you'll be ready for anything."

"What does *that* mean?"

"You see? You've got the wrong attitude. Can you be ready or not? Yes or no? If you can't accept that condition without asking questions, we'd better stop right here."

Ah, we were going *there*. The mind-bending territory of Asian paradox. Accept what comes. Regardless. The Western mind always seeks answers. It *needs* to find a logical balance. The Japanese mind can suspend belief when necessary. It can hold on to conflicting truths—without judgment—until things need to be explained.

If the day ever came.

I could do it only because I grew up on these shores.

"I'll be ready," I said. "And the second thing?"

"No matter what happens, we stay friends. I *am* your friend and you say you need this, but my advice would be to back down unless it's do-or-die mandatory. Is it?"

I thought about all that had happened in the last seven days. Miura, Hamada, the death of the third old trooper, the chase on the ferry, the Chinatown shuffle, Wu.

I considered for a long moment. Then I said yes.

Tommy-gun pursed his lips. "All right. Once I hit the start button, no matter what I say, no matter what *they* do, it's not *me*. Okay?"

Despite my resolve something went cold in my chest. "Okay. But why the table pounding, Tommy? You know me. You know what I've been through. What I can do. Why are you pushing this?"

He shook his head, sadness washing over his features. "It's a window onto a world I don't think anyone should ever have to look through. But if you've got no choice, then step in knowing. Because it's going to be like nothing you've ever encountered."

DAY 8

THE NEW DEVIL

TOMMY had reached his contact's assistant, who said the man we wanted was in South Korea for two days, and unreachable.

Unreachable.

Sounded very spylike and promising. I swallowed my disappointment. The upside was that Tommy and I had time for that long-overdue beer—after I attended Hamada's funeral in the early afternoon.

The police had released his body, so three days after the decapitation, the funeral took place. Yoji's body was still being held.

Leaving a skeleton crew at Brodie Security, the rest of the employees trooped over to a Buddhist temple in Koiwa in the eastern suburbs to pay their respects to one of our own. On the off chance that the killers might turn up to inflict more damage, we posted men at the gate and in the upper stories of neighboring buildings.

On the drive over to the temple, my mobile vibrated, and when I answered I was surprised to hear Tanaka-sensei from the kendo dojo on the other end.

"Hi, I just heard about the run-in you had with some of our people."

"Just?"

"I've been away on business, but let me apologize for what they did. We do have a rebel element in the dojo."

"Well, it was partially my fault."

"I heard that, too. Nakamura-sensei takes the intrusion seriously but he is more upset with how his pupils responded. Their actions fall outside the spirit of kendo. He's passed down punishment. Attention to your action he's left to the police. But between us, if you were to apologize in person, the matter would evaporate."

A lot is forgiven in Japan in return for a sincere apology and an exhibit of remorse.

"Maybe once my work is done, I'll do that," I said. "Does Kiyama feel the same way?"

"Of course. He's standing right beside me."

"Well, I appreciate the advice."

"You won't forget my request for rare swords? I'm always in the market for new specimens."

"I'll put you at the top of my list."

"Great."

We said good-bye and disconnected.

Even in death, the rest of the world carries on.

Flanked by relatives from both sides of the family, Hamada's widow and the twins sat stoically to the side of the traditional flower-bedecked dais, with the closed coffin underneath. Attendees approached, added a pinch of incense to a burning pile, and offered prayers.

The twins took it like men, but their eyes were red. They'd already cried it out. Every time I glanced their way, it tore me in two. Robbed of their father at thirteen. One day my Jenny might find herself on the receiving end of the same insurance policy—financially secure but with her biggest fear realized. Every step I took for Brodie Security in my father's shadow summoned up images of my daughter's anxiety. The idea haunted me. But helping others pulled me powerfully in the opposite direction. My father had built a smoothly oiled machine and passed half of it on to me. A Brodie family legacy. And, amazingly, I seemed capable of handling the work. As if it and the art were seared into my DNA.

The funeral went off without disturbance. All but Noda stayed until the end. The brooding detective disappeared minutes after offering condolences, his lips compressed, his bulldog face red with rage.

I wanted to follow him out the door, but I was duty-bound to remain. At least I knew without asking that Noda was out there fighting the fight.

At the appointed time I strolled into the *kushi-katsu* restaurant on a backstreet in Ginza.

Kushi-katsu are skewered morsels of seafood, meat, vegetables, and other edibles briskly breaded and deep-fried in a light oil.

As he had in Golden Gai, Tomita had secured us a window seat, this time overlooking a narrow lane with a famous tempura place across the street. Since we were meeting in a popular area, I'd waved off backup, a choice that circumvented what—I later realized—could have led to disaster.

Even with the decidedly high-end menu, Tomita went low: beer and yakitori—skewered chicken bits grilled over charcoal. Curious, but not unexpected, considering my host's pocketbook.

As soon as the waitress was out of earshot, Tomita plunged in, not with a thank-you for the Japantown story but a tease for the next one: "The, uh, guy got in touch early this morning. Called from Seoul and agreed to meet you day after tomorrow. I had to offer benefits."

"What kind of benefits?"

"You don't want to know. But from me, not you."

"I want to know."

"Future benefits. Everything costs with him. That's all I'm going to tell you. You okay with this?" I nodded and Tomita said, "Good, because there's a rule book."

"Let's have it."

"First, only when he says *no* does it mean *no*. Everything else is up in the air."

"Diplomatic tendencies?"

"Officially, that's what he is, yeah. There may be hope for you yet, Brodie."

"And unofficially?" I asked.

"You got what you ordered. One authentic Chinese spy. You owe me big for this."

Tomita had pulled off a minor miracle.

"You got it," I said, "if we can trust him."

"We can."

"How can you be so sure?"

"My sister-in-law married his cousin."

"So you're a relative."

"Hardly. But spies collect people, and the guy's taken a liking to me."

"And the cousin?"

"An entrepreneur."

"Ah," I said.

Asian entrepreneurs could be legit or shady.

"*Ah* about sums it up. You still want in?"

"Yes. And stop asking that. How do you get a yes out of him?"

"He'll say, 'I don't know what you're talking about.' Deniability in case of electronic ears. Everything else will depend on context."

"You do know some characters, Tommy."

"Glass houses, Brodie."

The skewered chicken arrived and we eyed it skeptically. Both of us seemed to have lost our appetite.

———

Tommy stood and stretched. "Restroom run. Be right back."

A minute later our third beers arrived.

Two minutes after that a handsome Chinese man in a stylish tan blazer over a pale-green Ralph Lauren knit shirt slid into Tommy's seat. His eyes were dark, narrow, and alert. They sat prominently in a face tanned and practiced at looking relaxed and nonchalant.

I started. "Sorry, you've got the wrong table. My—"

His smile was thin and cool, his look penetrating.

Son of a bitch. *No matter what happens . . .*

"Ah," I said. "You're not in Seoul."

"No." *No means no.*

"Bet you never even went. Since when do men in your profession give out their itineraries?"

"I don't know what you're talking about." *Yes.*

"You choose this place?"

"Still don't know what you're talking about." *Another yes.*

"The time?"

He nodded. *Which according to Tommy's playbook could mean anything.*

Tomita's unnamed spy had given himself some breathing room I'd not had. An edge he'd probably used well. I wondered how well.

I said, "You have me watched?"

He frowned. "Tommy told me you were an amateur. Maybe you're not."

"I'm the new kid on the block. Not a fool."

Dark brown eyes drilled into me without reserve. They probed, appraised, searched, cataloged, memorized. They sucked up every telling feature—strengths, weaknesses, where pressure could be applied, where it couldn't. I went into deadpan mode as fast as I could, which wasn't fast enough.

An eerie kinetic energy flowed between us. There was a physical sense of information being extracted bodily. From my psyche. The sensation was unnatural. Overpowering. Creepy. But very real. I'd heard of such powers but they usually resided with temple monks or mountain mystics. I raised my guard as high as it would go.

"A fool?" he said, the smile turning frigid, his lips stretching. "I suppose not. Just so you know, I've read your dossier."

"That's ridiculous. The Chinese embassy couldn't possibly have a dossier on me."

He gave a languid wave of his hand. "It does now. I ordered one as soon as I got off the phone with Tommy last night."

His Japanese was polished and polite. Worse, it was disarming and sincere, suggestive of camaraderie without stepping over the line. His linguistic ability was perfect. Frighteningly perfect.

A waitress sidled up to the table and my Chinese visitor ordered from the high end of the menu:

"Take away this yakitori, would you? I've seen better dog chow. You don't mind, do you, Brodie?" he asked, giving me a sideways glance but not waiting for an answer. "Bring us your best sashimi." He flipped rapidly through a menu. "Also some *shirako*, some Hokkaido *kani*, *kani miso*, and the kushi-katsu deluxe set. Plus a large flask of the Gyoku-ryu *daiginjo* saké, heated not chilled."

He'd ordered a world-class lineup of delicacies: top-of-the-line raw fish, cod milt, the most flavorful crab from Hokkaido, a soup or paste of the crab's organs, and Jewel Dragon saké, culled from the highest grade of the traditional brew. The skewered food set started with foie gras, duck, a rare Camembert cheese, rabbit, and lobster. A distinctly French twist on a traditional Japanese cuisine.

Once our server departed, I picked up where we'd left off. "You're a careful man." His mention of a dossier had started my nerves popping.

"I like to stay alive."

"I thought spies didn't kill each other anymore."

The saké arrived, my new host poured, we drank, and he refilled the glasses, urging me to drink up. After a third round, he set down his cup with a satisfied smile. "Who said anything about the other side?"

"Ah," I said. "I hear it can be hard on the mainland." Brodie, the diplomat.

His eyes darkened. "Survival requires infinite skill. Especially in China."

"Been true for a long while."

"It's another reason I like Tokyo. Compared to Beijing this city's benign. A baby could thrive here. But in China it only takes a single misstep and . . ."

Before the last word left his mouth, he had the saké flask up again to refill my glass, gesturing me to drink before he topped off my glass. I drank, raised my cup to accept the pour, then drank again, as local etiquette dictated. He waited a beat, topped off my cup once more, then refilled his own.

We'd just run through a double flask. He waved the empty bottle at our waitress to reorder.

The brew was brilliant and complex. Jewel Dragon bloomed when served warm, and we soon found the sweet spot as the temperature settled. The drink was nectar on the tongue, sensual and slightly smoky. Whatever else the man before me might turn out to be, he knew his drink. His connoisseurship allowed him to transcend the dogma that all high-grade saké must be chilled.

"One thing before we start," he said.

The intense stare was back.

"What's that?"

He pointed to the roof of the five-story office building across the street that housed the famous tempura shop. I saw a movement, then a flash of reflected glass. The hair on the back of my neck rose. I wanted to lean back, out of the area framed by the window, but it was too large. I'd have to get up and change seats to remove myself from the target area.

He noted my reaction. "You know a sniper when you see one. That's not . . . promising."

"I know a gun scope aimed my way."

"Security measures."

My anger surged. "What? No red dot dancing over my shirt?"

He made a sign. A laser dot appeared. "Better?"

"No."

He gestured again and the circle vanished.

It's a window onto a world I don't think anyone should ever have to look through, Tomita had said.

Too late now.

CHAPTER 49

THE sashimi arrived with the next round of saké, and my still-unnamed host took up the fresh bottle as a gesture of reconciliation and repeated his early offering.

We both drank. He poured for me, waited a beat for me to drink, refilled my cup then his, and drank. His eyes bored into mine, open and dark and revealing nothing. He offered more saké, again politely waiting and replenishing my cup before giving himself some. We drank more. The saké got smoother.

His eyes continued their scan of my every feature.

And then I got it.

It was a subtle move, which he'd used in the previous rounds as well. And I hadn't caught on. I was drinking twice as much as he was. He wanted me drunk. Or at least loosened up. And had chosen a seductive brew as temptation.

I drank out of courtesy, and because of the excellence of his offering—all the while expecting an apology for the gunman on the roof. Which hadn't come. The body language was there but little else. He played on convention, courtesy, and expectation to keep me drinking. This was a clever man. And dangerously subtle.

"Don't stand on ceremony," he said. "Have some sashimi. The fish is brought in daily and kept in tanks in the kitchen until ordered."

Fresh slices of raw fish beckoned from a large platter decorated with mounds of shredded daikon radish, shiso leaves, parsley, and minute purple flowers with teardrop petals.

"Looks great," I said, taking a few modest pieces.

"You won't regret it. The master has a great connection down at the market."

I selected a few pieces of glistening seafood and sipped some saké at a measured pace, giving myself time to think. *Window seat, long gun on a rooftop less than thirty yards away.*

I was pinned down. Even if I managed to avoid the sharpshooter, there was the spy across the table, for one. I glanced around the restaurant and another man looked quickly away. Well dressed. Flat Chinese brow. A female companion with her back to me. The trap was complete.

I took a deep breath to calm my nerves. "Thought Tommy vouched for me."

"He said you have no intelligence background. Is that really true?"

"I deal in Japanese art. I'm here on a buying trip."

"Art's a good cover. Gets used all the time."

"Not in my case."

He waved the finger and the red dot reappeared. "Aren't you forgetting something?"

My jaw tightened. "Brodie Security is an inheritance. I'm half owner and care about the people there, but art is my primary focus. Your 'dossier' doesn't cover that?"

"You're an investigator." The dot bounced around.

"A fledgling one. By default."

"Maybe you were turned. Maybe you got close to Tommy to get to me."

"I've known him for years. I've never heard of you. I don't even know your name."

"Except for your relationship to Tommy, all unprovable. Maybe someone who knows you two are friends persuaded you to approach Tommy to draw me out. Gave you some cash. Applied some pressure."

In his world trust was an elusive, oft-abused commodity. Treasured when steady, deadly when it was flipped on you. I felt sorry for this guy. I bet the number of sleepless nights outweighed the peaceful ones.

"You never know what's real, do you?" I said.

"I don't know what you're talking about." *Yes.*

"I wouldn't want your life. Ever."

He broke into a smile. Suddenly he radiated sunshine. All the hostility was gone. "That, my friend, is one of the few answers that won't get you shot." He waved his finger and the bright-red spot vanished.

With this guy you'll be stepping into an alternate universe. . . . Can you be ready or not?

CHAPTER 50

'D been allowed to step back from the precipice, so I wasted no time shifting gears.

I said, "You have a name?"

"Ten of them. Take your pick."

"Any of them real?"

"As real as anything else in this world. How does Zhou sound?"

A philosopher and a spy. Tommy-gun could pick them. "Old-school mainland. Why not? As long as your information is real."

"It will be."

"How do I know?"

His smile warmed even more. "Once I accept you, you're in."

The rest of the food arrived. Before I could protest, Zhou loaded a small plate with delicacies for me, then one for himself. To reciprocate, I filled his saké glass. With the bottle I motioned for him to drink, holding the flask ready to refresh his cup. His trick. He smiled with a bottomless charm, drank, then set his cup off to the side, out of reach, and politely relieved me of the flask, renewed my drink, and bid me to drink, immediately topping off my cup as soon as I took a sip.

He hadn't fallen for his own ploy, but I glimpsed a hint of curiosity in his look. Had I seen through his maneuver or was my gesture merely a polite echo of his?

I drank a second time, deciding to keep him guessing. Two could play at this game.

Zhou's smile was a blinding beam now. "I trust Tommy. He trusts you. Who could ask for more?"

Zhou waved down a waitress and ordered another flask. His voice intensified and softened. In it I heard compassion, understanding, and an offer of friendship. "You know, I haven't been in Tokyo long, but this is a great city, don't you think? The people are considerate, the food superb. You must love coming here."

"It is special," I said.

His smile widened. "I bet you see things. Meet lots of people. Do you ever go to museum openings? I hear the most interesting people attend exhibition previews."

"All the time," I said, relaxing now that he seemed to be heading into more open waters.

"It's got to be exciting. Getting an advance viewing of classic art pieces hundreds of years old. Especially something as unique as Japanese art."

"It is rewarding."

He nodded, desire lighting up his eyes. "I wish I could be involved in something creative. I really do. My work is so dull. You might think it glamorous but I spend most of my time chained to a desk. Filling out forms. Meeting boring businessmen and diplomats like myself. Attending endless embassy parties with the same old people. Dull, let me tell you. Good food and drink, and the occasional good company, like tonight, are the only things that liven up a very stale life. Believe me. I bet you meet much more exciting people."

"At times."

"Your world is so glamorous. Meeting VIPs from Japan and the U.S. at special events. Through your work. Do you have clients from Europe?"

"Some. I never would have thought you'd be interested in my line of work," I said, hoping to guide the focus back toward him.

"But I am. I work for a bunch of bureaucrats. *Drab* is their middle name. You want to hear a joke one of the party higher-ups told me?"

"Sure."

Finally, a shift toward neutral ground.

"Good. You can see how feebleminded they all are. Here goes: 'What's the price of a loaf of bread in Los Angeles ten years from now?'"

His smile was broad and congenial, telegraphing how sure he was I would enjoy this jest at his colleagues' expense.

I found myself returning the smile. "I don't know, what?"

"Twenty-five yuan."

He chuckled appreciatively, lifting his saké cup jocularly for a sip. His lips were parted in a grin, but his eyes were dark, penetrating tunnels ready to lap up every detail of my response.

Which was immediate. Despite my best efforts, I felt the blood drain from my face. Something slimy and repulsive tugged at my guts.

Bread would be paid for in Chinese currency because the People's Republic had invaded and conquered.

Zhou's quip was a brilliant piece of spycraft, and it scared the crap out of me. It exposed the listener's level of patriotism. Or corruptibility. If a person loved his country, he couldn't be anything but appalled. His reaction would be a mental knee-jerk he couldn't contain—as had mine.

Those of wavering loyalties would respond with appreciative laughter when the bait was dangled. Or nervous laughter if they were stepping for the first time onto Zhou's ledge. Whether a thin titter or a full-blown guffaw, the reaction would telegraph the listener's state of mind in a flash.

The joke struck such a gut-wrenching chord that I found it physically impossible to offer a covering laugh. I was outclassed and overmatched.

Two could *not* play at this game.

CHAPTER 51

Z HOU'S demeanor changed yet again.

His eyes dulled. The smile dimmed. The inviting flush vanished from his face. He was no longer interested in me on a professional level. I might lead a glamorous existence. Rub up against people from all walks of life and be able, on occasion, to supply him with a tidbit of useful information. But I was constitutionally unrecruitable, so I was no longer a man leading a desirable business lifestyle.

He radiated disinterest on a grand scale.

"So, Mr. Brodie, what can I do for you?"

I understood from his tone that this was my moment.

"You've heard about the home invasions, of course."

"I don't know what you're talking about." *Here we go again.*

"The prevailing opinion is that the Triads are behind them and some related killings, but I have it from a good source that it's not the Triads but spies pretending to be Triads. Is that possible?"

"Not if your source thinks it's Chinese spies."

"That's precisely what he thinks."

Zhou paused to examine my answer, before saying, "Please continue."

"My contact was certain. And if anyone would know, he would. His opinion is based on years of experience dating back to the war."

Zhou nodded distractedly, staring into the distance. "Go on."

"That's it. My people are tracking the Triad angle. This new contact contends it's you guys. He's seen it before. I got the idea he knew people who had been victims of such tactics."

"I don't know what you're talking about." *A yes. Wu was right.* "But in this case your informant is mistaken." *Setback.*

"Are you sure?"

His chest expanded as he weighed his reply. "Did Tommy happen to mention my position?"

I shook my head. "I only requested someone high up in the food chain."

"Good, Tommy was discreet."

He leaned forward, his eyes sliding left toward the table where the Chinese couple sat, then right toward the window. Zhou shifted in his seat to place his back more prominently toward the man, blocking a larger part of our table from view. Between the platter and the dish of crab, he traced some Japanese characters on the table. *You can go no higher.*

Then he sat back and said, "Our time is drawing to a close. Do you have any other questions, Mr. Brodie?"

"I need to make sure we are on the same page."

"I don't know if I can help you."

"Fine. Have your people ever gone after others in Tokyo using the Triad ruse?"

"I absolutely don't know what you're raving about." *A more emphatic yes.*

"So the home invasions are not your doing, or that of anyone you know?"

"No." *Definitely not.*

"How can you be so sure it's not a Chinese spy from, say, another camp?"

He shot me a look of impatience. "What do you know about Triad methods?"

"I've heard that they are sloppy, unpracticed killers, and use blunt blades."

His smile was cruel and bereft of charm. "True as far as it goes, but deceiving."

I didn't like the sound of that. "Deceiving how?"

"Triad leaders discovered long ago that hacking off body parts horrifies people. So what you call 'unpracticed' is actually calculated. They often assign the chopping to younger members, who have less experience. The act terrorizes the victim. The finished product terrorizes everyone else."

Product.

"My people like the method because it's easy to reproduce," Zhou added. "It doesn't require practice."

"You're saying you know the details about the recent home invasions and the approach used doesn't match yours?"

"On the contrary. I don't know what you're talking about." *Yes.*

Of course he would know. He would have investigated. Just to make sure one of his men wasn't freelancing.

"Okay," I said.

He smiled. "*Koroshi monku*, is it not? I love that Japanese phrase."

The phrase translated literally as "killer words." What it meant in most instances was that the reason or argument put forth was an end-all. It smothered any further resistance.

Considering Zhou's Japanese fluency, his bandying about of that particular image was no accident.

CHAPTER 52

THE saké gone, Zhou signaled the waitress and ordered a round of beer.

The order alarmed me. No one followed multiple rounds of saké with beer.

"So," I said, "just to be sure there's no misunderstanding, what we have here is a killer imitating a spy imitating the Triads."

"I have no idea what you're talking about." *Confirmation.*

"Makes my head hurt."

He chuckled. "Welcome to my world. Do you mind telling me your source?"

"I'm afraid I can't."

"You've already given me more hints than you should. You've been talking to a certain doctor who escaped our country years ago."

I spread my hands as a sign I had no further comment.

Zhou said, "That old man has been a thorn in our side for years. I'll give you fifty thousand dollars American if you tell me where he is. I can get the money in twenty minutes."

I didn't reply.

"Okay, one hundred and fifty. Cash. Sixty minutes."

I shook my head.

"How about this? We'll buy you a building in San Francisco. Four units. You just arrange another meeting with him, give me the location, and we show up in your place. You'll have your own place for that beautiful daughter of yours. A slice of San Francisco real estate worth several million dollars."

A chill ran down my spine at the thought that a man like Zhou knew about Jenny.

I cleared my throat. "Not my style, sorry. Even assuming we are talking about the same gentleman."

"We are." Zhou studied me. "Name your price. China is awash in cash."

I shook him off and he said, "When I meet resistance, I normally change the candy. I try power, revenge, or a Chinese honey trap. We have some international beauties. But I think you are like my friend Tomita. I can't reach you."

I stared at him, offering no reaction he could read.

He said, "The world needs people like you and Tommy. To protect it from people like me."

A disarming comment. Followed by the return of the thousand-watt smile. "May I be frank?"

"Refreshing idea."

He gave an icy chuckle. "You'd make a fine asset if I could turn you, but we're on opposite sides."

"Meaning?"

"Meaning we'll never be friends. But an enemy well regarded is better than an acquaintance whose loyalty you doubt."

It may have been his first genuine sentiment of the evening. "A matter of peace of mind, I'd bet."

His smile was tinged with a weariness he allowed me to see. "You are a very intuitive man, Mr. Brodie. Such a waste."

Our waitress brought two foamy mugs of Kirin lager. She set them down and left. Zhou pushed his mug toward mine until the glasses touched.

"This evening's on me," he said. "I require only one last thing. You must stay seated until you drink both the beers before you. Under no circumstances are you to leave before you finish. And not for at least ten minutes, even if you guzzle the beers. Don't take a toilet break. Don't call anyone. For a nonspy, you play the game too well, so I'm not taking any chances."

"There's no need—"

"Don't waste your breath. You have nothing to fear from me as long as you circulate none of what transpired here tonight other than the Triad information. Now I must leave you. I've signaled my men. Again, do not follow me. Do not leave prematurely. The shooter has orders to terminate you if move more than five inches out of your seat."

Anger rolled through me.

Koroshi monku of a different order.

CHAPTER 53

T WO beers and two cups of coffee later, I was still sorting through my cat-and-mouse session with Zhou when Noda called and suddenly my night was far from over.

I'd finished the beer at a leisurely pace, then ordered the first cup of coffee, staying well past Zhou's ten-minute minimum to avoid any misunderstanding.

Three minutes into the second cup my cell phone buzzed. "Got some news," Brodie Security's head detective said.

"Good or bad?"

"Hard to tell."

Noda preferred monosyllabic answers and, barring that, the shortest sentence that took him from question to answer.

"Don't be shy."

Outside of a mandatory information dump, he seemed incapable of stringing three sentences together unless a major emergency loomed.

"Found where Miura's key fit."

The key I'd dug out of the fractured kendo sword. "Serial number?"

"And shape. Mitsui condominium tower in Shakujii-koen."

The construction arm of the Mitsui conglomerate. Noda had made the rounds of all the big builders, starting at the top.

"That's a posh neighborhood," I said.

"Cost us a case of premium saké."

"Fair enough. Who lives there?"

"A woman. Sounds pretty."

"Got anything else?"

"An appointment to pay our condolences."

"Isn't it a little late to be making a call?"

Noda was quiet for a beat before he said, "The lady in question is, uh, accustomed to late-night visits."

"Ah," I said. "That kind of pretty."

The woman's name was Masami Saito.

She lived in the shadows and wouldn't be attending Yoji's funeral. She'd be eager for news, which was no doubt the lure Noda had cast.

The discovery astounded me. Mistresses weren't uncommon in Japan, but keeping a love nest with all the attendant accessories took a healthy money stream, which I was convinced my client's late son didn't possess. On the other hand, I'd seen Yoji's compulsion for nice things, and it looked like we were about to get a glimpse of one more.

Noda and I sat in a company car, looking up at a prestigious condominium tower built on prime property directly across the street from Shakujii-koen Station. The *koen* part of the name means "park," in this case a reference to an impressive urban spread of greenery, woodlands, and a pair of large ponds, each several city blocks long.

"Approaching grieving women seems to be becoming a habit," I said.

"Works that way sometimes."

A couple of months ago we'd sat in another company car outside the house of a woman whose husband had gone missing on the Japantown case. With the earlier visit to Yoji's widow, my tally had climbed to three.

"Probably a habit worth breaking," I said.

"We're not responsible for the death this time."

"Feels like it."

The tower lobby had a small office with a guard. A gleaming parquet floor bled to one of polished marble. Once out the door, a resident had only to walk ten paces to a taxi stand. Ten paces to the left brought her or him to a fleet of indoor ATMs and a mall with an upscale supermarket, dry cleaners, cosmetic kiosk, and hair salon. The train station was another twenty paces past the taxi stand. A prime location in a good neighborhood. For Yoji, the stop fell about halfway between his downtown office and his home in the burbs.

Convenience on all sides.

Propped up on the dash was one of the photographs I'd removed from Yoji's locker. The attractive woman I took to be a cousin or a sister. Looking pointedly at it, I said, "Anything else I should know before we go?"

"Yeah. Yoji was broke."

Not what I was expecting, but it would do. "Thought he might have gone over the edge."

"Why?"

"Career stalled. Wearing platinum cuff links when we first met. Lexus at the house. Pamphlets for pricey tropical vacations on the coffee table."

"Good call."

I waited. Nothing more was forthcoming.

I said, "Because?"

Scratching his jaw, the detective dredged up the facts. "Monthly fees for the sick kid took a third of his salary. Spent a third on drinking and clothes. Second mortgage on the house eight years ago from the same bank. Took more cash from a legal loan shark four years later at nine percent. Second one in January this year at twelve."

"Can't be cheap to keep a lady friend here," I added, though it was far less than Roppongi, Aoyama, and the other chic districts in central Tokyo where millionaires, company presidents, and politicians stashed their love interests.

Noda grunted. "Cost him more than the kid."

An image of Yoji's wife cradling her disabled son rose up before my eyes. Given her misplaced hysterics, she hadn't endeared herself to me, but my sympathies were shifting.

"Life insurance?" I asked.

"After the debt, about five years of living expenses."

I shook my head. The widow faced an indefinite future but almost certainly one of lack and poverty. Knowledge of the mistress could unhinge her completely.

I nodded at the photograph. "That the woman?"

"Yep."

"Maybe someone did the wife a favor. This thing was a time bomb."

Noda nodded. "Found an old flame on her side, too."

My ears perked up. "Boyfriend or secret admirer?"

"Don't know yet."

"A lover would make Yoji's killing what? A copycat murder by some-one who knew about his father's concerns?"

"Yeah."

"What a mess."

The case had just imploded. Who had killed Yoji and why? An ad-mirer of his wife or someone after information? The heavy beating Yoji suffered suggested the second, unless a lover or would-be Romeo with a white-knight complex had meted out punishment. But where did the Sengai come in? If anywhere? And what about the kendo thugs? And how, then, did Hamada's death fit?

I said, "Could the wife have been part of it?"

"Still checking."

"Well, at least with the insurance she can keep a roof over her son's head until this is straightened out."

Noda's grimace told a different story. "You're living in a fairyland. Bankers're drooling over the house."

"Body's not even cold."

"Cold enough."

"Sounds like Yoji might have been dead even before someone took it into their own hands."

CHAPTER 54

YOJI'S expensive tastes extended to women as well.

Masami Saito greeted us sheathed in a tailored suit of mourning. She was gorgeous, in her late thirties to Yoji's mid-fifties, with full-bodied black hair, big brown eyes, and pale almond skin with a shimmering translucence. She wore a pair of petite diamond earrings and a delicate gold necklace displaying a string of equally delicate diamonds with even better color. Japanese women do not go in for big jewelry but they zero in on quality. These sparkled with the brilliance of top-of-the-line Tiffany creations plucked straight off the Ginza.

"Do come in," she said with a wide smile and a bow, pulling the door aside.

We entered, then stepped out of our shoes and into the guest slippers waiting for our arrival.

She led us into the interior with a proprietary walk. The sitting room was not what I expected. Instead of a cozy, pillow-laden love nest in overly cheerful colors, the room had a pristine, understated elegance. A white designer sofa with a regal back and squared-off armrests was the room's centerpiece. Fronting it was a black lacquer table, also elegant and carrying a price tag, I knew, of a small automobile. Thick white wall-to-wall stretched everywhere underfoot. The large-screen TV and stereo were black to match the table. A broad picture window swept across the east side of the room, giving out on a stellar view of Tokyo proper.

Now we knew what Yoji's loans had purchased.

Saito pointed us to a seat on the couch with a practiced wave. "It's

wonderful to have friends of my Yoji visit. Please make yourselves comfortable. I'll be right with you."

Our replies trailed after her as she vanished into the kitchen.

We sat.

"Friends?" I said in an undertone.

"What else?"

"Someone has very good taste."

"Hers."

"Because?"

"Jewelry, furniture, clothes. All well coordinated."

"Come to think of it, Yoji's place was nothing like this."

"Can you price the painting?"

The solitary wall decoration was a black-on-white abstract oil painting by Lee Ufan, the Korean-born, Japan-based artist.

"Approaching a half million dollars, give or take, but a lot less six or
seven years ago."

Lee Ufan is an acquired taste, so most people wouldn't know what
the painting was worth. I did.

Noda grunted. "Retirement fund."

"Maybe she likes art."

Noda looked around the room. "Only piece of art I can see. Retirement."

He was probably right. Who knew how much money her lover had
left her? They would have talked about it. Maybe there was another
insurance policy tucked away in a safe deposit box, but I doubted it.
By definition, her position must still be tenuous. It would have been
buttressed over time. But time had run out.

"How's she going to live now?" I asked.

"Find another sponsor."

Saito returned carrying a black lacquer tray with two traditional tea
bowls and palm-size bamboo plates, silently setting the black tray on
her black table. In the bowls was a frothy *matcha* tea. On the plates,
wagashi—the traditional Japanese confection, often sculpted—were
cradled on a folded piece of handmade Japanese paper.

"So how do you know my Yoji?"

My Yoji. Present tense. It was the second time she'd used the phrase and, as with the first mention, her face softened as the words passed her lips. But there was a heaviness behind them.

"Through his father originally."

She inclined her head with a measured grace. "I'm so glad we have a chance to meet then." She nodded toward the pair of tea bowls. "This is a tradition of ours started three years ago, in our seventh year together. We bring out these bowls for honored guests. He would be pleased I'm still entertaining with them."

Her upper lip quivered.

"I'm sorry," I said. "We didn't mean to upset you."

"It's all right. I must get used to his not being around."

She knelt on the plush white carpet, bowed, set a bamboo plate with a tea confection before each of us, placed the tea bowls alongside the plate, and bowed again, this time repeating the standard phrase for us to partake of her tea.

I took the sweet into my mouth and let it melt on the tip of my tongue. Lifting the bowl, I placed it in my palm, rotated it in two small turns so the back faced me, then took a sip. Noda did the same. I took a second sip, then a louder final taste, and set the bowl down, rotating it back to its original position and bowing as tradition required.

Saito returned my bow then Noda's as he finished.

"A unique bowl," I said. "I don't think I've ever seen anything quite like it."

The tea vessel in question was bathed in a burnt-yellow glaze, with four colored stripes of red, blue, white, and black running around the outside. Inside the same yellow ran down to a startling circle of red glaze in the bottom that had revealed itself as the thick green tea disappeared.

The red disk was unexpected, and maybe that was the point. But the piece was garish rather than subtle. The color scheme did not mesh with Japanese tastes or, for that matter, with any of the sensibilities in Saito's apartment.

"They are hardly my style," she said, responding to my quick glance around the room, "but it would have hurt Yoji's feelings to mention it. I treasure them as another of his gifts."

"Along with the painting?" Noda asked.

Her smile cooled. "Yes, my Yoji was kind enough to buy that for me on our second anniversary. I've always been a fan of the artist."

Their second anniversary would have come around eight years ago, about the same time Yoji took a second mortgage on his house. Love on the installment plan. At a time when it had become clear the relationship was working.

"Lee Ufan does have his moments," I said.

"Yes," she said, flushing with pleasure. "My Yoji was very kind. He could relax here, you know. He and his friends."

There was a woman's possessive pride in her voice, even as she subtly shifted the conversation.

"Did they come here often?" I asked.

"We had a regular gathering. It was always so much fun."

"Oh? Who was that? Maybe we know them."

"Oh, I'm not very good with names."

I felt Noda's body stiffen at her first lie. There was no outward sign of movement or of a change of expression, but as we were sitting side by side on the couch, a vibration passed through the upholstery.

We exchanged pleasantries for a few more minutes, tossing out a couple more delicately phrased probes, but she ably avoided them with the smooth grace of the perfect hostess. We weren't going to get any more today, and maybe not during a subsequent visit.

Back on the street, Noda asked, "Any value in those bowls?"

I shook my head. "Not unless they have a pedigree. They did have some age on them, though. Did we learn anything from the visit?"

"Two things. She adored him."

"Okay. And?"

"You said the current wife was his second?"

"That's right."

"Yoji was grooming her for more than a plaything. Looks like he wanted to make her number three."

CHAPTER 55

IT might be nothing.

Because one in five Japanese households have tea bowls.

And yet I couldn't get the pieces out of my head.

I needed to follow up, even though the inside of my skull pounded from a late-night fatigue. I splashed water on my face, doused some ice with a fifteen-year-old Suntory whiskey, then collapsed on the couch and made the call.

Graham picked up on the second ring. "Hi, Brodie. Nothing new to report on this end. Appallingly, the Sengai painting has disappeared down a black hole."

A second sip of the Suntory snaked down my system. "Probably have better luck if we posted it on a milk carton. For what it's worth, I have feelers out on this end."

"It could travel. It's happened before. What can I help you with? I have a client popping around at the top of the hour, so I need to get away in the next few minutes."

Someone was shopping Pu Yi's treasure, using the lesser pieces of his stash as calling cards.

"Won't take long. It's a shot at the moon, but you're the China expert. I saw a curious pair of tea bowls in a woman's home tonight. They wouldn't fetch much from serious collectors, but the lady did have a pricey oil painting on her wall. It got me thinking."

I described the earthy yellow bowls with their four bright stripes and the curious red blotch inside. They were in the form of a Japanese tea bowl, but they were off somehow.

"Were the stripes near the top? Each about a centimeter wide?"

"That's the one."

"Blimey," Graham said. "First harpoon in the whale, mate. Those are the colors of the Manchurian flag. Yellow ground with the four stripes. You saw one of the Pu Yi tea bowls. One of the calling cards the treasure hunters were on about."

"They were ugly."

Graham laughed. "They were a knife to the heart. Remember what I said about the Japanese military taking pleasure in keeping the Last Emperor in his place? They made sure the bowls were brought out at state functions."

My God. The bowls' meaning hit me. When served with tea—as they would be at, say, a Manchurian dinner party—they proudly displayed the Manchurian flag. However, as the tea level dropped, the symbol of the Japanese flag—the red globe of the rising sun—emerged. No guest could fail to miss the significance: Japan was the power behind the throne.

Graham interrupted my thoughts. "Where exactly did you see the bowls?"

"The Sengai was at the wife's house. The bowls at the girlfriend's."

"The connection being some philandering husband, I presume. Talk to him, Brodie. Quickly. He's the one who can tell you if the treasure is a hoax or real."

I closed my eyes. "He's dead, Graham. Murdered a week ago."

"You neglected to mention that the first time around."

"I was being discreet."

"Then by all means possible continue to be so. When someone in our profession ends up in the morgue it's *always* about a tug-a-war over a whale. In more than two decades in the business, I've had occasion to say this only once before. Watch your back."

"What happened to the other guy?"

"He didn't make it."

DAY 9

TWICE AS HARD

HOW did Yoji wind up with two of the Last Emperor's tea bowls? I fell asleep juggling this and other questions, picking up the next morning where I'd left off.

Yoji had gifted his mistress with the bowls without—apparently—mentioning their lineage. Having snagged the Sengai in China, he most likely scooped up the bowls at the same time or on a follow-up trip.

But what did it all mean?

I knew Yoji's work took him to China. Had he stumbled onto Pu Yi's lost hoard? Was he killed for it? Or did an inflamed lover of Mrs. Miura's murder him to eliminate the competition, unaware that Yoji was in the middle of negotiating for relics of untold value? Or maybe the wife's white knight had his eye on the loot as well as the lady. *I'm thinking we should comfort a grieving widow.* If her love interest were a member of her husband's kendo club, that would go a long way toward explaining the attacks in the locker room.

Before I could explore these conjectures further, Takahashi from Kyoto called and sounded the alarm. Breathlessness edged my dealer friend's voice. "Brodie, your Sengai has surfaced."

"You're joking?"

"Wish I were. Right under your nose. At Chinzanso. Three o'clock this afternoon."

"*Today?*"

"Yes. In a private conference room. Attendance is being offered through prudent channels. I have a contact number that will get you in.

Well, not *you*, for obvious reasons, but whomever you choose. Do what you can. This sort of thing gives our profession a bad name."

Chinzanso is a luxury dining, banquet, and hotel facility in Mejiro, an exclusive pocket in northwest central Tokyo. Lavish surroundings would draw the big fish.

"Be happy to."

"You will find yourself in the company of the . . . slimier sort from our ranks. Some of them have fangs."

"Earlier you mentioned my growing profile. Are any of the people involved likely to recognize me?"

"No. Different circles. But be careful."

"Aren't I always?"

"Hardly ever, my friend."

CHAPTER 57

F ROM Shibuya I caught the Yamanote line north to Shinjuku, transferred to the Chuo train, and rode it four stops to Koenji, Akira
Miura's neighborhood. My shadow sat three seats away.

Since the ferry incident, I was rarely alone.

I chose to arrive unannounced, hoping my unexpected appearance
might jar something loose from Miura that hadn't occurred to him
previously. At the very least, I wanted to avoid prepared answers. I kept
the Brodie Security team in the dark as well. They should be prepared
by definition.

My knock was answered with caution, the guard alert, his partner
a pace back and to the right, a piece held alongside his leg. Neither
showed any surprise.

"Saw your approach," he said, making eye contact then scanning the
area to the left and right behind me. "Alone?"

"Yes."

He opened the door only enough to allow me to pass. In a lower
voice, he added, "I have what you requested yesterday."

"Good. Later."

He nodded then stepped aside. "They're in the den."

"Everything under control?"

"All but the wife. She spends most of her time in bed. Not uncommon unless it continues for much longer."

"If you think professional help might be the way to go, talk to
Officer Hoshino out of Shibuya. Under Kato. She may be able to set
something up, or arrange a referral."

I traversed the short entry hall and found Miura and his old army buddy Inoki engrossed in a game of *shogi*, Japanese chess.

They looked up when I entered and Miura asked, "Have you found something?"

"Yes."

I took a seat on the adjoining couch and filled them in on the Last Emperor's treasure and the art in Yoji's possession. I left his mistress out of my narrative. As I spoke, I watched Miura for telltale signs but he gave no indication of prior knowledge.

"Does any of this ring a bell?" I asked.

He shook his head. "I wish it did. Yoji never mentioned it to me. Looting was common during the war. By Japanese soldiers and all of the Chinese factions—Communists, Nationalists, local warlords, and even highwaymen. But imperial matters fell to the barons and dukes from the old samurai families in the top military spots, and of course Japanese princes from the imperial family. They rubbed shoulders with Pu Yi and his crowd. Not us."

"Inoki-san?"

His look was forlorn. "I was a sergeant. A glorified foot soldier."

"So neither of you has any idea how Yoji could have stumbled on the treasure? *If* he stumbled on it."

Miura slumped in his seat, puzzled. "Yoji never asked me about China, except once for a high school essay."

So much for the surprise approach.

I said thanks and left. The Brodie Security op joined me outside on the curb. I looked back at the house. No one was watching.

He handed me an envelope. "What do you want them for?"

"To stir the pot," I said.

CHAPTER 58

HOTEL Chinzanso Tokyo was the perfect setting for a Sengai to make an appearance.

Located in an enclave of the privileged, the Chinzanso complex sits on the edge of a highland plateau southeast of Mejiro Station, an area daimyo warlords and aristocrats once called home.

The district is also the site of Gakushuin University, where many members of the imperial family have been educated, including the current emperor of Japan, Akihito, and his father, Hirohito, known posthumously as Emperor Showa, who reigned during the havoc of World War II.

A later addition to the complex, the hotel started life as a Tokyo branch of the Four Seasons. Now run exclusively by Chinzanso, it is no less elegant. Afternoon tea is served daily in the lobby, and nearby display cases offer such ornate accoutrements as blended two-hundred-year-old Hennessy cognac in Baccarat crystal.

Whatever the nimble-fingered Jamie Kendricks might or might not know about Japanese art, the London dealer had been shrewd in selecting his Japanese partner. The lure of the hotel's premium comforts would draw wealthy collectors who expected no less.

Yet another sign that the slimeball was no fool.

———

I met Inspector Kato in the lobby.

"So you own a suit," he said.

"One here, one in San Francisco."

In Japan suits were still the visual currency of nearly every meeting in the land. Since I was lying low, I had someone from the office bring my outfit to Mejiro Station. I ducked into the closest coffee shop, ordered a drink, changed in the restroom, then grabbed a taxi for the short ride to Chinzanso, managing only a single sip of the alluring Sumatra blend before rushing out the door. I'd said good-bye to my tail as soon as I spotted the inspector.

"The one back home spends most of the time in mothballs," I added. "Do I look like a translator?"

That was the plan. Kato was a Zen monk with good cash flow who wanted quality art for his temple. A not-uncommon scenario in Japan. I was his lowly English-language conduit. For the ruse, the good inspector had shaved his head and donned his old monk's robes.

Kato considered my question. "A little more thuggish than I would like. The tie makes up for it though. Slim, tasteful, and a hint old-fashioned."

"*Vintage* is the word you want. You're a closet fashionista."

"Try observant cop."

"Any sign of Kendricks?"

Kato shook his head. "Nothing from passport control. If he's in Japan, he came with false ID or through a back door."

Two men with oiled hair and expensive suits walked by in the company of an obvious dealer type who had more oil in his hair than the other two combined. He hovered at their side.

Kato said, "I'm spread a bit thin. I brought three people with me. Everyone else is tied up with the ongoing home invasion investigation."

"Hoshino?"

"She's here. Out of uniform, like the others."

"Good. Did you see the car at the back of the lot?"

Kato nodded. "Yakuza. Most likely connected to the dealer Kendricks is working with. Watching their investment. But they won't get close. They'd spook the guests. We've got photos. Someone back at Shibuya HQ is working on a gang name."

"Good."

"You ready?"

"Let's do it," I said.

CHAPTER 59

THE bidding starts in five minutes, gentlemen."

For the auction, a spacious conference room had been reserved. At the front stood a podium for the auctioneer. Eight rows of ten chairs had been set out, but standing room at the sides and back was abundant. Slender women in long black gowns circulated among the fifty or so invitees with trays of hors d'oeuvres and champagne. Some guests sat. Most stood. Drink in hand. Dealers were attached to many of them. There was one other temple monk in residence. Which made sense, considering the artist and his theme.

The Sengai rested on a display easel next to the podium. Most of the clients had already viewed it. Kato and I stood in a short line and filed by. No one recognized me, or gave either of us a second glance.

Not surprisingly, the work looked even better than it had in the emailed snapshot. The painting depicted a chubby Zen monk, maybe even Sengai himself, skipping through a graveyard, doing a jig, a bottle of saké in one hand, while three roughly sketched tombstones seemed to sway in the background. It was a joyful, smiling, silly frolic. Uninhibited and not afraid to look foolish. On the side was an inscription that read

Above the sorrow, dance.
In the lingering merriment
infinity's echo.

It was Sengai's unabashed lack of pretense that captured the hearts of the people, and unwittingly earned him a place in history.

The auction started. Bids were open but circumspect. Kato and I watched from the side, halfway back, which gave us a good view of the action and the participants. I was the only non-Japanese in the crowd. Kendricks was nowhere in sight.

Kato put in two offers early on but was immediately outbid. After the second bid, he said, "Looks like this is going to fly."

"It should. The piece is superb."

"Think Kendricks will show?"

"Don't know."

"You're a dealer. What would you do?"

"Assuming I'd steal art and traffic it halfway around the world?"

"Assuming."

"I'd check out the action to see how much my investment was reeling in. But I'd wait until the second half."

Kato nodded and watched some more. We'd identified the organizing dealer. He looked slippery.

I said, "If Kendricks doesn't show, can you get his Japanese partner to give him up?"

"Normally, yes. That guy, maybe not."

The price climbed slowly. The pace was leisurely. The auctioneer stopped often to comment on some aspect of the work—the brushwork, the theme, how it compared to other Sengai paintings of some renown.

Fifteen minutes in, he broke for a preannounced intermission. The twenty-minute interval would allow bidders to seek refreshments, take a restroom break, and consult privately with their advisers. Several collectors stepped from the room with their consulting dealer to regroup.

There was still no sign of Kendricks.

Both the dealer and auctioneer circulated among the guests, chatting them up and tactfully rejuvenating interest where it had flagged. The auctioneer engaged Kato, encouraging him to bid again. The inspector-turned-monk assured him he was seriously considering it.

The auction resumed. Several new bidders joined the fray.

"How high do you imagine it will go?" Kato said.

"We're no more than halfway there. The auctioneer is massaging his audience better than most, and many bidders have come back inspired."

Kato nodded and put in another bid to keep his cover intact. His offer was soon smothered.

"Easy come, easy go," he said.

When an older collector in a dark tie entered the contest by bumping up the asking price by three ranks, the room came alive.

"Here we go," I said.

A palpable buzz electrified the gathering. Two other competitors jumped into the battle, stepping up the price in equal measure. Several tentative bidders seemed to deflate. A couple of others looked around quizzically. Hesitating. The price continued to scale up. Competing bids slammed into each other. The hum of excitement escalated. More of the opposition dropped out, and it came down to three men with big money and big egos. Inside two minutes the price doubled.

After each new bid, the auctioneer shot focused looks at each man in turn. His face was expressive but sectional. A raised eyebrow, a challenging smile, a query with widening eyes. One at a time. Judiciously placed.

All eyes bounced between the bidders and the auctioneer. The suspense had redoubled, and so did the price—again.

That's when Kendricks slipped in the back door.

———

Absorbed by the proceedings, Kato and I had let our surveillance lapse. The bidding war was as dramatic as a horse race with three steeds running neck-and-neck.

I cast the occasional look around, but I'd grown lax as the quest for the Sengai heated up. The interplay was exhilarating. Not wanting to miss even a second of the action, I tore my eyes away with great reluctance. I scanned the scene resentfully and too hastily. I caught Kendricks leaning against the back wall, and he caught me looking. And recognized me.

In a flash, he slipped out the door and was gone. Kato had seen the exchange, and murmured into a hidden microphone.

In five quick paces we covered the ground to the rear of the conference room. No more pretense. Out of the corner of my eye, I saw the hosting dealer frown. But it didn't matter. We knew who he was and where he lived. It was his British counterpart we needed to wrap up the deal.

As I reached the door, I heard Rie call from the corridor, "Mr. Kendricks, you're under arrest."

Kato and I bulldozed through the double doors at the same time. More than fifteen yards ahead of us, Kendricks barreled down the carpeted expanse toward Rie, who held her badge up high in her left hand.

Kendricks didn't slow. She was five-five and one hundred and ten pounds. Kendricks was beefy and broad, topping out at six feet and two hundred and ten. He towered over her by seven inches and a full hundred pounds. His limber pace indicated substantial athletic ability.

We were too far away to help, Kendricks too swift. The dealer was ten yards and closing. He didn't slow. If he couldn't dash around Rie, he would roll right over her. He shoved an arm out, ramrod straight, palm out. *Beefy and broad.* A rugby move. That would be his sport. Rie's badge fell to the ground. She relented and gave way. Without slowing, Kendricks swerved to dash around her, his shoulders relaxing as he saw a clear path.

Then Rie grabbed his arm and shirt, turned her hip into his, and the oversize sleazebag flew into the air, flipping over on his back and crashing to the floor with an impressive thud. Even from our distant position, we felt the floor underfoot vibrate. A classic judo throw, perfectly executed.

Kendricks lay in a disabled heap, groaning.

Rie turned to me. "Happy?"

DAY 10

JOY KILLER

COFFEE mug in hand, I was strolling from my glassed-in office over to Noda's when the elevator doors slid open and six Chinese men poured into the room.

Six armed men.

"Mr. Brodie-san," Lester Wu said with a stony glint in his eye.

The man to Wu's right held a pair of Chinese fighting sticks by his thigh. The man to his left had unleashed a six-inch blade and it glittered in the yellow glow of the office neon.

Our Chinatown guide-cum-frustrated-organ-harvester was back with what looked like a far more unsavory arm of the family association. I scanned the faces. They were not friendly. The shooters from the cemetery were among them.

I frowned. "Lester, what can I do for you?"

Around me, work continued to hum along. The transition to alert mode went unnoticed by our visitors. Small nonthreatening actions threaded their way into the flow of office activity. To my right, a woman staffer went to the copy machine with a sheaf of documents. At the back of the room, a male employee headed toward the restroom in the rear. All around me, randomly, one by one, staff members opened a desk drawer or reached for a bag or slid a box from a shelf, set it on their lap, and opened it.

Then they waited.

Inside thirty seconds, every Brodie Security employee was armed and ready. With batons, knives, pepper spray, fighting sticks, and maybe even an unregistered gun or two I didn't want to know about. All out of sight but within easy reach.

Lester said, "What you think, Mr. Brodie-san?"

The new recruits looked as cold-blooded as the cemetery triggermen. Family association or not, none of the men were doctors or dentists or merchants. No white-collar workers of any kind. Their faces had too many hard edges. Maybe some were construction workers or longshoremen by day, but clearly their extracurricular activities bordered on red collar rather than blue.

I said, "You know, Lester, in this day and age a phone works wonders."

"No funny funny," he said.

The elevator headed down again. Noda emerged from his office with a scowl and took up a position alongside me. His hands were jammed in his jacket pockets. There was bulk there. There would be weapons.

"You okay?" he asked.

"Yeah. Stay close."

"Not going out for soba just yet."

The man with the knife said something in Chinese to Lester and Lester said to me, "We want look around."

"No," I said.

"You call us, remember?"

And then it dawned on me. They weren't here to extract revenge or payment.

I'd rung them after I'd picked up the envelope at Miura's.

They were the advance guard.

"Okay," I said. "Only you. Your men stay back by the elevator. And they pocket their weapons."

Lester squinted at me, the damaged eyelid flickering. "I send my top man. We step back. Weapons stay."

Good for him. A matter of face. And he wasn't going to be pushed around.

I gave my unspoken assent, another matter of face, and Lester said a couple of words to the man at his right, who nodded, pocketed his weapon, then stepped past the reception counter. He made a tour of the office, opened the doors to the conference room, the washrooms, the storage areas. He glanced at the open desk drawers and the weapons everyone had close at hand. He looped back and gave his report.

Lester turned to me with a frown. "Man who went in back not there."

A quick glance confirmed that Noda thought the same thing I did: impressive. Lester's right-hand man had caught the move.

"Safety precaution," I said.

Unless we called him off, the man who'd headed into the restroom had gone out a trapdoor and would be bringing reinforcements from a smaller security firm we sometimes farmed out work to. The woman at the copy machine had her finger near a silent alarm running straight to the Shibuya Police Department.

Lester's searcher mumbled something in Chinese and Lester said, "How long before others come?"

"Two minutes," I said.

Lester raised his cell phone. "I'm calling an all-clear. He's coming up." He hit a preset button, said one word into the speaker end of the phone, and disconnected.

I gave the go-ahead nod to the seated woman in charge of office security and she picked up her phone to abort the backup maneuver. But the in-house staff stayed in alert mode.

The panel above the elevator showed movement. The light stopped at our floor and Wu emerged as the doors slid open. A cigarette dangled from his lips. Four more men flanked him. If things went south, there would be a serious rumble.

Last out were Rie and Danny Chang.

Rie stepped to the front. Danny followed. Eyes flicking over the scene, she was alarmed at the drawn weapons Lester's men brandished and the tense faces of the Brodie Security employees.

I said, "You could have warned me."

"And you, me," she said evenly, a veiled reference to her involuntary dive.

"Actually, I couldn't," I said. "There wasn't time."

"Same here," she said.

"Explain. "

This last was also a signal for everyone in the office to hold his or her position until I gave my own all-clear.

Rie said, "You called *them*. Lester insisted."

Her fragmented answer did nothing to defuse the situation.

Several Brodie Security staff stiffened noticeably.

Clearly, the standoff had rattled Rie. She wasn't thinking straight. As good as her instincts had been at the hotel, her mental acrobatics in a "live" situation still lacked breadth. Her explanation didn't allow us to step down the emergency level of the standoff. Lester's people bristled with a tense energy, ready for a brawl. Maybe even eager for one.

"Wu," I said. "It's good to see you again. Why don't you come in the back, where we can talk?"

"I am sorry to come like surprise storm. My people insist on these ways."

Danny chimed in for the first time. "With Uncle Wu we take only the risk we might offend."

I smiled coolly, showing my displeasure. Their approach was clumsy. Someone could have gotten hurt. But it would do no good to mention the lapse now.

"I understand, but next time try calling ahead," I said to Danny while looking at Lester. To Wu, I gestured toward the conference room. "Why don't you bring in your men? Mari, could you show Mr. Wu the way?"

The old doctor smiled. He said something gently but firmly in Chinese and the weapons disappeared. Mari filed past, followed by Wu, Lester, Danny, and the rest of the crew.

As Rie passed, I said in a voice only she could hear, "We even now?"

Her look was resolute. "Not hardly."

CHAPTER 61

FIRST things first," I began, once we were all settled in the conference room. "Thank you for coming."

As a sign of trust, Wu occupied the seat at the far end of the table, deepest into the room. To his right were Lester and his top man. To his left, Danny. Rie took a seat in the middle, a neutral position. I sat at the end nearest the entrance, with Noda to my right, Hamada's replacement to my left. Wu's following filled the remaining seats, the overflow standing along the far wall behind the old doctor.

Wu smiled. "I visit you this time as courtesy. My wish is big inconvenience for my people. They think only of danger but I hope good luck for ghost-spirits."

I considered the promise I'd made to help Wu, then of Zhou's extravagant offer if only I would finger the ancient provocateur.

"I talked to a spy as you suggested. He's looking for you."

"Many look. No one find."

"I'm glad you're well protected. The spy confirmed that the people I want aren't Triads or his people, although they have used the method in Japan before. What I don't understand is why you are both so sure."

"A spy who has knowing." Wu stubbed out the cigarette. "Ten years ago home invasions by Triads in this country shamed whole Chinese community. Japanese police very angry. They close our shops. They chain our warehouses. They take business papers so we can do no work. Even worse, Japanese customers stop coming because they are scared."

"I remember the headlines."

Wu nodded. "Very bad time. We understand police message. We

complain loudly to Triads. 'Chinese people pay you tribute money for protection, but your action make us loss.' Yakuza also push them. So pact made. Those kind of killings stop in Japan. This is how I know Triads not do new ones."

All of which echoed TNT's comments when the yaki visited me in the hospital.

I locked eyes with Wu. "The spy claimed it was not the work of any of his people, but you implied it was."

The Wu family patriarch shook his head. "I say you *find* Chinese spy because Chinese spy often do copying of Chinese Triads. Chinese spy in Japan know we have pact so know they cannot use method here. But someone copying spy maybe not know this. Or if there is rebel spy, or even dumb spy, it might still happen. Only higher Chinese spy can check these things."

I nodded. "Well, he'd checked."

"Okay, so we done about Triads. What is second question?"

On the table in front of me lay the envelope I'd brought from Miura's house. I withdrew a stack of five-by-seven photographs borrowed from the old soldier's private photo albums. They were crude black-and-whites. In them, Miura and his troops appeared in various groupings. No photo had less than thirty men. Some captured groups of nearly a hundred. One showed them in full dress uniforms, which were neat but ragged. The men looked weary yet proud. In another they wore standard uniforms and drank what I assumed was saké out of tin cups. A couple of prints were official "*kinen*" photos—for posterity.

I held up one shot and pointed at my client. "That's Lieutenant Miura," I told Wu. "Do you recognize anyone else?"

I passed the pile down the line. When Wu received them from Lester, he squinted at each one in turn. He went through the pile twice. His examination took nearly five minutes.

Five tense minutes.

When Wu glanced up his face was pale. "This man is one of *them*."

"Them who?"

"Black Wind. He is Young One. Man who shot me in river."

"Really?" I said, astounded.

Wu passed the picture back to me. I looked at the figure he'd indicated. The face appeared in the back row of a kinen shot, half hidden behind the soldier in front of him. Clearly, the man had attempted to avoid the camera. As it was an official photograph, he would have been required to stand before the lens.

I stared at the five rows of men, whose faces were impossibly small. I angled the picture until I found the best slant to catch the light.

Rolling goose bumps peppered my skin from scalp to sole.

It was Inoki.

The last man standing.

CHAPTER 62

"YOU'RE sure?" I asked.

Wu nodded. "He made many ghost-spirits. He almost kill me."

Good point. You don't forget a man who tried to kill you. When I'd dropped in unannounced on Miura with the news about the Last Emperor's treasure, I'd zeroed in on my client's reaction, turning to Inoki only as an afterthought. The old fox had had plenty of time to compose himself.

"Give me a second." I dug my cell phone from my pocket and hit speed dial. When the operative who'd handed me the photos answered, I said, "Can you talk?"

"Hold on." I heard him excuse himself, then a moment later he said, "Okay. What's up?"

"Don't argue, don't ask questions, just do what I say. How many of you are on duty now?"

"Three. One man from the last shift stayed to help with the wife."

"Perfect. The three of you grab Inoki and stick him in the den. That's got the window with bars over it."

"Whatever it is, you're too late. "

"What do you mean?"

"He's gone."

Damn. "Any idea of where he went?"

"No. Two men in their forties picked him up about an hour after your visit. He assured me he'd be more careful than Doi."

Cursing under my breath, I hung up.

Black Wind . . . special wartime ops . . . executions.

I saw it all now. Inoki was behind the home invasions. As a member of a wartime assassination squad, he was more than capable of carrying out such deeds. Of carrying out a *string* of such deeds.

He'd killed Yoji. And Hamada. And Doi. He or his men.

Wu looked alarmed. "You know Young One? He still alive? He is close?"

I nodded unhappily. "He was staying with my client." I looked at Noda when I spoke next. "He's gone."

Lester Wu said, "His name?"

I queried Noda with a quick glance. He shrugged.

"Tetsuo Inoki," I said.

Noda excused himself without a word. Lester mumbled some quick orders in Chinese and two of his men stood up and followed in Noda's wake.

"Young One is joy killer," Wu said. "He get much pleasure watching men die."

I nodded. He gets much pleasure *and* he was in China during the war *and* as a member of a special fighting force he would have been involved in all levels of activity. Elite fighters went everywhere. He might have had some exposure to the activities around the Last Emperor. He could have heard about the treasure.

"Thanks for the warning," I said. "One last question. Could the Young One have known that Chinese spies sometimes copy Triads to escape blame?"

"Yes. It is old Chinese trick. Government spies in China use this technique from last century, maybe longer. Black Wind traveled with Chinese collaborators. They talk many things."

It looked like we had found our killer.

But could we catch him? Inoki was already on the move.

DAYS 11 & 12

BANDITS AND WATER ELEPHANTS

CHAPTER 63

NODA didn't pick up Inoki's trail until late the next morning.

The ex-military assassin had skipped off to Miami in the company of two men with Chinese passports. Probably the same men who had picked him up in front of Miura's place. Probably the same men who had been spotted in Kabukicho the night of Yoji's murder. Probably among the three men who had attacked me on the ferry.

The trio had flown out of Narita on Japan Airlines the night before, but had booked the previous morning, with a time stamp earlier than my arrival at Miura's to talk about the treasure.

Inoki wasn't running *from* us but *to* something, and I had a pretty good idea what that was.

———

Ironically, only Noda and I made the evening flight.

When the time came to move decisively on the home invasion case, the MPD couldn't get their people out. Inspector Kato and his chosen backup, Rie Hoshino, tripped over red tape. So did the MPD's designated golden boy. No one seemed capable of expediting the required paperwork and the string of stamped approvals needed all the way up the chain of command.

So much for the long arm of the Tokyo MPD.

Fortunately, since my passport was lodged at Shibuya HQ, Kato managed to spring it with a phone call and a promise to follow up with the proper forms. But the document was released with strings attached:

the charges filed for the kendo club break-in stayed on the books and I would need to return to Tokyo.

"With luck we'll be a day behind you" were the inspector's parting words.

Jenny's parting words involved a desire for ugly reptiles. When I'd called my daughter, she'd surprised me with some esoteric knowledge of Florida fauna. "My friend said Miami has lots of iguanas."

"That's true."

A healthy population of the five-foot lizard lives in Florida, the off-spring of escapees or overgrown pets released into the suburban bush by harried owners. Their number had grown so large that when an unsea-sonably chilly weather front swept the region, the cold-blooded reptiles went into a false hibernation, lost their grip on their lofty perches, and fell to the ground in surprising quantities. Which delighted rabid Sunshine State watchers by producing yet another string of bizarre headlines, among them "Kamikaze Iguanas Fall from Florida's Frozen Trees" and "It's Raining Lizards."

"Can you bring me back a baby one?" Jenny asked.

"Do you actually know what they look like?"

"No, but Alan Peters has one in a glass box at his house and everyone says it's cool."

"So you like lizards?"

"It's a lizard? I thought it was like a turtle or something."

"It starts out cute and small and bright green, then gets big and ugly and wrinkly, with a sagging neck pouch."

"Yuck."

"You want two?"

She giggled. "No! Bring me something good though, okay?"

"Consider it done," I said.

Noda and I landed without mishap, traveling from the cooling fall breezes of Tokyo to the balmy September weather in Miami, via a transfer at the Windy City.

On the drive into town, billboards old and new informed us that we'd arrived too late for something called the Barnacle Under Moonlight and too early for the Dragon Boat Festival. The first involved live music at a nineteenth-century estate on Biscayne Bay, while the second, sponsored by a Chinese-American collective, featured an eggroll-eating contest and a platoon of boats decorated in dragon motifs. I could easily imagine Uncle Wu at the second event, lounging on the grass and enjoying the festivities of what he no doubt considered his extended family. I had no clue as to what Zhou would make of such an affair.

"You have the address?" Noda asked.

"Right here," I said, tapping my shirt pocket.

Our Miami affiliate had booked us into the Mayfair in Coconut Grove. The taxi driver knew the place, and thirty minutes later we pulled up to a monstrosity that looked like an art deco building with leprosy. Noda gave me a doubtful look but was reassured once he saw the lobby.

"Two days, señores?" a Cuban man with stark white hair and a beige fedora said from behind the check-in counter, a string of miniature potted palms lined up behind him.

"To start, yes. Any problem to extend if we need to?"

"No, señor. You want someone to see to your bags?"

"Not necessary. We're traveling light."

He smiled knowingly, and it took me a moment to realize the phrase had a very different meaning in a town that saw more than its fair share of contraband and sudden departures.

The second of which, as it turned out, we would unwittingly honor.

———

I awoke refreshed and ready for our morning meeting. At the front desk, a new Cuban in a black shirt and a red vest pointed us in the right direction.

During our taxi ride yesterday, we had taken in a good swath of the local color. Coconut Grove was an old Miami enclave of coffee-houses, restaurants, boutiques, and a gallery or two. Large shade trees lined its nicer streets. The district sported some of Miami's tropical pastels—aqua, mango, peach, and cherry—though whites and beiges predominated and there were only vague hints of the famous beachside art deco color palette.

Our affiliate was a two-man operation. One who had adopted the name "Fitch" was meeting us at GreenStreet, a local coffeehouse. He assured us we'd have no trouble finding the place or him. Fitch knew a couple of other Brodie Security employees, but not Noda or me.

GreenStreet was a comfortable European-style café with wooden tables, upholstered benches along the walls, and a few high-back love seats in tuck-leather red for the romantically inclined.

When I told the blond waitress who greeted us that we were meeting someone, she invited us to look around and floated away. At the back of the café was a table with a Japanese newspaper draped over the edge. The occupant was a handsome pale-skinned man in a white linen shirt and jeans. He watched the entrance while pretending to be engrossed in the *Miami Herald*. A Cuban coffee and the remains of an omelet rested in front of him.

We strolled over. "Fitch?" I said.

"Abercrombie."

He had black hair parted on the right and gray eyes with a mischievous sparkle.

"You can't be serious."

He broke into a grin. "Of course not. Got to have some fun on this job. Don't like to use the real name over open emails. Ken Durgan."

He rose, we introduced ourselves, shook hands all around, and sat. Noda's English was serviceable when it needed to be.

"You eaten?" Durgan asked. When I said yes, he ordered us Cuban coffee then settled in to study me. "I was really sorry to hear about your father. I've done several jobs with him and his team over the years."

"Thank you. I appreciate it."

"A good man and a real waste of talent. Been hearing good things about you, too."

I said, "Name like Durgan, can you get around Miami?"

He laughed. "You think you're the only one who can cross a cultural divide? My partner's name is Cruz. We both speak Spanish. With freelancers, we can reach into the Cuban, Latino, Jamaican, and Haitian communities for starters. Whatever you need."

"Any sign of Inoki?"

His grin grew. "Nothing says 'find me' like checking into the Biltmore. Your friend does not believe in keeping a low profile."

Noda said, "He isn't expecting visitors."

"Always the best way," Durgan said. "You told me he was some big-time military guy way back when. Can you give me more?"

"In some kind of special task force during World War Two."

Durgan raised an eyebrow. "And he's vertical and still killing people?"

"He's recruited help," I said.

"He did rent a two-bedroom suite," Durgan said.

"Do you know how many checked in?"

"No, there's been a glitch. My source saw the advance booking, but the norovirus knocked Maryanne on her pretty little can before your guys checked in so I don't have any more info. For obvious reasons, she's not going to call up and ask how many and what room. From her sickbed she's narrowed Inoki's suite to a couple of floors. Because of visiting VIPs for some conference, there's extra security so discretion is the byword."

"How many rooms?" Noda asked.

"About fifty," Durgan said, regret in his voice. "Which is why you'll want these." He distributed Biltmore name tags and passkeys. "We head back to my office, I can fit you with blazers and pants, too."

I said, "That's some connection, willing to give you ID and pass-keys."

His grin turned wry. "Those are from my personal toolbox. If Mary-anne knew about them, she'd never speak to me again. You need me along?"

"Better you come," Noda said. "This guy's full of surprises."

"Not to mention he has the habit of leaving bodies in his wake," I said.

CHAPTER 64

THE three of us strolled into the lobby of the Biltmore in slacks and blue blazers with small guns tucked unseen into the waistbands at our backs. The decidedly Mediterranean luxury hotel was a peach-colored monolith from a former age. It had a tall central tower and two outstretched wings that anchored the posh Miami enclave of Coral Gables with dignity and panache.

"We're underdressed," I said.

Durgan's eyebrows danced. "That's because we know our place."

Dress-up may have been routine for Noda and Durgan, but I felt stupid with a Biltmore name tag pinned to my lapel. My new name was Tony.

Built in the 1920s, the refurbished Biltmore was aging gracefully. Its lobby overflowed with subdued grays and browns. Oversize hardwood birdcages were set at studied intervals, a nod to the hotel's legacy years when colorful tropical finches were considered exotic and the height of elegance. The finches, sporting their rainbow hues, were still in residence.

"Okay, we all know the drill," I said. "Stay in touch."

Splitting the rooms between us, Durgan and I headed out. Noda took up a post in the lobby as a lookout, in case our prey left before we could track them down. We exchanged cell phone numbers, agreeing to call for a joint takedown the minute one of us found something, or meet back in the lobby in forty minutes' time if our search proved fruitless.

I decamped to my assigned floors. Adrenaline trickled into my system. We were closing in on Inoki. The Japanese authorities sought him for the home invasions, but I wanted him for retribution. Payback for Yoji and Hamada.

Now in his eighties, the aged assassin should have been a shadow of his former self, but he'd scattered bodies throughout the Japanese capital, with nary a single detective of the forty-thousand-strong Tokyo police force the least bit suspicious until Wu had singled out the trained killer in Miura's ancient army photo.

We proceeded with caution, but I was optimistic for the first time. With Noda and Durgan backing me, and Inspector Kato and his team on the way, I hoped to have the gray-haired butcher under wraps and on his way back to Japan before dinnertime. Or if delayed, by tomorrow at the latest.

I traipsed through the halls of the Biltmore, knocking politely on doors. Soft rose-colored carpet muffled my footfalls. I announced myself as a floor manager and inquired in rapid English about a missing piece of luggage. The blazer and the name tag were enough to quell any suspicion.

Most people weren't in. If they were, they usually opened the door long enough to respond. When my knock went unanswered, I moved on, planning to return later. We'd decided to put the passkeys into play only if we came up empty-handed.

Since Inoki was traveling with two Chinese, we were relying on an Asian accent to signal Inoki's presence, and the rapidity of the query spoken through two inches of wood to confuse them. We deemed it unlikely they would expose themselves to view by opening the door. A polite refusal with a telltale accent would trigger an apology and retreat, followed by a regrouping in the lobby and a three-man assault.

I crossed the sixteenth room off my list of twenty-five and proceeded to the seventeenth. I knocked and asked my question.

"Come in," a muffled voice said.

The door was ajar, as if they expected a maid or room service momentarily. I pushed it open and entered without thinking. Call it what you will—a slip, foolishness, or jet lag. In hindsight, it didn't matter.

It was too late.

CHAPTER 65

T HREE men were in the room. All were standing. Two of them held guns. One of them was Inoki.

"Welcome, Mr. Brodie," he said. "Do come in."

With my hand still on the doorknob, I took a half-step back.

Inoki straightened his gun arm. "No, no. All the way in. I *will* shoot."

Considering his record, the warning was hard to ignore, even in the hallowed halls of the Biltmore.

"How did you know?" I said.

Inoki smirked. "One of my boys saw your group in the lobby. We decided to wait for you. Come in and close the door, please."

Please. The polite hand of death.

The unarmed man stepped up, yanked me forward into the suite, and slammed the door, throwing the dead bolt. He patted me down and confiscated my firearm. He was Chinese, as was the third man in the room. Both were tall and thin and had choppy hair and bad complexions. They looked to be brothers, one in his mid-forties, the other a good ten years younger. Neither was among the three who had attacked me on the ferry.

"You should have dropped it, Brodie. I left your client alone."

There was an arrogance to Inoki's manner I'd not glimpsed during our encounters in Miura's home. His undercover work had trained him well.

"He hired us to protect him *and* find out who committed the home invasions."

"Did he? Well, now you know. Until . . . you don't."

Something sparked behind his eye.

"Is it worth all the killing, Inoki?" I asked.

A thick purple-gray tongue poked from his mouth as he considered how to reply. It slid over his lips like an overfed garden slug. "I'd forgotten how thrilling the action can be."

"Action?"

"The war in Manchuria was the ultimate playground. I took anything I wanted. Life, women, gold. But I tossed the money around without thinking about the future. I was far too young to consider funding my golden years. Youth can be that way."

"So the home invasions were what? A reliving of your glory years?"

The tongue pushed out his lower lip. "You mock, but you are closer than you think. Let's just say I rediscovered an old passion. Once we started in on the first family I found it hard to stop. My compulsion had returned. Particularly for women. Mind you, I can't take full credit. The Kuang brothers here helped."

Something in me shrank away from this man. He was damaged slime from a bygone era.

"Families with children, Inoki."

He scowled. "Who are you to judge me? At one time the government paid me well to do exactly the same thing. Miura's army buddies were old men. One was blind, the other wheelchair bound. Their lives were over."

"They were your friends, too. Maybe your *new* friends should remember that."

The older brother sneered; the younger one didn't react.

Inoki raised an appreciative eyebrow. "You're smart, Brodie, but that won't work. These two boys are like family. In Manchuria I belonged to an elite squad. We reported directly to the top field marshals. We performed various, uh, tasks. Often we were sent undercover to check up on the troops. I was assigned to Miura's unit for a time, but my loyalty was to my commanders and my own squad."

Which explained why he'd tried to hide his face in the old photograph.

I said, "So Miura didn't know of your dual role?"

"Never."

"Did he know about the Black Wind?"

Inoki grew quiet. "I haven't heard that name in decades. How could you know about it? The operation was highly classified and our code name was different. Only the Chinese peasants called it 'Black Wind.'"

I stayed silent.

Inoki searched my face. He raised his gun higher. "You want to tell me who told you?"

"Not particularly."

Inoki stared at me some more.

"Wu," he said finally. "*I* gave you the lead. The old quack is alive. I heard stories but never believed he could possibly survive the shooting at the river. I'm right, aren't I?"

I said nothing. I'd made a promise not to spread Wu's name around, and I'd kept it. But some circles were too small. The Chinese spy Zhou had peered into the shadows and seen Wu. Inoki divined more from even less. In his eighties, Inoki's mind remained facile. On many levels he was still a dangerous man.

The old fighter's interest in Wu waned. "Do you know how long I've been looking for Pu Yi's treasure?"

"Are you sure it belonged to the Last Emperor?" I said. "He died penniless."

"Oh, I'm sure. Overseeing its relocation was one of my last assignments. When Japan began to falter at the end of the war, Pu Yi's minders ordered my unit to spirit away half of the treasure as a precaution. Pu Yi's most trusted Chinese confidant accompanied us to record the entombment. We hid five wagons' worth in a cave deep in the mountains. On the way back bandits ambushed us. With our superior firepower, we made short work of them. But"—Inoki's eyes brightened—"Pu Yi's confidant caught a stray bullet." He grinned. "We brought back the poor man's body, and those of a few bandits to prove we'd been attacked. But after I shot Pu Yi's right-hand man with one of the bandits' guns, I altered the map. Pu Yi would never be able to find the caves.

"Then two weeks later the surrender came without warning and my war days were over. Worse, it was suddenly open season on Japanese. The Chinese were hunting us. And the Russians, too. Three of the four men who went with me to hide the wagons were killed the very next day. We had planned to drive south to the nearest port. The five of us could have pulled it off. But with three of my trusted friends dead, I slit the throat of the fourth in his sleep to keep the secret to myself. Everyone who knew the *real* location was dead except me. The treasure was mine.

"But alone I could not escape with five wagons. Immediately after the surrender China degenerated into chaos, so I decided to come back when the dust had settled. But then civil war broke out again between the Communists and the Nationalists and it dragged on for years. After the Communists won, they sealed the country. When China finally reopened in the seventies, I joined a tour and went alone to the cave, but the stash was gone.

"Tatters of my old Chinese network survived the war. Most of them were poor. I'd funneled funds to them over the years and they were grateful and loyal. These two men are the grandsons of my great friend Kuang." He broke off, looking at the two men fondly, then scowled. "This summer rumors of the treasure surfaced, so these two checked it out. The original caves were close to Anli-dong. The treasure had simply been moved to another location by one of the village peasants. Since he couldn't trust any of the local officials and had no way to move the goods overseas, he contacted Doi, from Miura's old troop. Doi! A man dumb enough to risk his life for some goldfish. But that was three years ago. Three long years and I only heard about it this summer. But even then, we didn't know about Doi.

"The villagers approached him on one of his charity trips to the mainland. They liked and trusted him. He's financially secure, so he didn't have any interest in it himself, the dumb sap. He went to his old lieutenant. Miura was away at a hot springs resort with his wife, but Yoji was there tending the house, and Doi told him the story. Since Yoji had some connections on the mainland through his company, he said he'd take care of it, but begged Doi not to tell his father because Akira had a weak heart. His heart was fine, but Doi didn't know that and agreed and they formed a partnership. It took three years but Yoji got the treasure out. The last installment shipped from Hong Kong in July. When we were together at the house, Doi told me some of the story out of earshot of Miura. But not the secrets, of course. When the idiot left to feed his goldfish, my boys beat the rest out of him."

"I'm confused. Why go after Doi at all? Didn't you get everything from Yoji before you killed him?"

Inoki looked startled, then barked with laughter. "You think we killed Yoji?"

"Didn't you?"

"No."

"And Hamada?"

"Who?"

Strange. His responses were instant and genuine.

"The men who came after me on the ferry?"

Inoki shook his head. "You're babbling, trying to rattle me. It won't work."

His rapid-fire answers unsettled me. If his group had no hand in those events, then there was an unseen party nearby. Another point in favor of Noda's white knight theory.

I said, "But what are you doing in Miami?"

Even before I finished the utterance, I suddenly understood.

Booked the previous morning, with a time stamp earlier than my arrival at Miura's to talk about the treasure.

He'd come for Pu Yi's stash.

The older Kuang, who had been antsy for most of our conversation, said something in Chinese and a conversation I couldn't follow ensued.

Inoki's look was severe. "My partner doesn't want me to tell you any more but I told him not to worry. You'll be dead soon. He agreed to let me answer your questions only if he could kill you himself. Hardly a fair trade, but in a leadership role you must sometimes sacrifice your own pleasure for the greater good. Do you know any kung fu?"

"No."

"Good. Then your death will be quick and painless. I've seen him snap spines. Now, where were we? Yes, Miami. Thanks to Doi, we traced Yoji's group to Miami. With Doi and Yoji gone, there's five left. None of them are ex-military. We'll take the treasure from them and kill any that give us trouble. But first, we must dispose of you."

Inoki nodded and the older brother lunged.

CHAPTER 66

INOKI had asked the wrong question.

I didn't know kung fu, but that didn't mean his native karate and judo wouldn't afford me a defense.

I soon discovered Inoki's confidence was misplaced. Kuang was mediocre at best. His skills were all gristle and no meat. He knew the basic moves and was strong. Against an opponent with little or no martial arts skills he was formidable. Against me, he had little chance.

Which put me in grave danger.

While I could fend him off, in winning I'd lose. Two weapons were trained on me. Once Kuang was down, retaliation fell to the firearms. They would shoot. I couldn't defend myself against bullets. My only defense was Inoki's so-called kung fu master. And it would be painful.

I let Kuang drill me once during each maneuver. I pulled back enough to blunt the effect of his blows, or deflected them with a last-minute block while letting him partially connect. To an observer, it would look like Kuang was slowly and painfully wearing me down. I grimaced appropriately. It wasn't hard. Kuang was powerful, and his punches carried an undeniable brute force.

Before each new clash, we circled each other. His two companions gave us a wide berth. By the eighth or ninth exchange, I'd positioned myself as I wanted, and when Kuang next pounced I let him in, then seized his arm as I dropped to the floor, planted a foot on his abdomen, and flung him over my head at his brother. I rolled over, sprang up, leapt after him.

Kuang collided head-on with his sibling. Both men went down, the forward momentum carrying the older Kuang another five feet beyond his felled relation. As Kuang the Younger regained his feet, I plowed a fist into his stomach, grabbed his gun, and sluiced behind him, yanking him upright by the hair and pressing the barrel of the captured weapon to his head.

Inoki frowned. "You're just delaying the inevitable, Brodie."

"This is a game changer, Inoki."

"No it's not."

I gave the old assassin the benefit of the doubt and made myself small behind my hostage. Even if Inoki's shooting skills had declined with age, a distance of ten feet wouldn't be a potent deterrent. Inoki was certainly confident. The muzzle of his weapon probed for a shot. As did that of the older brother, who had scrambled to his feet, red-faced, and snatched up my gun.

"I've got pressure on the trigger," I said. "You shoot me, I fall backward. My body weight will pull the trigger and your boy will be dead or a vegetable even if you hit the bull's-eye."

Kuang lowered his weapon. Inoki maintained his bead on me. The elder Kuang growled something at the old fighter in Chinese and Inoki let his arm fall.

"Here's what we're going to do," I said. "You decamp, I'll send your boy out after you."

Inoki shook his head. "No way you're leaving this room alive."

I scooted sideways toward the closest bedroom, dragging my hostage with me. I kicked open the door, took a flash-glance at the layout, then looked back at my audience. Neither had used the opportunity to advance, which was smart.

"Okay, alternate scenario," I said. "I scuttle into the bedroom, shoot this brother, then wait for the next of you through the door and put a couple quick rounds in him. That'll make it two dead and one-on-one. That's your second and last choice."

I kept my Japanese slow and clear so the older brother could understand.

They were quiet.

I said, "Does Junior here speak Japanese?"

"No."

"English?"

"No."

"Then give him a hand signal to wait and not struggle. No speaking."

His brother mimed a wait sign and convincingly conveyed the idea that all would be well, then whispered something in Inoki's ear.

The old special-ops soldier said, "My Chinese friend here wants to shoot you himself."

I solidified my grip on his brother, removed the barrel from my captive's head, and pointed it at the brother's heart. "Your move."

Kuang grimaced. "You bastard. How we know we can trust you?"

"Do I want to take your kid brother home as a souvenir? You walk out, you get him back."

"Okay. We go. If he no come out, I kill you. If not do today, I look forever and ever. Then I kill you."

I rolled my eyes. "You'll get him. Just don't point your guns at me again."

They backed toward the door, their eyes bouncing from me to my hostage.

Kuang reached for the doorknob and I said, "Set your pieces on the stand and clear out. Close the door behind you."

They placed their weapons on a polished mahogany side table, then walked out, shutting us in.

One battle won, though not the war.

I shuffled toward the front of the room, keeping the young Kuang between the entryway and me in case Inoki burst back in with a second weapon. Ex–military men rarely come to a war party underequipped.

At the door, Kuang began to squirm.

"Settle down," I cooed in English, hoping the tone would get my message across.

It didn't.

I pressed the barrel against his carotid and he froze.

"Good boy," I said, again in a soothing voice, but this time in Japanese. "This isn't rocket science. Stay still and you'll live. Bump me the wrong way and you may hit my trigger finger."

Since his brother spoke some Japanese, this guy might know a scattering of words. He only needed a few to get my drift. The next thirty seconds were crucial and I didn't want my charge panicking at the wrong moment. An ill-advised move could get us both killed.

With my head, I indicated for him to open the door, then pressed the muzzle deeper into his neck. "Slowly," I said.

He got the message.

He reached for the doorknob and pulled gingerly. I stalled the door's progress with my foot. I peered through the crack into the hall. No sign of either man.

"Okay, out you go," I said.

I yanked open the door and shoved Kuang into the hall, pivoting back against the wall as I slammed the hatch shut. I threw the dead bolt. I pressed my back against the adjoining wall.

I heard retreating footsteps, then a second later, multiple sets of footfalls approaching at a fast clip. I couldn't tell how many. A bullet came through the door at chest level.

Young Kuang called out something in Chinese. *Damn.* I didn't have to understand the language to know what that was about. I dove for the floor as two more shots came through the wall panel I'd been standing against a moment before.

I rolled onto my back, and from a prone position returned fire, sighting about ten inches below the two holes. I heard the older Kuang scream and then a lead-footed retreat.

But I couldn't tell how many of them had left. Or might still be out there.

CHAPTER 67

CALLED Noda.

"You been gone too long," he said. "You all right?"

"Walked into a trap. Inoki and two Chinese goons."

"They gone?"

"Not sure. Shots were fired. I hit one of them. Need you two to come get me." I gave him the room number and descriptions of the Kuang brothers.

Four minutes later there was a tap on the door.

"All clear. You still in there, Brodie?" Durgan said.

"Yeah."

"Alone?"

"Yeah."

"Hurt?"

"Only my ego."

"Okay, we need to vacate. Heads are poking out of doorways. Security's probably close. Come out slow."

A pro's answer. Durgan was worried I had a gun at my head and couldn't speak freely. I checked the peephole and saw neither man. I tucked my weapon in the front of my waistband where they could see it, turned the deadbolt, and strolled out with my arms loose at my side. A hand yanked me to the right. Durgan squatted two yards back to the left, against the opposite wall, firearm angled to take out anyone who came through the door after me. I looked at him. A few beats passed. Noda released me.

"Guess you're alone," Durgan said.

I nodded. "Appreciate the thought, though."

Durgan rose and studied the bullet holes in the wall and the door and shook his head. "Maryanne's gonna be pissed. Think it best we exit via the far stairwell."

We walked to the end of the hall.

"How pissed?" I asked.

"She's the assistant manager, home hacking her guts up. That damn norovirus is suddenly looking like a savior. Once we're clear, I'll need the badges and the blazers back."

We trotted down the stairs, and on the second-floor landing passed Durgan the Biltmore lapel tags. The blazers would wait until we left the hotel grounds.

"Can you find them again?"

"Five times as hard the second time 'cause they know you're looking. I'll need full details once we're clear."

At ground level we pushed through the stairwell door into bright Florida sunshine and a grassy area leading to the golf course.

"Back exit," Durgan said.

We strolled into a vast expanse of rolling grassland. There were palm trees and rosebushes and walkways. Farther on, there were fairways as far as the eye could see. To the right, beyond the rosebushes, was a roofed patio and poolside dining.

We turned toward the swimming area. Women in designer beach dresses or cover-ups lounged with men in knit shirts and trunks. Most of the women had colorful cocktails. Mojitos were prominent, with sprigs of mint and purple lilies spilling over the edge. The men had whiskey in crystal tumblers, or martinis.

Nary a beer in sight.

"This way," Durgan said under his breath. He turned away from the restaurant area and followed the covered egress that ran alongside the pool toward the front of the hotel.

I paused a moment to take it all in. The pool was the size of a small lagoon. Whales could frolic in it. Yacht crews could practice their regatta moves.

Tiled tables and wrought-iron chairs populated the patio. On the far side of the water were private cabanas for rent with lounge furniture and trellises and lush pockets of protective greenery.

As I gazed around, a familiar figure caught my eye. She sat three tables down in the shadows and sipped delicately from the straw of a raspberry mojito. Her pinky finger was extended in a ladylike manner.

On a cushioned chair, cradling her son in her lap just as I'd last seen her in Tokyo, was Yoji Miura's wife.

CHAPTER 68

MY, my. How quickly some recover from tragedy. Uninvited, I slid into the padded chair across from the widow Miura.

"Fancy meeting you here," I said.

Even as amazement flew across her features, recovery erased it. When she spoke, only a balanced poise was in evidence. "Mr. Brodie, this is an unexpected pleasure. Are you on vacation too?"

With her husband's body still in the police morgue, she was soaking up the Florida rays, most likely with a lover nearby. And she was looking good while doing it. Over a coral-red bikini Mrs. Miura wore an elegant full-length white chiffon beach dress that flared at the bottom. I looked around for her companion but couldn't pick him out. Probably out on the links.

"Call it a working vacation," I said. "Have you spoken to Inoki-san yet?"

"Who?"

A lame guess I didn't think would pan out, but I flung it at her anyway. She looked genuinely confused, which made sense. The Kuang brothers had gotten Yoji's playbook from Doi, which no doubt included a stay at the Biltmore for Yoji and his partners.

"Did your husband choose this hotel?"

She shifted in her seat. A pleasing feminine fragrance wafted my way. With an aimless smile at full wattage, her son watched a couple of kids splashing in the pool. His head lolled to the side, his eyes watchful but unfocused. His arms and legs and hands were twisted at unnatural angles that probably weren't all that unnatural for him.

"Yes, way back when. It was to be the first stop on our way to the islands. I told you about the trip when you first visited us." Her smile was faint but not without warmth.

During my visit to her home, her reference had been oblique. She'd whined about her fate and her future and her lack of a financial safety net, then threw a temper tantrum, neatly avoiding telling me the slightest bit of useful information.

Seeing my unmasked skepticism, she added, "After all that has happened, I just *had* to go abroad, so I came on alone. Well, not completely alone," she said, kicking up the wattage of her smile. "Ken-chan's my chaperone." She mussed the boy's hair. If he noticed, there was no sign. His eyes remained glued to the pool activity, their glazed aspect unchanged.

"And a fine chaperone he is," I said, my glance making a barefaced sweep of the table.

In front of her was a half-eaten lobster salad sandwich. In front of Ken, a child's plate of deep-fried chicken fillets and a glass of chocolate milk. In front of me sat an empty plate and an empty tumbler.

Mrs. Miura's smile flickered. "All my friends thought my coming here was just the bravest thing." She leaned forward to confide in me. "You know Yoji's original plan was to go to one of those Caribbean island places with all those native people in half-dress, but I'm not comfortable with that. I don't understand their culture or their music or anything, so I'll probably stay in Miami."

"You've come in Yoji's memory, then?"

"That's it, yes."

Her smile stabilized and I smiled along with her. Then dropped my bomb. "So you're not here with a boyfriend looking for the treasure?"

I lifted the empty tumbler and waggled it at her.

She blushed violently, which pretty much gave up the game, but she made a valiant attempt to extract herself despite the tell.

"You speak Japanese so well," she said with a winning smile, "but you are far too frank for a new acquaintance." She gave an infectious laugh. She flirted modestly. "Such a fascinating job you have. I bet you travel to places like this all the time. Miami's just routine for you, isn't it?" Unadulterated admiration seeped into her tone.

She'd shifted the conversation sideways. Glossed over my probe. There had been no direct denial of a lover. No curiosity about the treasure I'd mentioned. She'd glided magnanimously past both, forgiving my impertinence with a teasing look, then falling back on her womanly charms.

Which were potent.

Her smile grew fuller and more enticing. Her eyes brightened and locked onto me as if I were the most fascinating man she'd run across in ages. They extended a vague promise that was hard to miss. She *was* a beautiful woman. No less so than her husband's mistress, though higher up the age scale.

"My apologies. In my business you hear things," I said, leaving it open-ended.

Which is where it stayed.

And died.

Her smile stretched to the limit. Her jaw firmed. She shut down. "I find gossip and innuendo so degrading, don't you? And I guess you're still in the employ of *that man*."

Her eyes darkened with her last words and seemed to demand an answer—with a fetchingly arched eyebrow so I would know her to be serious but would not take offense.

"If I'm one thing, it's constant," I said, summoning up an engaging smile of my own.

It didn't work.

Her eyes flared. "Then it's just as I told you at the house. I will not, under any circumstances, help that man. I'm sorry, but that's just the way I feel. I don't really mean to be impolite, but we are on a real vacation and I will not have that man spoiling our fun. There's been so little of it lately."

"I understand."

"I hope you do. We need the break. Me more than Ken-chan, but even he, in his little world, senses the strain. He looks around for his father every day," she said, her smile sagging. I glimpsed genuine hurt.

My heart went out to the kid. He may have been only half present, as they say, but he immediately sensed the mood change in his mother and tilted his head up and back to stare adoringly into her eyes. He raised his hands in an attempt to stroke her cheeks but instead his appendages flapped and fluttered and slapped at her face. She bore his awkward caresses nobly, accepting the offering for a few moments before gently guiding his flailing extremities back down to his lap and kissing him on the forehead. He smiled sloppily and went back to gazing at the kids in the pool.

"I love Miami," she said, her eyes moist now. "Don't you? Sun, beach, fresh air, good food, nice people. I could live here forever."

The rhythm of her words was upbeat and syncopated. Ken perked up immediately. He rotated his head up at her again and smiled. She kissed his forehead once more. He looked back out across the pool and began rocking blissfully in her lap.

"Yes," I said. "I like it a lot. Are you staying at the Biltmore?"

She looked at her watch. "I'm planning to show Ken-chan the manatees. He has a thing for elephants, you see, and manatees are water elephants. At least that's what I've told him. He's all excited. So we have to be going."

I tried one last time. "Are you sure there isn't anything you could tell me? It could really help me find the . . . the . . . culprit."

"Culprit" sounded so false. So staged. I wanted to say *killer* or *murderer*, but to the Japanese ear, and mine in this instance, both words and any of their close substitutes sounded too blunt, despite the boldness of my earlier assault.

"You're sweet to ask," Mrs. Miura said. "Really, you are. Don't give up. I want you to find the man responsible. I just can't bring myself to help Yoji's father. He never wanted us to marry, you know. Did I mention that?"

"Yes, you did."

"Well, it's true."

"Water elephants, Mommy," her son said.

"He's got a perfect sense of time," Mrs. Miura confided. "I don't know why, but if you tell him 'two hours' he knows when the time's up. Say, I have an idea. Why don't you join us?"

"No, no, I—"

"Water elephants, Mommy," Ken said again, staring in my direction, his eyes wide.

Mrs. Miura gave her son a mother's special smile. "Ken is going to need another man around. I mean for today," she added, blushing. "You're strong. You speak Japanese. Do you want to come?"

"I'm flattered, really, but I've got people waiting for me."

She smiled brightly, imbuing her latest effort with another potent dose of womanly warmth and understanding. "Well, then," she said, hoisting Ken up as she stood and bowing briefly. "It's been fun."

I rose with her, then watched her walk away. Her smile held until she turned, fading in the half-profile to a mean frown she thought I couldn't see.

Mentally, I berated myself. I'd arrived at her table with sharpened claws, ready for the inevitable sparring. And yet I'd gained nothing but two distinct impressions. First, that even with a problem child in hand, she'd played me better than she had any right to and second, that there were deeper waters to be plumbed.

DAY 13

CHOKE POINT

I AWOKE to thunderous pounding on my door at seven thirty the following morning.

My initial thought was *Inoki has tracked me down*, but I axed the idea the next instant. The former Japanese special forces soldier operated in stealth mode. Announcing his presence was not his style. My follow-up thought was *The police want me for the Biltmore shooting*. After all, the hotel offered the city's premier lodgings, and an unsolved shooting might sully its five-star image.

Then an overbearing Japanese voice issued a command. "Brodie, get your ass dressed and downstairs in ten minutes. Orders from Tokyo."

Every trace of sleep evaporated. With the kendo club charges hanging over my head, I was at Tokyo's beck and call.

Then I heard a pounding on Noda's door and a repeat of the same one-sided conversation. The Tokyo police department's alpha watchdog had arrived, barking testosterone-infused orders into all corners to mark his territory.

Twenty minutes later I meandered out of my room. Since Rie was also scheduled to arrive with Inspector Kato and the MPD's boy wonder, a shower and shave were in order. I ran into Noda at the elevator, stifling a yawn.

"That was some alarm clock," I said.

Noda grunted. "Guys like that is why I never took a city badge."

"Guys like that ought to be taken out and shot."

We boarded the elevator. We hadn't conspired to arrive ten minutes "late." We just did. Neither of us took marching orders from loud-mouthed Japanese police bureaucrats who had no more authority in Miami than a polar bear. Even with the threat of the B&E charge in Tokyo hanging over me.

In the lobby the white-haired Cuban was back at the front desk. This morning he wore a lime-green shirt and a gray fedora. He smiled. "You have many friends, *señor*?"

"Ask me again in five minutes," I said.

He chuckled and busied himself with some paperwork.

The troops from Tokyo were lingering near the hotel entryway. Kato, Rie, the door banger, and a fourth man, of Latino descent. The MPD's hound dog wore a dark blue suit, white dress shirt, and muted blue tie. Probably the only tie in all of Coconut Grove. In the muggy Miami weather, he had to be uncomfortable.

"I'm Jim Brodie and this is Kunio Noda. Glad to meet you," I said in English. *Glad* might have been overstating the case, but polite has always been my watchword unless provoked beyond the point of no return.

"Inspector Shin Yano," the human alarm clock announced. "I know who you are, even though I'd be infinitely happier if ignorance were an acceptable option. We're officially checked in with the Miami police, so this is now *my* operation. You and your man"—he flung a disdainful chin wave in Noda's direction—"are to follow my lead. We've a liaison officer present, and I've agreed to clear everything through him."

"Very efficient," I said.

"Professional, as it should be," Yano snapped back, an official slap down to impress the local badge. Another condition for releasing my passport was that I accept leadership from whomever the Tokyo police department sent.

I waited for an introduction to the fourth man, but when Yano wasn't forthcoming I stuck out my hand. "Miami PD liaison would be you?"

"Juan Moreno. Yes."

We shook hands.

"Low man on the totem pole?" I said.

"In this dump on a Sunday? I climb five flights maybe I reach the bottom of the pole."

I smiled appreciatively.

Rie was proper and official in a navy-blue suit and white blouse that echoed her police uniform. I ignored her. If a dunking in the Sumida River could put a damper on her career, any sign of the friendship between us in front of Inspector Yano would torpedo it.

The minute I *didn't* look at her, relief suffused her features.

Yano said, "Have you made contact with Inoki?"

Yet another condition required us to give the inspector a full report of everything we might have uncovered in his absence. In hindsight, I might have conceded too much control to the MPD.

Noda preempted me. "Still looking."

"Was your Mr. Fitch not able to come up with anything?"

"Nothing."

"Have you had contact with anyone else concerning the case?"

"No."

"Do you have any new suspects?"

"No."

While Noda fended off Yano, I wondered about Durgan's progress. He'd called last night to say Inoki and the Kuang brothers had not returned to their suite at the Biltmore. Their belongings, which amounted to three wheeled pieces of carry-on luggage, remained unclaimed.

"From a reliable source?" I'd asked.

"Friend on the force."

"Good enough."

———

After Mrs. Miura had strutted off in her dazzling white beach dress to ready herself for her swamp romp, I'd rejoined Noda and Durgan in the Biltmore parking lot, and our man in Miami led us to one of his favorite restaurants, in an attempt to boost morale.

"You get shot at and live, that's a victory in our profession. You got to treat yourself. This one's on me. Best Spanish restaurant in town."

It was a nice gesture, and I accepted gratefully. While his partner and two others scoured Miami for any sign of Inoki, Durgan ordered up a feast at Los Gallegos, an untrumpeted tapas restaurant on a nondescript stretch of Bird Road.

Durgan grinned happily. "Finding your boy again is going to take time, but the good news is that in a town as small as Miami, three's an army. My tech guy will poke around online. The other two will spread the word. We'll have eyes everywhere. We're tracking three Asians. One's an octogenarian and the other two are brothers who could pass as twins at a distance. They might as well be hauling around the Hollywood sign on their backs. If they're dumb enough to show themselves in public, we'll nab them. Meanwhile, dig in."

The waiter brought a bottle of red wine, then a string of colorful home-style tapas—chorizo sizzling in a hot skillet, bacalao croquettes, garbanzo beans, garlic shrimp. There were worse ways to go.

"Sorry about the extra work," I said.

"Happens."

"Shouldn't have."

Noda grunted. I wasn't sure if the noise was a confirmation of my comment or an appreciation of the *calamares fritos* he'd just spooned into this mouth.

"Not your fault," Durgan said. "Nothing tougher than an old pro. Even one from the last century."

"Anything we can do to help?"

"Enjoy the tapas and let my boys do what they do best."

Ouch.

———

Yano was shaking his head at Noda's string of negatives. "Incompetence is a given when dealing with you guys, isn't it?"

Noda went very still. Given his profession, Yano should know how to read people. Especially fellow detectives. It didn't take a genius to see that Noda was not the kind of man you could insult and walk away from unscathed. If his stocky bulldog frame, gruff manner, and dark piercing eyes didn't clue you in, the scar bisecting his eyebrow should have.

My cell phone rang. I said, "Mind if I take this?" and hit the connect button without waiting for Yano's answer.

"Pack your sunblock," Durgan said.

"You found them and they're on the move?"

"Yep. Inoki and his Chinese bookends caught the final flight out last night to a certain tropical paradise." He told me the name.

Yoji's original plan was to go to one of those Caribbean island places with all those native people in half-dress, but I'm not comfortable with that.

Looked like Yoji's partners had stayed the course.

"Makes sense. Good work."

"You need backup over there?"

I stared ruefully at the Tokyo police contingent in the hotel lobby. "Thanks, but no. We have reinforcements big-time."

"If that's as bad as it sounds, I could run interference."

"Tempting, but I'll pass this time."

"Knowing what I know, I went ahead and booked you two for the next flight out. Usual procedure. Leaves in three hours. Work for you?"

"Perfect," I said.

"Anything else?"

"No. You do good work, Fitch."

"You already said that. And it's Abercrombie to you." He disconnected.

I shoved my phone back in my pocket, and Yano glared at me with knitted brow. "That was your Fitch?"

Ah, his shining detective instincts were on full display.

"Yes," I said. "*We've* got a flight out. I suggest you try to keep up this time." I turned to our liaison. "Moreno, it's your lucky day."

"How's that, *amigo*?"

"You're about to get the afternoon off." To Yano I said, "I hope you've brought your diplomatic chops. You're going to have to do your liaison dance with another police department."

"Police department where?"

"Barbados."

CHAPTER 70

RARELY does revenge arrive so swiftly and so sweetly.

With blank expressions, Noda and I watched Yano's face implode like a human sinkhole of despair. He would have to scramble if he wanted to book seats on the same flight *and* arrange for official police cooperation at our new destination.

But the worst was yet to come and we knew it, as did Yano.

It was a little after nine at night in Tokyo. His master was most likely out drinking and schmoozing and otherwise groveling his way to the top of the MPD power structure. Yano had no choice but to interrupt his lord's brown-nosing to enlist his aid in smoothing the pathway with the Barbados police. Otherwise, if things blew up, the designated golden boy would become the sacrificial tuna—scaled, sliced, and served up to the Japanese press and the Tokyo MPD higher-ups.

The corners of Noda's mouth flickered as Yano hurriedly pulled out his mobile and punched in a number. I suspect my expression echoed my partner's. Rie stepped behind her boss to hide her widening grin.

"What are you two looking at?" the MPD detective snapped at us. Fortunately for Rie, she and Kato stood behind Yano.

"Dog meat," Noda said.

Yano scowled and showed us his back. Rie popped to attention.

The Tokyo MPD contingent made the cutoff for boarding by ninety seconds.

Yano looked aggrieved but satisfied. Our plane had only one entrance. Boarding required all passengers to pass through the front part of the economy section, where we sat. Yano stopped by to say he'd see us on the other side, then walked smartly on into business class. Kato and Rie followed. Kato turned back and winked. Once her boss was looking forward again, Rie glanced at us and gave a half bow.

Signs of a thaw. Rie might still harbor some anger toward me, but to have an overbearing MPD babysitter who had contributed nothing to the case snap at Noda and me for no reason would make her madder still. After all, it was our joint footwork that gave the Tokyo police its first solid lead on the home invasions—Noda's digging around the edges to unearth Rie's Chinese connection; hers to get us to Chinatown; and mine in dredging up the old wartime photos for Wu to identify Inoki.

As they disappeared behind the dividing curtain, Noda said, "Good. We'll have some peace."

I dozed for most of the flight. The plane was filled with American and European tourists, and maybe three other Japanese. The rest were Barbadians, a warm people in a range of hues from white to a faint tan to coffee-colored to dark cocoa. They had ready smiles and a laid-back attitude I liked. The local term for it was *liming*, according to Durgan, which meant kicking back and enjoying food, friends, and life. Island life. A strong dose of waves and rays could do that to you.

Their accents, lively and musical, peppered my dreams.

———

Before I knew it the pilot announced our imminent arrival at Grantley Adams International Airport, eight miles from the capital city of Bridgetown. With eyes closed, I listened to him tell his captive audience that the island country was only twenty-one by fourteen miles, the same size as Montreal.

"For you Americans, it's about three and half times the size of San Francisco, or twice the size of Washington, D.C. For our European contingent, think one-quarter the size of London. But not to worry. Even as small as Barbados is, I won't miss the runway."

After allowing for a round of laughter, he offered a visitor's tip: "Should you be in the surf when a rain starts, don't bother leaving the water. This island paradise is that warm." More laughter.

True to his word, the plane touched down without incident. As the jet cruised to the arrival gate, the head purser came on the PA and asked everyone to remain seated once we docked while officials boarded to escort visiting VIPs from the aircraft. The procedure would require only a minute, and we were requested to be patient because "the island wasn't going anywhere." Still more laughter.

As soon as the cabin door opened, a contingent of Barbadian policemen stalked onto the airliner. They wore tan uniforms and stiff black caps. There were more frowns than smiles.

"That doesn't look good," I said to Noda, my eyes glued to the retreating figures as they headed to the front of the plane.

The police welcome wagon returned two minutes later with Yano, Kato, and Rie in tow. Two men leading, three behind. Walking proudly on the back of his heels, Yano was chatting gaily with the leader, who sported a toothy grin. As they turned to exit, Yano shot a haughty glance our way. Among other things, the look said that he would monopolize the police and elbow us from the case if he could.

Then they were gone.

"You see that?" I said.

"Yeah," Noda said.

"The MPD's plan from the start?"

Noda grunted. "Windup toys are preprogrammed."

The purser thanked us for our patience and said we could disembark.

Why bother, I thought.

A sentiment I would have been wise to heed.

CHAPTER 71

PASSENGERS lined up single file at Passport Control. A window opened up and Noda walked over and presented his documents. When the next position became available, I headed past Noda toward the waiting official. The inspector examining Noda's passport waved two armed guards over.

"Take this passenger to the waiting room," I heard him say.

"My passport's in order," Noda said, a challenge in his voice.

The guard nodded. "Just routine, my friend. We're interviewing all Japanese on your flight."

"On all incoming flights?"

"No. Only yours. They'll clear you in a couple of minutes, then you'll be on your way."

The Barbados police were no dummies. They were sifting our flight for sleepers from the Tokyo police. As the guards led him off, Noda avoided a glance in my direction.

I cleared Immigration without a hitch, took a seat in Arrivals, and settled in to wait for my chief detective.

Five minutes passed, then ten, then fifteen.

My phone rang. It was Durgan.

"No can do on the guns."

"Why not?"

"Outsiders with firepower on the island get manhandled badly if they're caught. Cops come down worse on the locals, so my connection balked, even after I offered twice the going rate. Publicized gunplay guts the tourist trade, which makes up nearly eighty percent of the jobs. They offered knives with ankle sheaths. Will that do?"

"I hate knives," I said. "We'll go without."

Durgan sighed. "It'll hurt their feelings to refuse, so just accept the weapons and leave them in your room. One of them will swing by your hotel shortly."

"All right."

Durgan was silent for a beat longer than he should have been.

"Something wrong?" I asked.

"Bad news on the wire."

"What?"

"Your Mrs. Miura. She disappeared yesterday."

"Disappeared how?"

"An accident in the 'Glades. The little kid, too. Presumed dead."

I felt something in my chest plummet.

Three people had taken out an airboat rental but never returned, Durgan told me. Five hours after departure, another boater found the capsized vessel in the saw grass. There were no signs of the passengers—Mrs. Miura, her son, and an unidentified Japanese man.

The police confirmed the identity of Mrs. Miura and her son through her credit card and a driver from the Biltmore, who had been waiting in the parking lot for the return trip. The Japanese man had arrived separately and his identity remained unknown. The police classified the incident as an accident, with an eye toward homicide since no unclaimed cars were left in the lot overnight. A local police expert added that if the bodies did indeed go into the water it was likely that the "alligators had tucked them away in a cubbyhole or under a log until they ripened and the eating was good. Gators are lazy hunters and not overly fond of human flesh, but if food is lying around they'll snatch it up."

I said, "Think there was a second boat waiting?"

"With all the action in this case, I'd have to go with a *yea*. Naysayers are few. If any bodies turn up, it'll be the wife and kid. The man's long gone."

I closed my eyes and inhaled deeply. Little Ken Miura. Glazed eyes, helpless on his own, but endearing nonetheless. Never a chance in this world, and wiped off its face in a flash. And only a year older than

Jenny, who was just a shade less helpless. My daughter wrestled with no disabilities, but children were children.

"Did this happen before or after Inoki left town?"

"After."

Which ruled his party out. Their involvement didn't make sense anyway. Most likely, the lover had turned on Mrs. Miura once he had a line on the ducats.

I thanked Durgan and hung up. My vigil for Noda continued. My phone rang again.

I hit the connect button and Rie said, "It's me." She was whispering. "Did they grab you?"

"No. Are you saying what I think you are?"

"Yes. That wasn't an official welcoming party. They were rounding us up."

"Are you okay?"

"For the moment."

"Are you still with the police?"

"Yes, but they confiscated our passports and cell phones. I'm in the ladies' room calling you on my iPod touch via Skype. The whole station's wired for Wi-Fi and it works in here, too."

"Are you in any danger?"

"No, it's not that. This is about control. Inspector Kato overheard two of them talking. They aren't going to let us out in public anytime soon."

Suddenly I was feeling a lot less secure.

"Is Noda with you?"

"No. Why? Wait. I hear voices. I'll call you back as soon as I can."

She was gone several minutes, then my phone chirped again. When I picked up, Rie's breathing was ragged. "I only have a minute. They're moving us to some VIP guesthouse. In the photo it's got three stories, sky-high colonnades, and a fifteen-foot-high grill fence. After they debrief us, I think they're going to sweep this whole thing under the rug."

"Is there anything I can do?"

"Nothing except stay away from the police. Oh, and I heard one of them say they're bringing Noda in. His Brodie Security business cards gave him away. They'll be coming for you next, unless you had the good sense to make separate reservations."

"We did."

It was standard practice at the office to book all hotels and plane tickets separately. Our affiliates were required to do the same. Until now, I never understood why we bothered.

"Got to go," Rie said. "Be careful, okay?"

"You too," I said into a dial tone.

She was gone.

The Barbados police had scooped up Yano, Kato, Rie, and most probably Noda.

On the off chance the ornery detective might bulldoze his way through, I gave him thirty minutes more, but he never emerged from behind the secure area.

I was on my own.

CHAPTER 72

I TOOK a taxi to the Accra Beach Hotel in Bridgetown, where Durgan had booked rooms for us. In hindsight, I wish I'd taken the Miami detective up on his offer to help. He would have made it through the police dragnet at Immigration, and I'd have backup.

Too late now.

I checked in. The town was a pleasant mix of modern colonial and tropic island pastel, salted with a healthy dose of tourist eye-pleasers. Sun and music and bright smiles greeted you wherever you looked. Fluttering overhead in prominent places was the Barbadian flag—two broad vertical bands of royal blue at the sides, with a swatch of bright yellow in the middle overlaid with the head of a three-pronged trident, symbol of the country's British heritage.

The Accra, like the Biltmore, was Mediterranean and, in its beach-side setting, nearly as monolithic, though it topped out at four stories. It was a shade lighter and a third of the price. For that you got as much sunshine, more palm trees, long stretches of white beach, but wicker instead of burnished antiques. Nor were there finches in the lobby. But the bed was firm and the shower was strong and hot. Since I wasn't here to soak up the rays, I had all I needed.

The front bell rang. I checked the peephole. No one. Cautiously, I inched the door open. On the floor was a fruit basket. I glanced up and down the hall. No one. Right. I scooped up the basket, closed the door, and threw the dead bolt. I brought the basket to a table and unwrapped it. Under the fruit were two knives with six-inch blades and Velcro holsters. On the bottom was a handwritten note.

*Welcome to Barbados, Mr. Jim. Certain arriving passengers
from Miami, Florida, America, have two places. Hotel rooms
in Bridgetown and rental in Turtle Beach. Beach house is most
private. After we have eye contact on them, we call you.*
            —A friend of Fitch

I was pleased. Either digitally or through the good-old-boy's net-work, Durgan's people had unmasked Inoki's movements, and eyes-on was due shortly. The idea of two rentals was confusing, but once a visual sighting was confirmed, I could deal with it. The only hitch was whether Noda, Kato, and Rie could untangle themselves from the authorities' preemptive embrace. The local constabulary could keep Yano as a consolation prize.

I called Durgan. "Got the fruit basket. What else can you tell me?"

"You're in an island paradise, man. Brilliant stretches of beach, a nice people, relatively crime free. Their major exports are sugar cane, rum, and cricket stars."

Everyone this close to the equator was a comedian.

"Pretty much got that on the flight over," I said.

"Get a chance, try the fish fry. How do the knives look?"

"Like I could carve coconuts."

"That's probably what they're for. Not much trouble if you're caught toting them."

"For a native."

"Yeah, you might not pass."

"Great."

I told him about the welcoming party and Durgan whistled. "It's a classic Bajan protection maneuver. Comes from the top."

"Are my friends safe?"

"Perfectly. Just neutralized. They'll get a lot of agreeable head bob-bing, silly-ass smiles, no answers, and when the authorities have cleaned up things the way they like them, your people will be ushered out the door with even more smiles."

"Will the local police go after Inoki?"

"Based on the snippet you got from the lady cop, I'd say no. They want to suppress any possibility of a spectacle. They keep the parties apart, they get no explosion. Is Noda with you?"

"They nabbed him too."

"If you can wait, I can catch the first plane out tomorrow."

"Can't. Your people here, what can they do?"

He paused. "Shaun and Orin? They're long distance. Paper trail, shadowing. No up close and dirty."

"I was afraid of that," I said.

CHAPTER 73

SHOWERED, shaved, dozed, and nabbed my cell phone on the third ring at ten minutes to nine. Outside it was dark.

"You ready, Mr. Jim?"

"Name the place."

"Come to Oistins Bay Gardens. Everyone know de place. We find you."

All the clerks at the front desk knew Oistins. So did the first cabbie I asked. In fact, mentioning Oistins was like saying the Champs-Élysées in Paris. You had to be dead not to know it. The taxi shot out to the water's edge, then veered onto Highway 7 and rolled along the moonlit waters of the Caribbean Sea for ten minutes before exiting the main road for a couple of quick dashes down smaller streets.

I paid the fare and strolled over to Oistins, which turned out to be a giant outdoor fish fry and continuous beach party. Street stalls served snapper, flying fish, and mahimahi, aka dolphin fish. Flames flared from giant barbecues. Clouds of white smoke wafted by. You could get your seafood blackened, grilled, or fried and served with chips, potatoes, slaw, or salad. If you didn't want fish, you could order shrimp or chicken or chunks of beef. Bottled beer was plentiful and cheap, as was the amber-colored local rum. Syncopated reggae, perhaps the only import, floated over from a stage I couldn't see. Food in hand, people swayed to the beat.

At a picnic table halfway in, a pencil-thin man of about twenty-three made eye contact and nodded at me once, then sauntered toward the waterfront. I trailed after, ten paces behind. On the beach, moonlight took over. My guide turned right and headed west. Holding hands, couples meandered by in both directions. College kids were chugging down drinks and whooping into the night. There were families at the water's edge, with young kids frolicking in two inches of warm water.

Underfoot, the sand was soft and white. A bottle of beer dangled from the hand of my guide as he strolled along, just another local enjoying the evening. We walked on without closing the gap between us. The festivities receded. Out on the briny blue, rolling over foot-high swells, a pair of solo kayaks paralleled the shore.

A discreet sign said we were headed toward Turtle Beach. A waist-high retaining wall edged the sand. Where a clutch of tall palms plunged the wall into darkness my guide set down the beer, stretched, and made a wide U-turn, heading back the way we had come.

As he drifted by, he mumbled, "Beer yours, Mr. Jim."

I rambled by the wall and looped my hand around the bottle. From a safe distance away, I uncapped the beer, took a sip, and casually peered into the foliage. Shades of black over black layered the vegetation under the palms.

"Come sit de wall, Mr. Jim," a voice from the shadows said.

The sea licked the shore forty feet away. No one was within earshot. I edged a few feet closer but remained standing.

"This will do," I said. "No one's around. Why don't you come out?"

"Good where I be, Mr. Jim."

"Any particular reason?"

"Everytin' easy on Barbados. Police find de people easy. Better no one see me wid you."

"Fair enough."

"Thank you, Mr. Jim."

I'd come quite a distance from Oistins but strains of steel drums reached my ears.

"What have you got for me?"

"Move into de shadow, Mr. Jim."

"What?"

"Move into de shadow *soon*."

I stepped into the shade of the overhanging palms and sat on the wall. From the beach, people would see a silhouette, but nothing more.

The beer signaled I was just another happy-go-lucky partier. As my eyes grew accustomed to the darkness, I could distinguish the outline of a man about nine feet back. He was tall and lanky and dark like his partner.

"See you de lovers wid matchin' reds, Mr. Jim?"

Along the water's edge maybe fifty yards back, a red-shirted couple strolled toward us.

"Yes."

"And way back, dere is man walking dog? Den de family? Den man wid hat?"

His night vision was far superior to mine, and mine wasn't bad. I peered into the night maybe two hundred yards down the shore. I could barely make out the dog. I took his word that the group walking together was a family. I couldn't tell. Beyond them, a few inches high from my perspective, was another figure. He may or may not have had headgear. He may or may not have been a *he*.

"Daz de one, Mr. Jim."

CHAPTER 74

HE was a silver silhouette in the moonlight. A solitary senior out for an evening stroll. Floppy beach hat, beige shorts, and a dark-blue collared shirt. Flip-flops.

As he drew closer, I saw that it was indeed Inoki. I stayed in the shadows, where I remained just another late-night partier. I sipped my beer. I rocked on my perch, luxuriating in the warm tropical evening. When he'd moved some fifty yards beyond my stony seat, I peeled off and followed in his wake. The ocean covered our left flank, a wavy line of tropical vegetation our right.

The Kuang brothers were nowhere in sight.

Away from the hot spots, beach activity tailed off. Foot traffic dwindled to couples, dog walkers, and the stray beachcomber. The gentle rhythm of spent waves lapped the shore. To my right, the retaining wall gave way to an undefined edge of sand and a growing number of cottages and beach homes. Then the quality of the lodging began to improve.

A half mile from Oistins, Inoki climbed a short set of stairs onto a patio fronting an elegant villa. I lost sight of him, but a minute later the beachside estate lit up with a warm yellow glow.

I approached with caution. I eased open the small gate at the top of the stairs without a sound, then shut it behind me, using both hands to muffle the latch mechanism. The patio had a profusion of lush potted plants and luxury lounge furniture. A beveled glass table on a marble pedestal sat in the corner with a prime view of the water. There was a four-foot-long bed of flowering plants along the left wall, and an over-size barbecue along the right.

Behind a sheer white day curtain, Inoki moved through a spacious family room that could accommodate a cocktail party for forty without effort. Stuffed leather chairs and polished wood side tables were strewn casually about, with plenty of space in the center to stand and mingle. Floor-to-ceiling draperies, gathered and secured, edged French windows that could be thrown open onto the patio where I stood.

As if that weren't enough, natural coral-stone walls framed the room, hung with tasteful original oils by local artists. The painting selection impressed me, but the room's centerpiece stole the show, if only for its drama. Crossed and hanging over an L-shaped leather couch were a pair of eight-foot-long antique tridents, yet another nod to the island's British heritage.

Inoki tipped some Bajan rum into a crystal tumbler, trickled in some soda, snapped up the remote, and settled in on the couch to watch a ninety-inch screen.

Sure, that's what I'd do. Come to paradise, then spend the night watching television. On the other hand, the guy was in his eighties.

I crept down a small walkway off the patio along the side of the house, which took me by a state-of-the-art kitchen. It gleamed. There was a cooking island with marble countertops in olive and gray. There were a pair of stainless steel refrigerators and a professional oven. Fresh flowers from the garden sat in a purple vase on the counter.

Beyond the kitchen was the first of four bedrooms, two with king-size beds, two more with twins. More full-length drapery and coral stone. Large Caribbean tiles throughout. There was egress from a central hallway through a back door at the end. I turned the doorknob. It was locked. The bedrooms were dark but I could make out suitcases in two of them, and clothes hanging in an open alcove, but nothing else of interest.

I returned along the far side of the villa. A small window looked in on the family room and I caught Inoki in profile, turned toward the screen.

He sipped his rum.

He watched what looked like a beach movie.

All was normal. Inoki had found his wonderland. On the coffee table in front of him was a bowl piled high with guava and mango and star apples. And in the far corner, tucked behind a table and visible only from this angle, was a waist-high stack of rustic wooden crates. One box was open, its lid tossed aside. Inside were a flood of palm-size Chinese gold ingots and a scattering of jade trinkets. In another, two dozen scroll paintings, rolled and tied, stood upright. The haft of a sword peeked out from behind the boxes.

Son of a bitch.

Inoki had also found his treasure.

And he was alone.

Returning to the patio, I came full circle. I pulled open the access door off to the side of the French windows.

I entered. The door swung shut behind me.

Inoki looked up. There was no surprise on the old assassin's face. No emotion. He said nothing. He went back to watching the tube.

Something wasn't right.

Get out of here, Brodie, the voice in my head screamed.

I turned but it was too late.

From the darkened hallway leading to the bedrooms in the rear, a figure emerged with a 9mm Smith & Wesson pointed at my chest. He held the chic "half-and-half" model, glistening silver steel on top, black polymer along the bottom of the barrel and the grip.

"Say good-bye to paradise," the gunman said.

I edged toward the door.

"Won't do you any good," said the man I knew. "There's three of my people out there."

CHAPTER 75

SOMETHING inside me shut down.

In a crowd he might not have caught my eye. One on one, there could be no mistake. He had dyed his jet-black hair reddish brown and grown a moustache, also dyed. His cheeks were flushed with good living and maybe a shot or two of the same rum Inoki was coddling. He wore an expensive silk shirt that lay on his skin lightly. Almost caressing it.

I stood face-to-face with a new and improved Yoji Miura.

He'd pursued the perfect life he'd promised his wife and son while I stalked the darker corners of Tokyo in search of his murderer.

I couldn't put into words the torrent of emotion flooding through me. Because for the last eleven nights, I'd gone to bed with a single goal foremost in my thoughts: nail Yoji's killer. Now only one word escaped my lips before my verbal dexterity deserted me.

"You're . . ."

Miura took great delight in my astonishment. "Alive and well and enjoying life? Yep."

"Then who . . . ?"

"Was the poor fellow beaten to pulp in Kabukicho? A black-sheep cousin."

Incoherence was unlike me. I'd survived worse, and come out better. But Yoji's body in Kabukicho had been the flagpole on which I'd raised my outrage. I'd borne the shame and the guilt of his death even if, technically, it was not mine to bear.

My passion for justice had been boundless. That passion had caused me to butt heads with the staff of Brodie Security. That passion had dragged me down a long and grueling road—bludgeoning myself with blame as I consoled his parents; sucked up the reproaches his wife had flung in my face; suffered a severe beating at the kendo club; fought for my life on the Sumida River; agonized over Hamada's death and the future of his wife and the twins; swallowed my pride in front of my daughter as Rie berated me for my conduct; endured a poisoning in Chinatown; faced down Wu's gunmen in the Chinese cemetery; braved a sniper's laser targeting; sparred with a dangerous and paranoid spy; defused a showdown in Brodie Security with Lester Wu and his over-eager thugs; and barely escaped from a trap set by Inoki and the Kuang brothers in Miami.

That passion had bashed and abused me but I'd stood up against each and every blow.

And now my resolve had brought me here.

My face went through contortions that would have sent my daughter scampering from the room with a frightened whimper.

"He was a homeless wreck," Yoji said. "He'd been disowned by the rest of the family long ago, drinking and gambling and unable to hold a job. I laid out money like bread crumbs and he waddled along obediently. After a year or so, I put him in a modest apartment where I could keep an eye on him, and supplied him with enough to eat and drink and gamble. It was the least I could do before the clueless bum repaid me in the only way he could."

Still the words wouldn't come but Yoji required no prodding.

"Because I was the front man in China, I needed to disappear. The rest of my team was faceless. Once we made the play for the treasure, I knew people like Inoki would come hunting for me. There's more of them out there, but none of them made the jump to Miami, our choke point, or here. We lost them in Kabukicho. If Doi had kept his mouth shut, Inoki never would have found us."

I recovered my voice, though it was hoarse. "So the Kabukicho killing was planned from the start?"

Yoji nodded. "When the home invasions happened, my father's worries gave me the idea of hiring a detective agency in the hope that a professional's confirmation would accelerate the police acceptance of the body as mine. So I slipped your card into my cousin's wallet. It worked."

I closed my eyes. Despite my anger, I had to hand it to him. It was a brilliant plan. Yoji had played up his father's feebleness. He'd opposed the use of Brodie Security. He was the reluctant but accommodating son. Then came the beating, which was so brutal we had all fixated on the pulverized body and never looked beyond it.

And seeing the cuff links broke my heart. In shock, I'd identified him without hesitation. His wife identified him. His father identified him. The dentistry charts identified him. The list was overwhelming. And in the process I unwittingly provided the independent validation Yoji sought.

"You guys did a job on your cousin. The face I get. But what about the arm and the rest of it?"

Yoji held up his right hand. "Couldn't fake this, so the arm had to come off."

There was a faint, irregular discoloration about the size of a nickel on his palm. A birthmark. You had to look hard to see it, but people close to him would be familiar with the blemish.

"Did your father know?"

"Neither of my parents was brought into the loop. That's why the arm had to go."

"How did you get the charts to match?"

"Easy. I found a hungry dentist. Then two days before Kabukicho, my liquored-up moron of a cousin stumbled down some stairs and chipped his two front teeth, so we had to knock them out."

Which explained why they weren't at the scene. "And the Triad thing?"

"Once we read about the home invasions, we knew someone was looking for the treasure, but we didn't know who." His glance strayed to Inoki's lethargic form in the corner. "But I thought, why not link my cousin's death to them? If the police bought it, great. If not, nothing lost. Inoki did us a great service."

Clearly Yoji was a natural-born strategist.

"Your cousin have a name?"

Yoji's grin vanished. "Why?"

"Seems more respectful."

"He was a besotted simpleton who'd pickled all his brain cells long ago. By the time I found him, he was living in a cardboard box under a bridge in Kanda. I gave him twenty months of a better life before putting him out of his misery."

"Like you did your wife?"

Yoji waved the gun. "Watch your tone, Brodie. She was a beauty. Always had been. But after Ken was born she soured. Complained constantly. Wanted more money. For her and the octopus boy that came out of her. They're both better off now."

"You still haven't told me your cousin's name."

"He has no need for a name anymore," Yoji snapped. "And in a few minutes, neither will you."

"Is Ms. Saito around? I'd like to say hello."

Yoji's jaw dropped at the mention of his mistress. I wanted him off balance and babbling. If I could unsettle him, maybe I could get close enough to disarm him.

He took a step back. "Forget the mind games, Brodie. They won't help you. Nice trick finding her, though. Only this time your cleverness has gotten you killed. You and Inoki."

I glanced over at the former special-ops guy. He was still hunched in the corner. His eyes were dull. He was deflated. He'd given up. I wondered what caused the transformation. This was not the man I met in Miami.

"Not quite," I said. "Don't forget my people and the Kuang brothers."

"Was that their name? Didn't know that."

Was.

"Where are they?"

"Now *that's* a fascinating story. You'd be surprised what you can learn in this place if you spread some money around. There's a little-known spot about a half mile offshore the locals call Shark's Cozy. For some reason sharks congregate there. No one knows why. Currents, maybe. Or warm water. Or good feeding. You toss in a hunk of beef trailing blood and they show up by the dozens. In seconds. It's quite spectacular. You see fins racing toward you. The water's so clear you see their big triangular noses, too, and their pointy white teeth as they tear into the food. When you throw a person in, I'm told the screams are like nothing you've ever heard. The water turns red and frothy. With two bodies,

I bet it looked like tomato soup. *Thick* and frothy. Gives a whole new meaning to Chinese takeout."

Yoji chuckled and Inoki turned pale, shrinking into himself. That's what had taken the fight out of the old soldier. There'd been a clear fondness between the ancient assassin and the Kuang brothers. *These two boys are like family.* With their execution, Inoki had lost everything—the treasure and his support. And his will. He was trapped on Barbados with nowhere to go, even if he did escape from the villa. Yoji's people could hunt him down before he could get off the island.

A second choke point.

And then I pulled together the threads of the trap.

Welcome to Barbados, Mr. Jim. Certain arriving passengers from Miami, Florida, America, have two places.

The beach villa had been a setup. Inoki hadn't just been strolling on the sand. Yoji's people had lured every last one of us to Barbados. Inoki had booked his usual accommodations for three—the hotel rooms. Then, unbeknownst to him, Yoji's team had reserved the beach house in Inoki's name, corralled him and his two Chinese protégés, baited the trap for me, and choreographed the moonlight walk.

Yoji's men shadowed me shadowing a complacent Inoki, the old soldier obediently following orders, holding out a last-ditch hope for the Kuang brothers.

My captor saw my mind racing furiously and filled in the remaining blanks without any prompting. "Half my team was monitoring Inoki in Miami when he made his play against you. Truth be told, I was sorry you showed up. I felt a little guilty deceiving my parents, but liked the way you and your people were working so hard for them. You were very loyal and I was touched. We did try to warn you off."

"You mean in the locker room?"

"Yes. Most people would have backed off after a thrashing like that. But you didn't, so we mailed your friend back in pieces."

"*Your people* killed Hamada?"

"And sent some freelancers after you on the boat."

A dousing in ice water could not have shocked me more. Hamada had died on my account. Inside my head I heard a howl.

I said, "Why didn't you just come after me first?"

"You have a whole company behind you. The ferry attack was supposed to draw blood, not kill."

Brodie Security had functioned as a cover and a curse. And while Noda and I struggled to decipher the events, everything else had fallen Yoji's way. His team had trapped Inoki. The Barbados police had swooped down on my backup. Even his wife was gone, courtesy of an unseen lover. The lover had . . . *damn*. How could I be so dense?

Yoji was grooming her for more than a plaything. Looks like he wanted to make her number three.

There was no mystery man in Mrs. Miura's life. The empty tumbler at her poolside table wasn't a boyfriend's. It belonged to Yoji or a minder on his team. The mistress was not in the market for a new sponsor. For both women, it had always been Yoji. The quiet handsome man. The charmer. The self-deprecating and apologetic manipulator who had visited Brodie Security.

Yoji couldn't bring both of them to his new tropical paradise, so he kept his wife waiting in luxury in Miami while he arranged her accident. Her professed distaste for the Caribbean islands played perfectly into his plans. He simply substituted the Everglades for Shark's Cozy.

"So you planned your wife's death, too?"

"Housecleaning."

Something inside me shuddered.

"Like I said, Brodie. I do like you."

I froze. When a guy like Yoji starts dealing out multiple compliments, what he's really doing is steeling himself for the next act. A self-prescribed dosage of reverse psychology to build nerve. Whether it's a beating, a double cross, or pulling the trigger, I'd seen it far too often not to recognize the signs.

I'd made no progress on my plan to distract him. He was too sly. I needed to think of something.

Anything.

Fast.

Then the front door opened, and my situation nosedived from bad to worse.

CHAPTER 76

YOJI looked toward the door.

Much to my amazement, Kiyama strolled in. He was the last person I'd expected to see in Barbados. The wallflower. The quiet kendo practitioner who had listened to me converse in the dojo with his boisterous friend, Tanaka-sensei.

Kiyama had been timid and withdrawn. A man with an endless reserve of polite. He'd struck me as anything but adventurous. Certainly not the type I'd peg to travel nine thousand miles from the comfortable nest of his Tokyo home to the edge of the Caribbean Sea. Tanaka—the overexuberant sword collector who had enlisted my services to track down specimens stateside, first at the dojo, then on the phone—seemed a more likely candidate.

Kiyama carried a pair of sheathed long swords. I could distinguish the outline of a compact handgun in his trouser pocket.

"So it's done?" Yoji asked.

Kiyama nodded.

Still the quiet one, I thought.

Yoji turned to me. "The dentist got greedy. He wanted a bigger payout. We invited him down for his money and a vacation on us. Kiyama and Tanaka took him for a swim instead. Makes you wonder how much more those sharks can eat."

I had nothing to say to that.

Yoji chuckled. "Brodie, you're an art dealer, so you can appreciate our haul. Look at it! Carved jade, scroll paintings, three koto by master swordsmiths, porcelains, silver plates, and bronzes. Our end comes to twenty-one million dollars American, and change. With six of us left, that's three and half million each. Clear and tax free."

The more Yoji spoke, the more jubilant he became. His dream was literally stacked in front of him. I looked at Kiyama. There was no joy, no triumph, no exultation. Not a single syllable of exuberance came from the wallflower. I began to wonder about him.

Yoji noticed, too. "Kiyama-san, aren't you excited?"

Kiyama nodded.

Yoji laughed, shaking his head in mock reprimand. "Look at you. You've got treasure. You've got freedom. You'll be the co-owner with Tanaka of the best sword in the public domain in all of Japan, and you look glum."

Kiyama's jaw line hardened. He bowed his head. As always, his response was submissive. Except for his stiffening features. I felt a coldness I couldn't explain sweep through me.

Yoji remained oblivious. "Everyone thinks that Tanaka is the better fighter because he has the higher kendo rank and was given the title of sensei. The man has an ego bigger than the Tokyo Dome, so we indulge him. Kiyama, kind soul, has always deferred to his *sempai*. Accepted a lower rank, no title. Even though his sword work is superior. This is the Japanese way, right, Kiyama?" Yoji grinned with the pride of an older brother.

Sempai is the higher position in a vital Japanese relationship known as *sempai-kohai*. Literally, it means senior-junior but in its fullest form the concept involves a mentor-novice attachment that lasts a lifetime. Often the senior member paves the way for his young follower, who, in turn, assumes a host of chores at the behest of his senior. The arrangement works well as long as neither member abuses his position.

I faced the new entrant. "I'm surprised to see you here. I expected Tanaka but not you."

Kiyama finally spoke. "Tanaka was part of our group."

It was the first time I'd heard his voice. It was low and firm and even, in a supremely confident way. There was nothing of a deferential "younger brother" in his tone now.

"Was?" Yoji said, his cheerfulness slipping a notch.

Kiyama shrugged. "There's only one sword with the emperor's inscription."

"But the other two are by Masamune. A swordsmith with a higher rep doesn't exist."

"But the emperor's sword tops them, and Tanaka tried to pull rank."

"Then you get the other two."

A frown crawled across Kiyama's features. "And listen to him boast about having the *best* sword until the end of my days? I don't think so. I've put up with his obnoxious ways long enough."

The mask is coming off, I thought.

"But two Masamune koto," Yoji said. "That's nearly as good."

"With Tanaka, *nearly* means nothing. You know that. So we fought for it."

Yoji was confused. "But how? Where would you find bamboo swords on this island?"

"We made do with what was at hand." Kiyama rattled the weapons in his right hand.

Yoji laughed nervously and looked toward the door, expecting Tanaka to walk through it at any second. "You're kidding, of course. Tanaka would never agree to fight his little buddy."

"I insisted."

"But you're . . ." Yoji paused, confused. "He doesn't know that . . . he . . . we are all friends."

"Were," Kiyama said simply, without any change of tone or expression.

I looked at the two weapons the younger man held at his side and didn't need to ask about the outcome of the duel.

CHAPTER 77

YOJI continued to look expectantly at the door.

"Tanaka-san, get in here," he called. "I know you're out there."

I looked over at the treasure stacked neatly in the corner. The grip of only a single sword protruded. The kohai held the two missing weapons.

Kiyama said, "He's not coming back."

Yoji shook his head stubbornly. "The others wouldn't allow it."

"After they trailed Brodie here, I told them to go into town and celebrate. Tanaka and I had just returned from taking care of the dentist. Once they left, we fought. Now it's just you and me. Plus Brodie and the old man."

"The joke's stale, Kiyama."

"You're right. I'm sorry. Now finish your work. You have to deal with Brodie. Everyone else has got blood on his hands."

I moved into the opening. "You don't have to kill anymore. You've won. Just take the treasure and go."

Yoji turned to Kiyama. "He's right. What can he do?"

Kiyama scoffed. "You're listening to *him*?"

"We can tie him up or something."

"He's got a whole fleet of detectives working for him. Kill him, then we'll feed him to the sharks and walk away rich."

"He did look after my father."

"We have all committed. You're the last. Think about it while I take care of old business."

I grew still. The balance of power had changed from Yoji to Kiyama.

Kiyama's was a quietly forceful presence. Cool and calculating. Still not a big talker. But armed with the world's deadliest steel.

Kiyama marched over to Inoki and dropped one of the swords at his feet. "Let's see if you still have your stuff."

"What?" Inoki said.

"Stand and fight, or die where you sit."

Inoki studied Kiyama. The old soldier gauged his opponent's resolution in a manner he'd probably done a hundred times before—but usually from a superior position, with a superior weapon, and superior backup.

Inoki rose reluctantly. He unsheathed the classic blade as Kiyama pulled his. They faced off with a pair of sabers pounded out by some of the best swordsmiths in Japanese history.

Under direct threat, Inoki came alive. After the first parry, it became apparent that Inoki's fencing ability would not fare well against the younger man's aggression. Kiyama set to toying with him, but it was a risky game. From Wu's story, I knew Inoki was a crafty fighter, and as I watched the match unfold I saw the old fox's eyes narrow as he sought a break in his adversary's defense.

But Kiyama was too good. He wove in and out of Inoki's advances with ease, pressing the ancient combatant back into a corner when he chose but not moving in for the kill. Kiyama wore Inoki down. Occasionally he nicked him and withdrew. Kiyama grew so confident that he countered many blows with the spine side of the blade with ease.

The kendoist was focused and intent. His eyes burned. He, too, had come alive. I recalled Inoki's words about his time in China: *The war in Manchuria was the ultimate playground. I took anything I wanted. Life, women, gold.*

But that was then. Now, in a new country, in a new century, this was Kiyama's moment.

The younger duelist pounced.

Japanese swords are made of hammered steel, refolded and pounded over and over again. They are dense and heavy. With the faceoff easing into its fourth minute, the octogenarian was having trouble keeping the tip up and in Kiyama's face. His breathing grew ragged. His guard dropped and gaping holes in his defense opened up.

What happened next is the grist of nightmares.

In a full-tilt frontal attack, Kiyama sliced off his opponent's sword hand. The appendage fell to the floor with a dull thud, still gripping the weapon. Blood spewed from the end of Inoki's arm. His other hand went automatically to the wound. He staggered but remained upright.

Kiyama rocked back on his rear foot, appraising his work with a connoisseur's eye, then his blade flashed—and in one smooth, well-placed stroke he took off Inoki's head. The severed body part rose to accommodate the passing steel, then resettled on the stump, misaligned by maybe half an inch.

Inoki blinked. His eyes found mine. His mouth opened and closed like one of Wu's ghost-spirits. Then the life-force dissipated and his remains tumbled over.

My heart stuttered in my chest. Was that how Hamada had lived his last moment? Was this what the sword-wielding kendoka had in mind for me?

CHAPTER 78

ORTUNATELY, I'd made my move before Kiyama began his butchering. When the triumphant swordsman turned to face us, blood spatter streaking his clothing like a proud warrior's ceremonial sash, a surprise awaited him.

Kiyama cast the same appraising look over the new arrangement. His eyes narrowed. Then his gaze grew calculating rather than flustered, and I knew my escape plan would fail.

The fencer's voice was tinged with a fatalistic regret. "I knew you couldn't do it."

Yoji said, "This is different."

"But it isn't. If you could do it, you would have pulled the trigger as soon as he came at you."

Under normal circumstances, Kiyama's take would have merit, but a real-life sword fight to the death unfolding before your eyes was a riveting event—and about as far away from normal as you could get.

"Isn't it enough that I uncovered the treasure and got it here?"

"You need blood on your hands."

Once the swordplay had begun, I'd inched toward Yoji. When the third parry drew Yoji's full attention, I moved inside his defenses and twisted his gun arm up and away before he knew what was happening, plucking the pistol from splayed fingers.

The playboy businessman grimaced. I raised the barrel to his head, stepped behind him, and snaked my free hand under his arm and across his chest, tugging him against me as a human shield, from which position we both watched Inoki come apart. It was at times like this that my speed served me well.

Kiyama eyed me closely. "Did Yoji tell you how Hamada died?"

"No," I said.

"Just like that," he said, tossing his head cavalierly at Inoki's motionless form. "Except Hamada didn't have a weapon. Five of us cornered him."

"You're lying," I said. "It wasn't a clean cut."

Kiyama's grin was brutish. "Oh, the first cut was clean. We went back with a cleaver to make it look like Triads. Hamada was my first tameshigiri. This was my third."

Meaning his former friend Tanaka was his second.

Yoji squirmed in my grasp, trying to break loose, but my martial arts training allowed me to hold him in place, despite his workouts at the kendo club.

"Why don't you let him go, Brodie?"

"Not likely," I said.

"You will in the end. You've got nowhere to run."

I said nothing, preferring to watch his weapon.

"Do you know what I discovered today?" Kiyama said pleasantly. "What they say about the best koto blades is absolutely true. For Hamada I used a gendaito. Modern swords do an adequate job, but when you cut with a koto it's like passing your hand through water."

He flicked the weapon so it caught the light. "A graceful shape, too."

I listened but held my tongue. I wondered if I could put him down before he came for me. The Japanese saber is long and deadly and razor-sharp. If my shot went wide or I didn't knock the fight out of him with the first bullet, he could still charge. He only needed to connect once with his finely honed steel to maim or kill. Problem was, you could pump a handful of 9mm slugs in a charging adult male and not slow him immediately. Even fatally wounded, Kiyama could get in a few strokes—and one was all he needed to inflict serious damage, if not kill me outright.

So it was a standoff and he knew it.

"Give it up, Brodie. Inoki didn't suffer. The mind goes into shock. There's no pain. Just a realization of death, and death."

I edged away. If I could circle around, I could reach the hall leading to the bedrooms, then scramble backward with Yoji as a shield, away from the patio, toward the rear of the villa. The problem was that Yoji had shut the door and both my hands were occupied. The second I moved to open it, I'd lose control of my captive and Kiyama would rush in. I'd be cut down before I could get through the door.

Kiyama read my glance and sneered. "Not enough time to make it out that way. The only path is through me."

Then the sneer faded. Kiyama grew quiet. His body firmed the way a martial artist readies for action. He raised the sword.

I knew instantly—as one fighter sizing up another—that Kiyama didn't see this as a standoff. He saw only a challenge. Another victory to be gained. And his rapid-fire glance gave away his strategy.

He is planning to cut off my arm.

With decades of kendo under his belt, his control would be superb. Especially at his level. He could probably sever the arm and still pull up millimeters short of his friend's chest.

Then a series of new calculations flickered across his features. He was amending his plan—and the revision was worse than I could have imagined.

———

In any martial art, the years of practice are all about teaching the muscles to move faster than the mind can think. My training served the same end. Which is why I could predict Kiyama's next move.

First, I saw naked ambition. At his feet was all the money in the world. So what was left for a supremely confident fighter? He was computing the ultimate angle for the ultimate strike.

One for the history books.

A double tameshigiri.

He planned to hack off my arm *on his way to slicing all the way through Yoji's torso.*

In the sword-fighting journals of old, there are records of multiple tameshigiri. Double- and triple-body cuttings with one stroke. The record is supposedly seven, though some experts say the claim is dubious. But whatever the numbers, the settings were always staged. The moves prearranged. The dregs of society were bound and gagged and staked into position for the amusement of a handful of bloodthirsty samurai. Otherwise, the chance to cleave multiple bodies with one stroke never surfaced. Not even on the battlefield.

But right here, right now, cornered as I was, with my arm wrapped snugly around Yoji's chest, Kiyama saw the opportunity of a lifetime—with the sword of the millennium.

All this I understood in a blink of an eye as his feverish glance gauged angles and distance.

I pointed the gun at Kiyama and pulled the trigger.

The hammer clicked on an empty chamber.

CHAPTER 79

KIYAMA'S sneer grew colder. "Yoji chases skirts and he's a hell of a strategist. That's why he was able to extract the treasure from China. But he doesn't have the stomach to kill. The box of ammunition in his bedroom is full."

I took another step back, dragging Yoji with me.

Kiyama cocked his wrists. His sword inched higher. His stance shifted and firmed. He tracked my arm obliquely, making final calculations in his head.

I feigned a move to the right.

The sword was in motion—and coming. It would catch me in its swing no matter which direction I took.

The arm was all but gone.

Then my training kicked in. I shoved Yoji hard in the small of the back with my other hand. He stumbled forward and into the descending weapon. One of the world's sharpest blades met his skull before the weapon could complete its sweep and take my limb. The steel wedge cleaved the head down to the jaw line, then its momentum stalled.

Kiyama tugged at his weapon, but it wouldn't budge. I flung the empty gun at him. The weapon clipped him in the chin and he grunted in pain. The sword sprang loose.

Kiyama grinned. He took a moment to wipe the bloodstained steel on the flap of his shirt.

I jumped onto the couch and lifted one of the tridents from its perch on the wall. I pointed the three-pronged pike at him.

"Smart," Kiyama said. "Won't do you any good, though."

"We'll see," I said.

The trident was eight feet long.

I looked down at Yoji. "Too bad you had to kill him."

"Don't be naive. I was going to do it anyway. I just wanted to see if he had it in him to finish you. Thirty years of kendo, but couldn't pull the trigger. Worthless."

There it was. Kiyama had played the modest companion for decades without aim or purpose. A closet sociopath with nowhere to go. Then the treasure came to light and gave him purpose. The repressed personality emerged from hiding and began spinning its web.

I firmed my grip on the trident. I jabbed it in his direction. Kiyama glided away, both hands on the hilt of his sword. The good news was, he didn't attack. The bad was, he was analyzing the problem like a professional. Not as a threat, but as an intriguing obstacle to overcome.

Won't do you any good, though.

In my heart, I knew he was right. But I needed something, and an eight-foot spear was an agreeable option. My only option. The problem was that the sword was far more lethal. I couldn't let Kiyama connect. Which meant I couldn't let him control the action.

I needed a defense and a counterattack, or it would be a massacre.

Not a massacre like the one in the locker room, where I'd taken a collection of blows before I collapsed. No. This time one blow would kill me outright, or damage me in a way too gruesome to contemplate.

I attacked with the trident. Straight away he halted my forward thrust by sliding his weapon between two prongs. Metal clashed. A sharp ping on his end, a dull reverberation on mine.

Kiyama's ears perked up at the sound.

Then he backed off and circled.

I looped around the other way. Then I lunged. Kiyama rolled sideways. He brought the Japanese cutlass over and down on the neck of the trident and lopped off its head.

Just like that the forked end clattered to the tile floor and lay still.

I fell back, stunned.

Kiyama nodded to himself.

His weapon had *glided* through the trident's soft iron body. I'm not sure it even slowed down. I should have guessed. The perfectly sharpened edge of the Japanese sword has been forged in high temperatures, folded and pounded and refolded, two layers becoming four, four becoming eight, eight to sixteen, and on and on until dozens of microthin layers were stacked on one another, each time pounded flat before refolding. Reinforcing the steel. Building strength and an invincible cutting wedge.

I recalled a videotaped demonstration where a Japanese blade had been clamped vertically in place, then a .22 was set up ten yards back. A bullet flew straight at the upright sword. The round was halved.

And that was steel on steel.

I held a decorative instrument forged of low-grade iron. Probably with more impurities than a fallen angel. That's what Kiyama had heard when he'd tapped the koto against the trident. That's why he'd countered with such assurance.

I was in trouble.

Won't do you any good, though.

My position of strength was an illusion. And I faced a shrinking time frame. In a couple of moves Kiyama would figure out how to penetrate my weakened defense.

We continued to circle. He watched for an opening. I jabbed the air between us with my truncated pole. Once, twice, three times. He took the bait with the fourth, attacking with the same overhead looping maneuver and chopping off another foot. The momentum of his strike carried the rod down and away. I gave my weapon free rein, rotating my wrists back toward me. The end of the trident skidded off the tile floor then carved a sideways U in the air and slammed into Kiyama's ribs before he realized what I was doing.

He grunted and dropped back.

The ricochet blowback had inflicted a measure of pain, but as an experienced jouster Kiyama absorbed the discomfort with no more than a twitch.

He zeroed in on the trident again. I backed away. My eight-foot weapon had been whittled down to five. He advanced. I jabbed the air with my truncated pole to retard his latest push and lost another segment. He retreated quickly as the trident curled around and missed his abdomen by inches. I stormed in, plowing the end of the rod into his stomach. He doubled over, soaking up the blow and bringing the sword up from below and halving what remained of my weapon.

I was left holding a two-foot length of what amounted to soft pipe.

Kiyama straightened stiffly. "It's over," he said.

I didn't argue.

CHAPTER 80

FOR a second time I considered a dash through the long hall. But Kiyama would be on me the moment I reached for the doorknob at this end.

There was nothing to do but face him down, or die trying.

The once impressive trident was now a two-foot length of malleable metal. I could wave the fragment about but it was only a threat if I could get close enough to bash a part of Kiyama's anatomy before he could take a swipe at me with his four-foot weapon.

So I did the unthinkable. When his sword came around in a long looping overhead swing yet again, I rushed him, eyes glued to the arm wielding the blade. The trident clattered at our feet.

The trick was in the timing.

As the koto neared its zenith, I surged forward and pinned Kiyama's forearm up with one hand, his wrist with the other. The downward arc of his stroke ground to a halt. I raised my knee and smashed my heel into the meaty part of his thigh.

He began to topple backward, but my double grip on his arm kept him upright. A miscalculation on my part. By the time I released him and eased off to avoid the downward course of the saber, he'd regained his balance and hobbled away, favoring his injured leg. His look darkened.

He began to run some new strategies.

I was now weaponless, and Kiyama had learned the hard way not to raise his sword too high.

Was I a one-trick pony?

Kiyama thought so. He unleashed another drive. I scooted out of range, barely avoiding the tip of his blade.

He was limping noticeably. Moving slower. His loss of speed had allowed me to evade his last sweep. I wasn't so lucky with the follow-up. I escaped the core of his offensive, but in the return stroke the steel tip raked my right side. A streak of red darkened my shirt.

Then Kiyama doubled back without warning and the koto grazed my upper thigh. I winced and a pulsing pain rocketed through my nervous system.

Kiyama was taking me apart piece by piece. Attack and retreat. A nick of the blade here, a flick there. Even with his hampered ability, he only had to wear me down as he'd done with Inoki. I could steer clear of him for a while, but time favored his new strategy. I was weaponless. The hall door was closed, as was the front entrance. I couldn't get through either exit before he could strike. So I could only circle. Until I ran out of steam. All he needed to do was drain my energy reserve. Slow my reflexes.

Before I could regroup, he released a fourth assault. I scrambled away—and slipped in a pool of Inoki's blood. My feet went out from under me and I skewed across the floor on my belly, colliding with Inoki's corpse.

The old soldier's sword lay right before my eyes. Why hadn't I noticed it earlier? I swept up the haft with my right hand and rolled over.

Kiyama corrected his course and darted in for the kill.

Coming out of the roll, I straightened my arm and the sword bounded upward of its own accord. I was horrified to see the severed hand still clinging to the hilt. Kiyama's glance went automatically to the bloody appendage, and in that second of distraction he took his eyes off the killing part of my weapon and ran right into my rising blade.

It pierced his stomach. He screamed and collapsed onto the sword. The emperor's koto flew from his hand and banged harmlessly against a French window. His body slumped on top of me, then tipped sideways as I released the haft.

The kendoka's eyes found mine. He said my name, and I could see he wanted to say more but he never got the chance.

CHAPTER 81

IT was the voices that woke me.

I must have blacked out.

My head throbbed. I'd banged it in the fall but only now felt the pain. Kiyama's arm was draped across my chest. I brushed it aside and struggled to my feet. I was weak and drained. My wounds stung. I'd lost blood. The room spun.

I shot a look at my would-be executioner. He didn't stir. He was dead.

I surveyed the scene. Inoki and Kiyama lay at my feet, in a widening pool of fresh blood. Yoji was sprawled near the kitchen.

In taking out Yoji and Kiyama, I'd avenged Hamada's death. It wouldn't bring him back. It wouldn't comfort his wife or the twins. But it soothed something strident and primal inside me and complicit in the makeup of all those who worked at Brodie Security. Gladiators on the field occasionally fall, but those left standing take care of their own. Then the loud voices on the beach startled me again. Footsteps pounded up the stairs, drawing closer.

Everyone else has got blood on his hands.

I dove for cover.

———

Quickly, I did the calculations.

The team had numbered seven to start. Dropped to six after Doi's death. Five after Kiyama had slain his longtime kendo pal Tanaka. Three after Yoji and Kiyama had fallen.

The trio of voices was boisterous and inebriated. They were laughing. Talking among themselves. Sloppy footfalls pattered across the patio. The door flew open. I heard the sound of people crossing the threshold—then a stunned silence.

"What happened?" one of them said.

"They're all dead."

"There's blood everywhere."

"Police?"

"Can't be. Otherwise—"

"—they'd be here, waiting," I said.

I rose from behind Kiyama's prone body, my clothes slathered in blood.

The horror in their eyes reflected a primordial fear well beyond mere surprise. In my blood-drenched clothing, I must have looked like a phantom rising.

Except for one hard fact. I'd dug out the gun from the dead swordsman's pocket.

The first man to see it reached for his own weapon.

"Don't do it," I said.

He did anyway and I shot him.

The others turned and fled into the night—and ran right into Noda, Kato, and Rie climbing the steps. Brodie Security's chief detective cold-cocked the first one out the door and Rie curtailed the progress of the second with a serviceable kick to the unmentionables.

"It's about time," I said.

"Noda called Durgan in Miami and got the number of your Barbados contacts," Rie said. "They led us here."

"Where's the watchdog?"

"Indisposed," Inspector Kato said. "Your buddy here accidentally bumped into him going down the police station steps."

Noda ignored the comment, instead glancing at my garb, the bodies, then frowning. "Too bad we missed the festivities."

Rie's takedown groaned.

"Not all of them," she said.

EPILOGUE

I WAS due back in Tokyo to clear up the matter of the kendo club, but after the Barbados incident Inspector Kato assured me it would be only a formality.

With the pressure off, I pushed my return flight to the Japanese capital back a few days to spend time with my daughter. I walked through the front door of my San Francisco apartment with a basket of coconut-filled chocolates from Miami under my arm, and a stuffed baby iguana as backup. Jenny swooped in on me, then on the gifts, after which I listened to a euphoric retelling of her soccer achievements. Last came the revelation she'd been saving.

"It worked," Jenny said, hopping up and down in a childlike jig, pigtails flapping. "Just like Ms. Deacon told us."

"What worked?"

"She said swimming was for fun and emergencies. The fun part was playing in the water with friends and stuff. Emergencies were for safety. She said a surprise might come and if it did we should be ready to do whatever the surprise wanted us to do. That's what life-guards do, and they're the best swimmers ever. My surprise came on the ferryboat. Something was wrong, wasn't it?"

Jenny had never laid eyes on the men who attacked me.

"Yes, but it's all finished now. No need to worry."

"I'm not worried. The world keeps spinning. Did you forget?"

"Uh, no."

"Your work is exciting, Daddy. Like a soccer game. I decided there can be good and bad and exciting when the world is spinning. Three things, not two. That's what I wanted to tell you before, but I had to get it right in my thinking."

This sudden reversal—from trepidation over the danger inherent in my work at Brodie Security to its embrace—what did it mean? Was it normal? Was it healthy?

Jenny continued her energized bouncing. The pigtails rose and fell. "I think the ferry and the river were exciting. Maybe that's why Grandpa gave you his company."

"You might have something there," I said cautiously.

My daughter beamed up at me with a smile full of discovery and joy and no trace of the anxiety for which I was always on alert. In the ongoing trauma of her mother's death, this could be a favorable step forward.

"Can I do what you and Rie do, Daddy?"

That stopped me. "What do you mean?"

"You know, the fighting stuff."

"You're big enough to start with aikido, I suppose."

Aikido was about self-defense and deflecting an attack.

"But you do judo and karate and tae whatchamacallit. Kids do those, too."

"Tae kwon do. How about judo like Officer Hoshino?"

"Yeah!" she said, and threw her arms around me.

I was puzzled by the shift in my daughter's attitude. I had not the slightest clue as to whether it was good or bad, but at least for the moment balance had been restored.

The day after I arrived back in Tokyo, I received a call from unexpected quarters.

"Do you know who this is?" Zhou said when I answered.

I was unlikely to ever forget the spy or his rooftop sniper.

"Yes."

"I see you used what I gave you."

"I did."

"You are talented. Perhaps dangerous."

"Not to you," I said.

"Good to get a confirmation. You have accomplished what you wished. I don't suppose you care to tell me where I can find the old man?"

"Sorry."

"I'll leave the offer open for a year. Think about it."

"I won't."

"Didn't think so, but had to try."

"Don't we all," I said.

———

I met Rie at her favorite java hideaway, Chatei Hatou. The coffee maestro was as precise in his pour-over as ever. We took the same table at the back of the shop. No one was within earshot.

Rie had made a clean escape. As a woman officer in the Tokyo Police Department, not only did she have to work twice as hard but she also had to be twice as careful. I was aware of the first but had never considered the second. Miraculously, there had been no fallout over the ferry incident. No one had heard of her involvement, or if they had, they kept it to themselves.

Rie took a sip of her Venetian coffee and sighed with satisfaction. "We have to stop meeting like this."

"I'll pretend you didn't actually say that."

"Speaking of pretending, shouldn't we finish our argument?"

"I took enough of a beating in Barbados."

"You look perfectly fine to me. Before we begin, I want to thank you for suggesting me for the Sengai auction."

"You didn't disappoint."

"Inspector Kato was kind enough to credit me with the arrest."

"You did slap on the cuffs."

"You didn't have to ask for me."

"You're welcome," I said.

Rie cleared her throat. "I'm willing to accept that you did what you thought was correct on the ferry if you agree that it could have cost me my job."

"I could do that."

A furrow darkened her brow. "But it was more than that, of course."

"Sure," I said.

It was also about equal footing. How far she had come. Pride of job. Face. I mentioned all of those and more.

The furrow went away. "Then it's finished."

"May it rest in peace and never rise."

"Coincidentally, I've wrapped up my biggest case." Her smile was faint.

I prefer one distraction at a time.

"I know a good French restaurant in Kamakura," I said. "But it'll have to be soon. I fly out the day after tomorrow."

"I see."

"Is that a *yes*?"

"What do you think?" She bent over and kissed me on the cheek. "I have a confession. The reason I never mentioned my judo was because I wanted to retain some of my feminine allure."

"It was never in question."

"You are a gentleman, but I've seen the effects it has when I mention both kendo and judo on a date. When added to my occupation, men run away."

"I saw your takedown at the auction. Even with that, I'm still here."

She leaned over and we kissed. No cheek this time. It was light and lingering but not too long. This was, after all, Japan. Public displays of affection were frowned upon.

When we broke, I said, "But I reserve the right to toss you in the water again should the situation warrant."

She punched me. Playfully but hard. And damn if it wasn't a judo move.

The last call I made about the case was to Tommy-gun Tomita.

"What are you ringing me about now, Brodie? You already gave me the home invasion story."

"Like I said, that was only the appetizer. You ready for the main course?"

I figured the sensational solution to the Tokyo murders would pave the way for a release of larger scale.

"I'm always ready. If there's an update on the Last Emperor's treasure, I'd be happy to run it."

The authorities were fighting over the haul. The Barbadian government had impounded the stolen valuables until they could "complete their investigation," the end of which remained indefinite. The Japanese government had laid claim to the whole lot as "historic artifacts." When Tommy-gun's story broke, the Chinese chimed in by insisting their "national treasures" be returned to them, which in their definition included the Japanese items. Not to be left out, an ever-watchful contingent within Brodie Security had filed for a finder's fee, which all three countries universally dismissed, despite our role in bringing the treasure to the public notice.

"Forget that," I said. "What I have is even better. It's about people killed in the night in the middle of a war. People the world has forgotten."

"Old war stories are like ten-year-old dried fish, Brodie. Still around but inedible."

"This one is about innocent men, women, and children killed by a joint Japanese-Chinese expedition. There is only one eyewitness left."

"Name?"

"He lives in hiding. He is under constant threat. I can introduce you. The rest you'll have to clear through his people. You're also going to have to jump through security hoops."

"Is it worth it?"

"Only if you're a real journalist."

"Talk to me."

So I gave him the remaining details and the contact information. At the end, I told him I needed it done big.

"Maybe this isn't dried fish. If it pans out, I'll get it on the wire services worldwide. It'll rattle cages. Thanks."

"No need to thank me. It's a promise I made."

I thought about my excursion to Chinatown with Rie. I thought about all the precautions. The poisoned tea. The evasive maneuvers. The showdown in the cemetery. I thought about Wu's heart-wrenching story, his guilt, and his dedication to bettering conditions for future generations, while keeping a promise to past ones.

"Brodie? You still there?"

"Yes."

"Anything else?"

"Only this: He's waiting."

"Who?"

"Close enough."

Two separate chance meetings with Japanese war veterans were the inspiration for this book. Each man, in his own way, was not unlike the senior Miura.

When I returned to Japan to stay several decades ago, many veterans were still alive, and hopeful. Back then, if you stayed long enough to learn the language, you might run across these former soldiers—survivors haunted by the secrets they bore. A defeated nation had turned away from its military men at the end of World War II, and forced them into a soul-suffocating silence.

For years no one wanted to hear their stories. For years no one wanted to remember. Those few who attempted to speak out were soon silenced by embarrassed relatives or friends, or chastised by employers or government officials, sometimes severely.

Decades later, when China first opened its doors, and long before prosperity started to emerge in the bigger cities, many veterans returned to the villages their troops had occupied, and tried to undo some of the damage. The onetime conquerors brought gifts and food and money.

It was all they could think to do. This book is for them. And to anyone, anywhere, willing to extend a hand across the water.

Part of the fun of writing a novel of this nature is weaving factual gems about Japanese culture into the plot. This time around, some Chinese background seeped in as well.

Here's what's true. Everything about the Buddhist monk Sengai (1750–1837) and his art is accurate. By all accounts he led a stimulating and fruitful life. At the age of forty, he became the 123rd abbot—you read that number correctly—of Shofukuji, the first Zen temple in Japan, and retired in 1811 at sixty-one. The happy-go-lucky monk eventually became known for his receptivity to visitors and for dashing off an ink painting whenever a guest asked. They were pieces to inspire and enlighten, or at least point the way. Sengai's masterwork *Circle, Triangle, and Square* (sometimes called *The Universe*) is perhaps his most famous painting. It is housed in the Idemitsu Museum of Arts in Tokyo, which owns the largest collection of the artist's efforts. The drawing at the core of this story is fictional but conceived in the spirit of the painter-monk's oeuvre.

The history and lore about Japanese swords are also accurate. The best Japanese blades command respect around the world. Practices for testing them mentioned in these pages are based on historical documents. Of course, most tests were not of the nature described here. The firearms test is factual. I was not able to confirm whether a koto sword passed between the "cousins," although many items were exchanged, so people well grounded in Japanese history assure me it is well within the realm of possibility.

The tea bowls mentioned in these pages exist. I have seen one and have been informed there are more. As for the other Chinese objects in this narrative, scholars have documented the extensive collection of Chinese art assembled by the Qing Dynasty (1644–1912), as well as the organized transportation of thousands of trunks of art and other treasure in advance of the Japanese invasion. In addition, with the weakening of the Qing Dynasty, there were reports of massive amounts disappearing, much of it likely under the watchful eyes of the more powerful eunuchs in the Forbidden City, possibly beginning decades earlier.

During the war years, looting in China and throughout Southeast Asia was rampant not only by Japanese parties but also by many other local powers, from warlords and other warring factions to bandits and local politicos. The existence of substantial hidden treasure troves has been the subject of endless speculation and sparse reportage, though thorough documentation remains scarce.

All the history and lore about kendo is factual. The legendary tenth-dan kendoka Moriji Mochida (1885–1974) is a revered figure in the field. The Nakamura Kendo Club is a fictitious dojo, meant to be representative of the many dojos throughout Japan. The martial art is alive and well and plays a positive role in the mental and physical training of those who practice it, regardless of age.

Delving into the varied and quixotic history of Yokohama was a pleasure. All the facts about the Japanese port city, an easy thirty-minute train ride from Tokyo Station, are accurate. The city itself is vibrant, with a thriving Chinatown that plays host to residents and institutions from both Taiwan and mainland China. The Chinese cemetery was at one time the serene yet frayed-around-the-edges place depicted in these pages, although improvements are made periodically. The waiting dead were still on the grounds during my initial visit to the cemetery a number of years ago.

Wu's adventures in China as a young doctor are fictional. His more arduous escapades are symbolic of the many atrocities of the time. His village, too, is imaginary, although it was drawn with a careful eye toward the records of similar villages from the same period. Chinese historical references, whether in the narration or a conversation between characters, are accurate.

Chinese "family groups" serve useful functions around the world. I'm told their structures vary depending on the size of the Chinese expatriate population. The back alleys of Yokohama Chinatown are there to this day, as are shops similar to the ones sketched in *Tokyo Kill*, although periodic spurts in prosperity tend to lessen the number of "colorful" stores and alleyways in the area.

The spycraft in this book is based in part on an accidental encounter I had with a Soviet spy in Tokyo during the last days of the Cold War. From what I can gather, aside from the fact that a spy's arsenal has been enlarged to encompass the Internet and digital paraphernalia, face-to-face exchanges remain vital, and the underlying techniques unchanged.

Kazuo Takahashi, the fictional Kyoto art dealer in these pages, voices a lament dear to many Japanese I have talked with over the years, and one I thought worth recording.

On a lighter note, Gyoku-ryu, or Jewel Dragon, the saké of choice in the spy sequence, is shelved under the Tamagawa brand, which has a history of some one hundred and seventy years. The bewitching drink is conjured up at Kinoshita Brewery, in Kyoto Prefecture. The coffeehouse Chatei Hatou is a treasured hideaway for java hounds. It is tucked way down a side street in Shibuya, not too far from the Shibuya Police headquarters.

Following the alcoholic trail, the Golden Gai, a long-time stalwart on the late-night barhopping circuit in Tokyo, does exist. At one time the area was pretty much the exclusive domain of certain closed-knit groups, but the demographic has gradually shifted. As one of the last "untamed" locations in the valuable Shinjuku property market, the beloved drinking district has had developers drooling over (and scheming against) it for decades. As of this writing, the core section has held. Ironically, the Gai's new status among tourists, which is also responsible for yet another shift in the district, may, with some luck, be responsible for saving it.

Bridgetown is the capital of Barbados, and the Accra Beach Hotel, Oistins Bay Gardens, and Turtle Beach are all actual destinations.

As many longtime residents of Miami know, the Biltmore, the Mayfair, GreenStreet, and Los Gallegos are real places. GreenStreet is a Coconut Grove institution. Once a modest coffeehouse for locals, a makeover put it squarely on the tourist trail as well. Happily, the old coffeehouse still puts in an appearance in the quieter moments of the day.

ACKNOWLEDGMENTS

I mentioned in *Japantown* that it takes many hands to launch a publication, and the observation remains true in this second outing. And once again, I have been extremely fortunate in the people who have helped.

Sarah Knight, my hard-charging editor at Simon & Schuster, offered timeless advice, and her insights were as sharp as ever. Others on the S&S team continue to amaze me with their effort and expertise: Lance Fitzgerald champions foreign rights sales for the series; Molly Lindley worked to finish up some essential final touches; Jae Song produced a stunning jacket for *Tokyo Kill* that lives up to its predecessor; the production team of Lewelin Polanco, Kathy Higuchi, Anne Cherry, and James Walsh performed their magic during the final stages with admirable precision; Elina Vaysbeyn and Meg Cassidy are handling marketing and publicity for the book; Lauren Pires helped launch the audio book for the first Jim Brodie book; Kaitlin Olson helped with vital last-minute essentials. Asian sales manager Jill Su ably traversed Asian cities in support of the series and pulled off some minor miracles. And once again Jonathan Karp, Richard Rhorer, and Marysue Rucci lent their support to this book.

Robert Gottlieb, my agent at Trident Media Group, has been a stout voice of support from the outset and has never wavered. Erica Silverman, also of TMG, along with Brian Pike of CAA, placed the Jim Brodie series with J. J. Abrams's Bad Robot Productions and Warner Bros. for a television drama. Also, a hearty thanks to Greg Pulis for handling the legal tangles. Back at Trident, Mark Gottlieb and Adrienne Lombardo lent their able hands to various aspects of the publishing process.

William Scott Wilson, renowned author and translator, and his wife Emily Wilson, teacher and editor, offered a guiding hand around

Miami, as well as some memorable evenings and sights. Their gracious hospitality allowed Jim Brodie to follow in our footsteps. Their son Henry gets extra credit for being a good sport and granting permission for me to sit in on his kendo practice, in order that I might see how the traditional Japanese sport is practiced stateside.

One of the benefits of moving into a new arena—for me, the world of fiction—is the chance to meet new and interesting people, and make new friends. That has come in many forms and from many different directions. Among the most welcome of these new encounters has been the support of the International Thriller Writers (ITW), which really proved the "international" aspect of its name by welcoming this Tokyo-based American writer to their annual ThrillerFest in New York City with warmth and graciousness. Among the many people in this organization I've been fortunate enough to meet are Kimberley Howe, Liz Berry, Anthony J. Franze, Jenny Milchman, and Melissa MacGregor, as well as a large number of established and talented up-and-coming authors too numerous to name—you all know who you are. And additional kudos to Anthony for his sage advice and friendship.

I owe a deep debt of gratitude to Shigeyoshi Suzuki, a Japanese Renaissance man and longtime friend, who knows traditional culture inside out and makes an ideal sounding board for my various plot lines and themes. For *Tokyo Kill*, I bounced ideas about Sengai and the Japanese sword off him. He also dug out some obscure historical details I requested with great good humor.

For a memorable afternoon photo shoot in the Shibuya area of Tokyo, I once again want to express my thanks to Ben Simmons for the portfolio of author photographs he took. The portraits he snapped on that sunny afternoon have seen publication far and wide, mostly with the photo credit intact. Please accept my apologies for the times when it did not appear. A partial selection of Ben's work, as well as a link to his homepage, can be found on my website in the "Contact/media" section.

The legacy of the Japanese sword is long and complex, and a quagmire for the uninitiated. I knew something about the subject and still found myself sinking up to my knees at times. Paul Martin, sword expert online and off, generously provided a safe path through this historical quicksand. His is an amazing story, and his work in the sword world continues to grow. Author and sword expert Nobuo Nakahara was also instrumental, and graciously offered his expertise.

Japanese saké is an endlessly fascinating topic, with an equally endless variety of offerings. To help me select a tipple that fit the character, dishes, and mood of an extended sequence in this book, I called on the services of longtime friend, author, and saké brewing master Philip Harper, who graciously worked with me to find an appropriate drink. In the process he may have inadvertently become the first literary saké sommelier in history.

For backing Jim Brodie on his Caribbean journey, my gratitude goes out to Joyce Abrams, Marilyn Knight, and Jean Sealey. They double-checked Brodie's steps on those sandy shores.

For timely feedback on the Romanization and spelling of Chinese names and terms, I'd like to thank Jun Ma, Ge Gao (Simon Gao), and Jiali Yao. Their help was invaluable, their answers swift. Many thanks to each of you, wherever you may be at the time of publication.

For their support of *Japantown* and its debut author, many thanks to the following bookstores, their owners, and staff: to all the people at The Mysterious Bookshop, in NYC, and The Poisoned Pen, in Scottsdale, Arizona, for their graciousness and for selecting *Japantown* for their book clubs; to Steve Kott and Taeko Kobayashi of Good Day Books in Tokyo for their enthusiasm from the very beginning; to Barry Martin and Mary Riley of Book'em Mysteries in South Pasadena, California, for two memorable afternoons of book talk; to the people at Mysterious Galaxy, in San Diego and Redondo Beach, California—a great crew and great stores; to Diane's Books of Greenwich, in Connecticut, for taking the Jim Brodie series under its wing; to Mystery Mike Bursaw and George Easter for their interest in the series and their warm welcome at Bouchercon; and to the staff at The Avid Reader in Davis, California, for their enthusiasm.

For much-appreciated help along the way, I wish to extend my thanks to all of the following people (in no particular order): to the inimitable Joan Hansen, as well as Cindy Woods, Katee Woods, and Jan Wilcox, for their warm welcome to the Men of Mystery event; to Ethel Margolin, "your greatest fan," for rallying round the troops; to Victoria

Magaw, for encouragement, support, and introductions to people in the Los Angeles Public Library system; to Jane Cohen, James Sherod, Sherry Kanzer, Leslie Chudnoff, Barbara Lockwood, Karilyn Steward, and Kerrie Mierop—all either with the LAPL or supporters of library events; to Beth Ruyak and Jennifer Picard for a great interview on Capital Public Radio (CPR) in Sacramento; to DeKristie Adams for helping to set up the radio interview; to Peter Goodman, publisher and editor supreme of Stone Bridge Press, for advice, support, and a place to stay; to John S. Knowlend for suggesting the name Tokyo no Tekken; to Mark Schreiber for his encouragement and for tracking down the answers to a couple of questions I had regarding the Tokyo police; to Kimberly Tierney, aka @kimiecat, for enthusiasm from the outset and for hosting a Cat's Meow author's night at Biscotti Tapas in Yoyogi-Uehara, Tokyo; to Shukla and Arnab Sakar for a memorable book event on the other side of the Pacific in Westhills, California; to Alan Brender, longtime friend in Tokyo and now dean of Lakeland College, for extending a hand and a good meal during a very dark hour; to Roger Grabowski for hosting an event at the Tokyo campus of Lakeland College; to two very special, long-lived book clubs—the SGPVJF Book Group (of Pasadena and the greater Los Angeles area) and the Bay Bridge Book Group (of San Francisco and the East Bay communities), for their wonderful hospitality, interest, and great book talk; to Rochelle Kopp for generously helping to lay tracks on which S&S could build; to Karen Catalona for a special guided tour and for introducing me to her friends working for the SFPD and the court system; to Maddee James and her crew for my well-designed website, which draws a continuous stream of compliments; to Michael Wyly and Lue Cobene of Solano Community College for arranging a pair of bracing events at the school; to Steve Turner, a British friend in Tokyo, for offering a second pair of eyes for all sorts of supplementary material when a fresh set was desperately needed; to Erin Mitchell for graciously lending a helping hand at the right time—on more than one occasion; to Räiner Perlitz, all around good guy, architect, coffee pro, and Japan enthusiast for pointing me in the direction of the Chatei Hatou in Shibuya; to founding editor of the *Kyoto Journal* John Einarsen for his enthusiasm and support; to Gavin Frew for his unfailingly sharp eye;

to Richard Auffrey, on Twitter as @RichardPF, for advice on the fly; to Adrienne K. Di Giacomo for help from the desert sands; and to Mika Saito, a talented Japanese designer and now also a specialty farmer of Japanese tangerines (*mikan*) in Ehime Prefecture, Japan, for creating the wonderful bookplate on my website.

I want to thank all my supporters on Twitter who have sent me encouraging and/or entertaining messages, retweeted comments, and favored posts, and in general been such a great bunch individually and sometimes in groups. Barring glitches on the site, which do occur, I believe I see each and every one of your messages and respond to as many as I can. Occasionally one slips through the cracks, for which I apologize. All much appreciated. In like manner, I wish to thank my Facebook followers on both the Author and personal page for their support and comments and for coming along for the ride.

A special thanks is due to longtime friends Naoko and Hideo Horibe for their friendship over the years, and for many memorable evenings in Tokyo and abroad in Cambodia, France, Belgium, Germany, and Switzerland. Bits and pieces of our travels have found their way into the first two books and will no doubt surface in future efforts.

Thanks to Mio Urata and Ayako Akaogi for applying their talents to translating the Japanese section of my website. And a special nod of gratitude to all my Japanese publishing colleagues who showed up for the memorable surprise launch party/*bonenkai* (year-end party) in Tokyo's Marunouchi district.

I owe a large debt to my brother, artist Marc Lancet, and his wife, Annette De Bow, a speech pathologist with a golden touch, for hosting me not once but twice during the book tour in Northern California for *Japantown* and while I put the finishing touches on the present volume. Their guest room became a home away from home.

And last, as before, family rallied around. So, many thanks to Bob and Lenny Lancet, Scott and Rosaleen Lancet, Marilyn Firestone, Melbourne and Teresa Weddle, Lilllie and Jose Reines, Margie and Mike Wilson, Debbie and Tom Herzfeld, Lincoln and Choi Lancet, Linda and Bruce Miller, Stuart and Wendy Firestone, as well as the next generation: Daryanna, Daniel, Evan (with her endless supply of stickers to decorate my computer), Bob and Christine Wilson, Hayley and Eloise Miller, and Lloyd and Lindsay Miller. On the Japan side are my wife Haruko, daughter Renee, son Michael, and the extended family: Hozumi and Masako Horiuchi, Masaharu and Hiroko Nagase, Hirotake Nagase, and Chikako and Shinya Ishioka, with their latest addition Yamato.

To each and everyone above, and those not mentioned who have hosted events, offered words of encouragement, and lent support, my deepest gratitude and thanks.

ABOUT THE AUTHOR

Barry Lancet's *Japantown*, an international thriller, won the prestigious Barry Award for Best First Mystery Novel; was selected by both *Suspense Magazine* and mystery critic Oline Cogdill as one of the Best Debuts of the Year; and has been optioned by J. J. Abrams's Bad Robot Productions, in association with Warner Bros. His second book, *Tokyo Kill*, is a finalist for a Shamus Award for Best P.I. Novel of the Year. The third entry in the Jim Brodie series is *Pacific Burn*.

Lancet moved from California to Tokyo in his twenties, where he has lived for more than two decades. He spent twenty-five years working for one of the country's largest publishers, developing books on dozens of Japanese subjects from art to Zen—all in English and all distributed in the United States, Europe, and the rest of the world.

His unique position gave him access to many inner circles in cultural, business, and traditional fields most outsiders are never granted. Early in his tenure in the Japanese capital, he was hauled in by the police for a noncriminal infraction and interrogated for three hours, one of the most heated psychological encounters he had faced in Japan to that point. The run-in fascinated him and sparked the idea for a mystery-thriller series based on his growing number of unusual experiences in Japan.

Lancet is based in Japan but makes frequent trips to the States.

For more information, please visit http://barrylancet.com/ or look for Barry on Facebook and Twitter (@barrylancet)

Turn the page for an excerpt from Barry Lancet's
next Jim Brodie adventure,

PACIFIC BURN

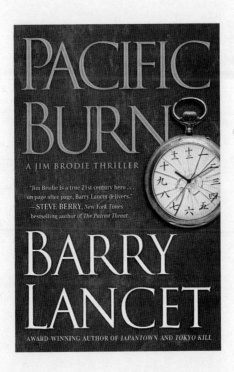

CHAPTER 1

SAN FRANCISCO, 7:05 A.M.

The phone call came far too early to herald anything good.

"Feel like taking a ride?" Detective Frank Renna asked when I picked up.

"Got to get Jenny ready for school soon, and I have a high-end client coming into the shop first thing today. She's eager to drop big money on an Oribe tea bowl."

Oribe was a sometimes brilliant Japanese ceramic style named after Furuta Oribe, a sixteenth-century tea master and samurai. I sold the distinctive green-and-white pieces and other Japanese antiques out of my shop on Lombard, west of Van Ness.

"Nice to see you making headway on the diplomatic front," Renna said, "but move it to the back burner and pack your daughter off. This is important. We're heading out to Napa."

"Are we now?"

"Yeah. There's a Japanese kid we need to see. He doesn't speak English."

"So put a phone to his ear and I'll talk to him. No reason we need to drag ourselves out to wine country."

"Kid's gone into shock and he's babbling. He's driving the local badges up a wall."

Renna was a lieutenant with the San Francisco Police Department, and a friend. He'd been instrumental in getting me a consulting job with the SFPD as their local Japan expert, which last came into play with an incident in Japantown. But I wasn't on call and received no retainer. Our arrangement was on a case-by-case basis, clearly a detail that seemed to have slipped Renna's mind.

"Isn't there a Japanese speaker closer to Napa?" I asked.

"None in their department, and they don't have anyone on file. That's why they need you."

"How do they know the kid's Japanese?"

"Because that's what his father was."

"Was?"

"Yeah. There's a body, too."

Ten minutes after Renna's call, I was waiting outside in the morning fog, ungloved hands snug in the pockets of a down jacket.

I watched brief shafts of faint red light penetrate the fog. Heard the sound of a car engine approaching. Saw, finally, a boxy vehicle emerge out of the cottony whiteness and ease to the curb. Renna had arrived in a dusty unmarked SFPD car that looked exactly like a dusty unmarked SFPD car.

The passenger-side window buzzed down.

"You're doing a good imitation of something the cat *wouldn't* drag in," my friend said.

"I was up until seven talking to Tokyo," I said. "Finalizing details for the shows. Fell into bed five minutes before you woke me."

The mayor of San Francisco had launched a Pacific Rim Friendship Program to improve the city's relations with its Asian neighbors, and Japan was up first. I'd rebuffed City Hall's first two advances to be their liaison, accepting with reluctance only after the big man himself called to press me into service.

"Coffee up," Renna said, passing over a cup of Peet's dark roast as I collapsed into the front seat. "It's all downhill from here."

He urged the vehicle back onto the road. "You get Jenny off to school?"

"Neighbor upstairs will drive her."

"Client take it well?"

"Wife said her husband would be furious, but we rescheduled for later today, so I squeaked by. Listen, I get the babbling kid bit, but why are *we* on the road? It's Napa, not SF."

As was his habit, Renna rolled imaginary marbles from cheek to cheek while he considered the question. "A Napa bigwig rang our dear mayor, and he rang the chief."

"So this is another favor for City Hall?" I said, wondering if they weren't pushing the boundaries.

"Not even close. The mayor hoards his political capital. He called my boss. I'm under orders. You're doing this for me. Since Japantown, everyone thinks I'm your goddamn social secretary."

"I could live with that," I said.

"You do recall we're cruising over marshlands soon, right?"

Overhead, a sign announced our approach to the Golden Gate access road. Our route took us over the bridge into Marin County. We'd pass the monied Marin communities of Mill Valley and San Rafael, cross the reedy marshes edging the upper fringe of the San Francisco Bay, then head north to Napa.

"Yeah, so?"

"You piss me off, I'll toss you into the muck and you won't be living with anything. You'll be lucky if your bones surface in a decade or two."

"Probably less painful."

The lieutenant grunted. "Hard to argue that."

I took a sip of the coffee. A hearty Italian roast rolled over my tongue. It cut through the early morning chill, but made not the slightest dent in my exhaustion.

"I've got to close my eyes for a minute," I said. "Can you handle the drive alone?"

"Sure. One thing first, though. Napa guys sent you a present."

"Am I going to like it?"

"Wouldn't think so."

He stretched a finger toward the face of his smartphone anchored in a dashboard cradle, but before he could tap the screen, my mobile buzzed.

An unknown number. "Hold on a sec," I said, then into my phone: "Hello?"

"Is this Jim Brodie?"

"Yes."

"Sean Navin. We haven't met yet but you're on my blacklist."

That was a first.

Before I could reply, Navin said, "You canceled on us this morning. No one does that to me."

"Sarah already rescheduled."

"I'm cancelling it."

"I normally don't—"

"Save the excuses. I'm sending my wife to one of your competitors."

I closed my eyes. There goes the Oribe tea bowl commission I sorely needed. The loss was going to hurt.

"Sorry to hear that," I said. "As I explained to Sarah, it's an emergency."

"Time is money, Brodie. You play fast and loose with my time, I spend my greenbacks elsewhere."

In his voice I heard none of the goodwill I'd earned over the last couple of years. Quality art from my shop decorated his home. Some of the rarities I'd tracked down in distant corners of Japan.

"I regret it happened, Sean. If there was any way around cancelling our appointment, believe me I would have found it."

"You made a bad decision and it's gonna cost you."

"So you've told me. Do what you have to do," I said, and disconnected.

So much for squeaking by. His wife was a valued customer, but mind games from an overbearing husband I didn't need. Life was too short.

Renna glanced my way. He'd pieced together enough of the conversation to know that I was going to pay for this morning's excursion.

"I'd pegged you for more diplomatic," he said.

"Husband kept twisting the knife. Got a feeling he was enjoying it."

"A lot of those types around."

"Yeah. Too bad. His wife was a regular. You were saying?"

"A present from the Napa boys." Renna punched the smartphone screen. A recording began.

"Can you tell us your name, son?" a clearly annoyed adult male voice said.

"Mondai attara Jimu Burodi-san ni denwa shite kudasai. Mondai at-tara Jimu Burodi-san ni denwa shite kudasai. Mondai attara Jimu Burodi-san ni denwa—"

"We hear you, kid," the man said through what sounded like gritted teeth. Then: "I'm telling you, Dick. That's all the little guy's said since we got here."

Dick gave it a shot. "Hiya son. I'm Officer Richard Kendall. Can you give us your name? Just your name?"

"Mondai attara Jimu Burodi-san ni denwa shite kudasai. Mondai at-tara—"

"See? Repeat loop," the first man said.

"Considering the circumstances, can't say I blame him."

The dispatch ended and Renna said, "Still want to close your eyes?"

"Got to."

"Sweet dreams."

They were anything but.

In the recording, the babbling kid had been asking for me.

CHAPTER 2

When Renna eased off the gas pedal, I woke instantly—alert and recharged. Looking out the windshield at what lay before me, I froze in midstretch and said, "You can't have the right place."

Renna had swung into the parking lot of the di Rosa Preserve, an art complex on prime vineyard land in Napa Valley.

"Afraid I do."

My heart rate kicked up a beat. An incoherent child was one thing. A crime scene linking my day job—art—to police business elevated this early morning summons to a whole other realm. Renna, the sly bugger, had held out. The crime/art combination, as he well knew, had proved poisonous three months ago in Tokyo.

"You could have told me," I said, a rebellious rumble rising in my throat.

"And make the trip harder? No thanks."

"You didn't know for a fact that I'd refuse."

"You saying you wouldn't have?"

"This is not what I expect from my social secretary."

"So fire me."

Rene di Rosa had been the son of an Italian aristocrat and a St. Louis heiress. He came west and purchased four hundred and fifty acres of neglected Napa farmland before the area became legendary for its grapes. Then he replaced free-ranging cattle and fields of barley and oats with wine varietals, and eventually molded the place into the first highly respected Napa Valley winery. Later, he divested himself of his prized vines and turned to collecting Northern California art with unbridled passion.

"You understand what the kid was saying?" Renna asked.

"Sure."

"So give me a translation."

"'If there's a problem, call Jim Brodie.'"

Marbles began to roll. "The Napa cops laid down bets for and against a message along those lines. The distortion made it hard to tell if what they heard was actually your name."

"It was. The Japanese language has a second alphabet that allows speakers to render foreign words into Japanese, but it's not precise."

"Convenient."

"Eye of the beholder," I said, staring at the art preserve up ahead.

"Maybe he's not talking about you," Renna said.

"He is."

"Did you recognize the voice?"

"No," I said, "but I think I'm about to."

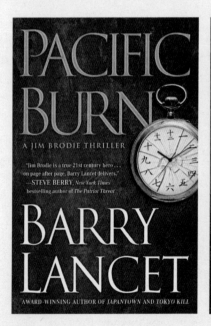 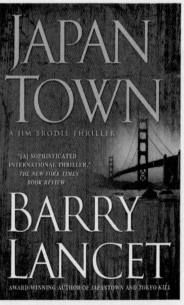